DEDICATION

To the "Qs" in our lives.
The quiet mentors who make us who we are.

Thank you.

THURSDAY

Micah's soul stilled as he stared hard at the email from his dad.

L. M. N. O. P. R. S. T. U. V…

There was no Q.

Q was missing?

Quinn was missing. Quinn Magary. Friend. Advisor. Sometimes government agent. Though whose government and which agency would always be in question.

And Dad wasn't going through official channels to report it.

He emailed back. *How long?*

Ten days. Lunch at Sadie's? One. Sending rep. Wendell Smothers. Green suit. Blue tie.

Micah looked at the clock. Ten o'clock. Which gave him three hours to round up the Knights and assemble them at…who acted as Sadie this week? Micah gazed at the calendar. Fifth month, second week. Micah. Himself. Three hours denoted urgency. Three hours meant drop what you're doing, cancel your plans, and gather. A Knight of the Octagon needed help. One for all, all for one. Right down to the dog.

Micah nudged Mialma. The oversized black lab

sleeping under the desk came to life. She snorted, sneezed, stretched, and rose. Micah emailed back. *K. Love you.*

Maybe it seemed less than manly to end his emails with "Love you." The murder of Jeremiah Acosta, one of the founding Knights and Micah's best friend, was still too close to ignore. Micah patted Mialma on the head. "Let's go, girl. I gotta round up the troops." The dog yawned and climbed up on the couch. She would wait for the command to follow him out the door.

Micah sent a group text to Tav and Luke. *Sadie's. One p.m. N-O-P-R-S-T.*

Luke texted back. *K.*

Tav's response came moments later. *K. Final. There when done.*

Micah's eyes narrowed. That's not how they played the game. When one called, the group came together. Quinn was missing. Quinn needed help. None of them would be where they were if not for Quinn. They *owed* Quinn...

And Quinn would say, "I don't need help from a bunch of college boys. And girls. Stay in school. I'm fine."

Micah closed his eyes and prayed. *Lord, we formed the Knights under You. Show us what You want in this. You know where Quinn is and what he's doing. Direct my thoughts and my steps. And especially my words. Everything from You, Father. All from You. Amen.*

* * *

Micah watched the young man approach the house. Casual attire. Jeans, pullover shirt. Black sports coat. Maybe Micah's age, maybe a year younger. Twenty-three, then. Shaggy dark hair below his collar. Walked with purpose. Micah watched the man's face. Eyes sharp, focused. Scowling. Not happy to be here? Micah would discover soon enough.

Micah pulled open the door before the man could knock. "Welcome. Micah."

"Wendell." *Who names their kid Wendell? Old family tradition?*

Micah motioned for Wendell to come inside. "Nice jacket."

Wendell nodded. "The green goes well with the blue tie. Are we done playing spy games?"

Micah didn't react. Externally. "I suppose. My father insisted on the formality. We'll take it up with him when he gets here."

Wendell's face drew down. "Kurt Andres is coming?"

"Kurt Andres stays here when he's in town." He wasn't, but Wendell didn't need to know that detail right now.

Micah moved to shake Wendell's hand. Wendell reached out and grasped Micah's. Strong grasp. But thin fingers. Small nails. Micah pointed to the living room. "Have a seat. Luke will be here at one. Tav will come when he's done with his final."

Wendell took a chair across from the window.

Micah asked, "Drink? Cola, citrus, water, tea, coffee?"

Mialma wandered in from the bedroom. The dog ambled to Wendell, stuck her nose in his lap, and bumped his fist. Wendell reached out and scratched her ears. Mialma went belly-up and wiggled. *The Mialma seal of approval. Except she only asks for belly rubs from certain people. Certain kinds of people.*

"Water." Wendell looked at the clock. "Done with a final? I thought you guys were tight. Drop everything and come running."

"How long have you been with Quinn?" Micah handed Wendell a glass of water with ice, then sat across from the young man.

"What does that have to do with it?"

"Answer the question. How long have you worked with Quinn?"

"About eight months."

"How well do you know him?"

Wendell's eyes narrowed. "Well enough to know he's missing."

"Right. What has he told you about us?"

Wendell sniffed. "You're two over-aged college kids and a slacker."

Micah grimaced. *I hear you, Quinn. I'll start school. Soon. I promise.*

Wendell continued. "You think as individuals but work as a team. You can navigate your way out of a paper bag."

Micah smiled. Quinn's favorite phrase.

Wendell continued. "He's called on you to help him in the past. None of which answers why your other guy isn't coming."

"Quinn repeatedly told us, 'I don't need help from college kids. If I do, I'll call you. Until then, stay in school.' He's missing. We'll help."

Wendell drank from his glass. His eyes narrowed, but he reached down and scratched Mialma's tummy. "We'll see."

Micah debated. *Go for it.* "Are you undercover?"

Wendell didn't look up. "Why do you ask?"

"Observation. Intuition. Spirit inspiration."

"What spirit?"

"Holy Spirit."

Wendell shook his head. "Bible thumper."

"Christ follower. But doesn't answer the question."

"What's it matter?"

"It matters because I need to know who I'm working with."

"You're working with Wendell Smothers. That's all

you—"

"—need to know. Heard it before. Not true. I need to know if you're more invested in protecting a secret identity than finding Quinn."

"I'm here."

"Didn't answer the question."

Wendell snorted. "Persistent bugger, aren't you?"

Micah gave a straight-lipped smile. "That's me. The persistent one."

"And the slacker."

Micah nodded. "Which is what Quinn calls me. And will until I get registered for college. But he knows what's kept me from enrolling."

"Care to share? Since we're getting to know each other?"

"Quinn should have told you if he's told you anything about us."

"The boys you found, right?"

Micah shifted in his seat. "Quinn would never say we found the boys."

Wendell nodded. "Fine. The boys who found you. Ben and BB. What kind of name is BB?"

"Quinn would have told you that as well. Is this a test or a diversion to keep from answering my question? Are you undercover?"

Wendell sat up and eyed Micah. "Yes. Why does it matter?"

"If we're working together, we may travel together. I have…principles…about arrangements."

"Meaning?"

He again glanced at the slender fingers. *Spell it out.* "If you're a woman, we can't room together."

Wendell's eyes twinkled. "Is that what's bothering you? I assure you, it won't be a problem."

"It would be for me." Micah sat back in his chair. "But we'll have to deal with the issue when we come to it, right?"

"If we come to it."

"Right."

The backdoor opened. Mialma gave a happy "woof" and jumped to her feet to greet the intruder. Luke called from the kitchen, "Honey, I'm home."

The lanky man walked into the living room. His eyes widened as he saw Wendell. "Oops." He grinned at Micah. "Sorry, bro." He extended his hand. "Luke Vaughn."

"Wendell Smothers." The agent returned the handshake. "You're the youngster of the group, right?"

Luke grimaced. "That's what Quinn always reminds me." He jerked his head to Micah. "As if him telling me isn't enough."

Micah grinned. "Speaking the truth in love, Luke."

Luke popped back into the kitchen, grabbed a soda from the fridge, and joined Micah and Wendell in the living room. He looked around. "Boys still in school?"

"BB has tutoring after school. Ben will be with the therapists until four. We've got time."

Wendell set his glass down. "You still haven't explained the name BB. And no, Quinn didn't explain it. Used the name as if it were a matter of fact."

"BB stands for 'Ben's brother.' When we first met up, that's what he said to call him. His official name is Louis, but he wants to change it when he's old enough. Until then, we call him BB."

"Not many kids want their identity tied to their siblings."

"True. BB's not many kids."

Luke popped his head in the hallway. "Tav here yet?"

"Finishing finals."

"Yeah, I know. Just thought he'd be done by now. He's

aced everything in class so far."

Wendell raised an eyebrow. "What's he studying? What are you studying?"

"Tav is an engineering major. I'm still undecided. Going for pre-med right now, but it may change."

Wendell looked at Micah. "If you go, what will you study?"

Micah bristled. "When I go, I'll study tax accounting. I'm a tax preparer now and want to be able to become a consultant eventually."

Wendell raised an eyebrow. "Actually work in your field? What a concept."

Micah snorted. "It happens. What about you? What's your background?"

Wendell hesitated, then took a drink of water. He set it down. "Majored in criminology."

"Working in your field. Nice concept."

The front door burst open, jarring against the wall. A tall figure in a motorcycle jacket and helmet flew in the hall. He banged the door shut, locked it, and rolled into the living room. He peered out the front window, then closed the blinds. Only then did he take off his helmet. Tav Vaughn had entered the room.

Micah's eyes widened. "What's going on?"

Tav breathed hard. He took a moment to catch his breath. Luke came to his feet and moved to his brother's side. "What's the matter? What happened?"

Tav sighed, sat, and admitted, "Someone followed me."

Wendell cocked his head, skepticism on his face. "What?"

Tav nodded. "They picked me up coming out of the garage at school. White sedan. No logo or front license. I watched them for about two miles, then did a four-corner right turn. They followed me all the way. I beat them at the light, but they caught me at the next one. Doubled back and lost them."

Micah sensed the group exhale. Until Tav continued, "Then, about three miles down the road, there's another sedan. Dusty brown. Same no logo, same no license. They tailed me for a mile or more. I jumped on the freeway and got off at Seventh. Got back on the same exit, and they stayed with me. Got off on Tenth. Doubled back, got off at Third, swung around the traffic circle, and hit Fifth. By then, they knew they were made and raced off. I didn't see anyone else, but I sure took the scenic route getting here."

Wendell leaned forward. "Lone driver?"

"Passenger in front. Both cars. Males, all of them. Caucasians. Dark hair. Passenger in one car wore a hat. No logo on it, either."

Wendell grimaced. "You seem pretty sure of your identification."

"If being with Quinn has taught us anything, it's to be observant. Pay attention to the details."

Luke nodded. "Which is how we won the Magary game. Paying attention to details."

Micah added, "And the Lord's grace."

Tav slipped in an "Amen."

Wendell ignored the affirmation and pressed Tav, "Why would anyone follow you?"

"I don't know."

"Do you expect to be followed?"

"No."

"Then why did you even notice?"

Tav turned to Micah. "Who is this?"

Micah swallowed a chuckle. "Wendell Smothers. He's the one Dad sent. He's Quinn's intern."

"Then you know Quinn insists we always be aware of

our surroundings."

"Why does Quinn even know any of you?" Wendell's voice carried incredulity.

Tav eyed Wendell. "Why does Quinn know you? You work for him. So do we. Sometimes. You tell us he's missing. Let's get to the matter at hand. Then we can see if someone following me is connected." Tav leaned forward.

So Tav took control. Good enough. Micah sat back to listen.

Wendell tapped the table. "Quinn left ten days ago. Said he'd be gone about three days. Had an assignment in Hanford. Be there and back by Monday."

"And he never made it back."

Wendell nodded. "Right. I spoke to the powers that be, and they all said the same thing. When he's unaccounted for the entire month, they'll consider looking into it. But until then, this is standard operating procedure."

"But you're not satisfied with it."

"Quinn's never late, never gone without reason. This isn't right."

"And Kurt Andres, Micah's father, agreed with you." Tav motioned to Micah.

Wendell nodded. "He's the only one who did."

"And he directed you to us."

Wendell corrected, "He said you could help. I thought it was worth a shot. Now I'm not sure I shouldn't go this alone."

"Except what does Quinn say?"

"'Never go alone.'"

Tav leaned back on the couch. "Right. Hanford. Any idea what his business was there? Not exactly a booming town."

"Not exactly a hotbed of crime, either."

Tav glanced across the room at his brother. "Luke?"

Luke typed into his phone, then came back. "Hanford. Central Valley. 2022 population 58,470. 18K households, 3.09 persons per house. Median income $68K. Per capita income $27K. Poverty rate is about fifteen percent. Population density of 3300 per square mile, encompassing seventeen square miles. What else do you want to know?"

"What do they do for a living there?"

"Top three are healthcare and social assistance, public admin, and retail trade. Top wage earners are, wait for it, public admin, finance and insurance, and transportation and warehousing."

"Crime?"

"It gets a D- for safety. But most of it is your assault, theft/burglary, vandalism, and drug variety. Nothing a major crime team would be looking at."

Tav shrugged. "You're not narrowing it down." He stared at Wendell. "Give us something to start with. Anything. Any phone calls? Suspicious packages? He win any lotteries?"

Wendell shook his head. "Nothing. 'I'm leaving. I'll be back in three days.' That's what I've got."

"Then I guess we take a field trip to Hanford."

Wendell's skepticism returned. "All of you?"

"All of us."

Wendell shook his head. "Who do you people think you are? Spies?"

Tav smiled. "No. We're Knights of the Octagon. We're ready for anything."

Micah added, "Because we get into most anything since meeting Quinn."

Luke's eyes narrowed. "Remember at the award ceremony, how Quinn wore his dress uniform? Marine, right?"

"Yeah, so?"

"So Lemore Naval Air Station is not far from Hanford. The Navy and the Marines are part of the same branch."

Wendell chuckled. "Do not let Quinn, or any Marine, ever hear you say that."

Luke ducked his head. "Forgive me. But it could give us a clue to go on. Does he have any old shipmates or brothers-in-arms in the area he might want to visit?"

Wendell's eyes took a faraway gaze. "There might be. I'll dig through his records and see what I can come up with. It still shouldn't make him ten days out and no communication."

"Granted. But we need to start somewhere. We could ask those friends if they've seen or heard from him. Then take it from there."

Wendell chewed his lip. "That's good thinking. I might not have come up with that idea. I've never seen him in uniform."

Micah cleared his throat. "If you remember, he made himself very clear about us not commenting on his manner of dress."

Tav grinned. "Words to the effect of 'as you value your life,' right?"

Micah nodded. "Exactly. He doesn't like to advertise his past."

Wendell snorted. "Or his present."

"That, too." Micah felt for Wendell. He couldn't imagine working for Quinn. Not full-time. It would be exhausting.

But would any of them have the chance to work with him again? They had to find him. One way or another. One for all...

A knock at the door interrupted the meeting. Micah looked out the front window. A tall, stern woman stood on the porch, briefcase in one hand, clipboard in the other.

Micah called over his shoulder, "Everyone, on your best behavior. The principal's here." He opened the door. "Hello, Ms. Phelps. How can I help you?"

The woman smiled. Somewhat like a snake that knows it's caught its prey. "Mr. Andres. I thought I'd drop by for a welfare check on BB and Ben."

Micah waved for her to enter. "Then you're in the wrong place. The boys are at school. As you are well aware."

"Yes, but I like to verify what goes on behind the scenes, you know?" She gazed around the room. "Are we having a party?"

Micah maintained as much professionalism as he could. "A search party. A friend of ours has come up missing. We're gathering information."

"Does this friend go missing often?"

Wendell stepped forward. "Almost never. Wendell Smothers, DHS. Does Mr. Andres require permission to have a gathering in his home?"

Ms. Phelps's eyes fluttered at the acronym. "Of course not. I merely inquired."

"Your tone indicated otherwise."

Micah wanted to warn Wendell off but couldn't think of a way short of kicking the man. Person. Agent. He intervened. "You know Luke and Tav Vaughn. They're certified caregivers for Ben and BB."

"Yes, I have them on my list." She checked the clipboard to be sure. "I see them here often."

"I want my boys to be comfortable, Ms. Phelps, with anyone they're around. If I should have to be gone, I don't want Ben to be surprised or dismayed in any way."

"I agree."

"Would you like to examine the boys' rooms to see if they continue living in a safe environment?"

Ms. Phelps nodded. "Yes. As you get closer to

permanent placement, we want to ensure we provide the best possible home for our children."

The mental crossing of swords exhausted Micah. He led the way to the closed back rooms. "I can't vouch for the neatness of the environment. I can for the cleanliness."

Ms. Phelps's eyebrows raised. "And the difference is?"

"Neat means everything in a specific place. Clean means no dirty laundry on the floor, no accumulation of dust under the bed, no used dishes left on the dressers."

Ms. Phelps nodded. "I agree." She softened. "We're on the same side, Mr. Andres. We all want what is right for the children."

Even when they disagreed on what that was. Micah opened Ben's door first.

Ben was meticulous with his belongings. Everything had to be folded and wrapped, and placed. Granted, some of the placement might be on the floor or under the bed. But he placed it all with the greatest of care.

Ms. Phelps walked around the room. She laid her hand on the pile of rocks on top of the chest of drawers. Micah warned, "Touch, but don't move. Ben is very precise in how he stacks things."

The woman gave an actual smile. "Yes. I've seen Ben in action. His ability to perceive the differences in the placement of items is remarkable." She looked at Micah. "Ben is remarkable. You're a fortunate man to have him for a son, Mr. Andres."

"I'm a fortunate man to have him find and accept me, Ms. Phelps."

She walked out and closed the door. Micah hoped the good vibes would last after opening door number two.

BB's room. Micah trailed behind the Children's Services agent. And prayed.

His heart stopped. BB's room was as immaculate as

Ben's had been. Ms. Phelps scowled at Micah. "Do you allow BB any freedom in his own room?"

"Of course I do. It's his room. Other than keeping it clean, I don't interfere in how he keeps it."

"Then how do you explain this orderliness?"

Micah shrugged. "BB's an exceptional kid on his own. He likes to know where things are." He paused, then added, "He also likes Ben to come into his room. Ben can't stand confusion and disorder. BB keeps his room neat so Ben will feel comfortable."

Maybe not *this* neat, but hey... Micah continued, "We're working to grow as a family, Ms. Phelps. We're all trying to get along. Which means making compromises for all of us."

Her eyes narrowed, and the corners crinkled. "Does that extend to your bedroom as well?"

"It extends to the remainder of the house, including my office and my bedroom. But we maintain an 'open door' policy at all times. I'm aware I don't have the same freedoms with my 'sons' as a natural father might have. So we're more careful." And restricted. A restriction Micah chafed at but obeyed. Side hugs.

Ms. Phelps closed the door to BB's room. "I wouldn't want anyone investigating my room, either, Mr. Andres." Together they walked back into the living room. The CPS agent shook hands all around. Her narrowed glance at Wendell said the jury might still be out on his presence. But she would allow it this time.

She left, and Micah closed the door behind her. He waited until she climbed into her car, then smiled at the room. "Well behaved." He glared at Wendell. "Except you. I could have introduced you as another friend, and she wouldn't have been any wiser. But DHS? Now she's going to think I'm under investigation for something."

Wendell shrugged. "She'll get over it. Or I'll send her an official letter from headquarters."

Micah groaned. "Don't do me any favors, please. Let it go."

Wendell sneered.

* * *

Wendell returned to the office to check out the names of veterans in the Hanford area. Luke and Tav returned to campus. Micah picked up the boys. BB flashed the papers he'd completed, careful not to block Micah's line of vision of the road and traffic. Micah nodded. "Good work. Another week of tutoring, you'll be with the rest of the class."

From his shotgun position, BB glanced over at Micah. "Could I do two weeks and then be ahead?"

"You want to? I have no problem with you being in tutoring if you're getting a benefit out of it."

"I am." BB dropped his gaze, then admitted, "I like learning new stuff. I like learning, period. Didn't get a lot of it in my old life. But this is kind of fun."

Micah chuckled. "As long as you maintain your attitude, I'll keep you in tutoring for the rest of your academic life."

BB smiled. "I'll hold you to that." He lost the expression. "What did you hear about the adoption?"

"We've got a court date. I got the call this afternoon. One month. You've got one month to change your mind, then it's final."

BB grinned. "I don't think I'm gonna change my mind in a month."

"You never know. I know I won't." Micah glanced in the backseat at Ben. "Ben, do you want to have me for a dad?"

Ben nodded. Once. Micah knew the boy rarely repeated himself. One motion was enough.

Micah hesitated. "I'm going to pull Ben from school tomorrow for a field trip. We're going to take the train to Hanford." He glanced over at BB. "You want to come?"

BB shook his head. "I think I'd rather stay in school."

Micah shook his head. "I'm sorry. You can't be my kid. No kid of mine will ever be interested in school. Just no way."

BB chuckled. "Guess you'll have to get used to it." The boy stared at the floorboard. "Of course, if you don't get in school soon, I might pass you."

Micah sighed. "I'm going, I'm going. What is it with all of you? Quinn is on me. Tav and Luke are on me. Now you're on me."

BB shrugged. "Someone has to be. You're avoiding it. You said you needed to get everything about the adoption straightened out. It's done. It's been done. You could enroll anytime and start a semester from now. But you keep making excuses. Why?"

Micah bristled. "When did you become the adult?"

"When I see you ducking the issue. What's wrong, Mick? What are you afraid of?"

"I'm not afraid." Micah paused. "Okay, I am afraid. I'm afraid of proving my mother right. I can't cut it. I can't be more than I am." He frowned over at BB. "There. I said it. Okay?"

"Now that you have, do you hear how stupid it sounds?"

"Maybe." Micah turned into the driveway. "I'll think about it." He parked the car. The trio walked into the house. Micah's phone pinged. He looked at the encrypted text. Wendell had information. *Ten names. Divide and conquer.*

Micah texted back. *How many in walking distance to train station?*

??

Taking train with Ben tomorrow. How many in walking distance to train depot?

Three. How will you get home?

Ride back. Train every two hours.

I come with you?

Sure. Meet here or at station?

Station.

See you in a.m.

Micah searched for Ben in the house. The boy had wrapped himself around Mialma's neck, in his silent way telling the patient angel about his day. Mialma nuzzled and woofed and did everything dogs do to make a hard day better.

Micah joined Ben on the floor. "Buddy, we're going to take a trip tomorrow. I want to take you on the train. No, Mialma can't come. She's not certified yet. But there will be a new friend with us. You will meet him in the morning. We can get ice cream, too."

Ben's head perked up. His eyes shone brighter. He grinned. Micah put a finger to his lips. "Shhh. Don't tell BB. He might be jealous."

BB called from the kitchen. "I can get ice cream here. I don't need to ride the train." The teen entered the living room carrying a half-gallon container of Oreo Fudge and a spoon to prove his point.

Micah sighed. "Right. Forgive me." He took a second glance at BB. "You haven't told your social worker I let you eat out of the tub, have you?"

"And ruin a great thing? Of course not."

Micah wiped his hand across his brow. "Whew. Thought I was in trouble for a moment."

BB laughed. "I'm a Knight of the Octagon. I know how to keep a secret."

Micah dropped the play. "Quinn is missing. He's late

from an assignment. We're going to Hanford to check with some old military mates to see if they've seen or heard from him."

BB frowned. "How long has he been gone?"

"Seven days. Had a three-day assignment and hasn't come back. His intern became worried and contacted Dad, who contacted me."

"Who's the intern?"

"Wendell Smothers. Sharp guy."

"Yeah? With a name like Wendell, he better be."

"Some parents are cruel."

"I hear you."

BB put the ice cream back in the fridge. "What are you fixing for dinner?"

"I thought I'd grill burgers tonight. Tav and Luke will probably come by."

BB snorted. "Of course they will. They're college students living in student housing. Where else would they go?"

"Nowhere." Tav and Luke may have won the Magary challenge with Micah, but they had decided to wait to invest their portion of the million-dollar winnings until after college. Living in student housing was frugal. Right. Except they spent almost as much time living at Micah's as at the university. Which suited Micah fine. Having help learning to live with eight-year-old Ben and fifteen-year-old BB mattered. They were all growing together. One for all and all for one.

BB brought Micah back to the matter at hand. "What do you think happened to Quinn?"

"I don't know. His superiors say not to worry unless he's been missing thirty days. Wendell isn't comfortable with the idea. Thus we're going looking."

"You think taking the little guy is a good idea? If Quinn

is in danger, then taking him…"

Micah shook his head. "If I thought for one minute there would be trouble, I'd…" He trailed off. Maybe he should think for a minute. A long minute. Micah studied Ben side-eyed, then glanced back to BB. "What do you suggest?"

"Leave him with me. I'll skip school." He laughed. "Yeah, I know. Me, skipping school. What a concept. But I can do it and stay with him. We could take the bus to the Amazetorium. He loves it there."

Ben nodded with vigor. One nod, but with vigor. Micah sighed. "Gonna change the adoption date. You'll adopt me. You're more the adult."

BB grinned.

* * *

FRIDAY

Micah watched a young woman approach the station. She picked her way around the discarded papers, soft drinks, and men experiencing homelessness who littered the approach to the waiting area. Her features were familiar. Eerily reminiscent of Wendell Smothers. Could this be him in another undercover disguise? Or in "his" real persona? Or someone else entirely? He'd know if they introduced themselves or approached him in some way. No other reason for a fine-looking woman to talk to him. Not in this lifetime.

The young brunette stared at her phone and the train station sign. She glanced around. Finally, she did the unthinkable. She walked to Micah. "Pardon me, sir. Is this the Hanford line?"

Micah nodded. "Yes, it is. Ms. Smothers?"

"Why would you think that?"

"Beautiful women don't approach me for no reason."

"Except I wanted to know if this was the right line."

"Siri or Alexa could have given you the information." He pointed. "Love the new disguise."

She shrugged, gesturing to the wraparound skirt and blouse. "Something I threw together at the last minute." She sat on the bench a respectable distance from him. "And it's Wendy."

"Wendy. Micah. Still the same." He raised his eyebrows. "You have the names we're investigating?"

She handed him two names with photos. "I found a fourth. All within walking distance. I sent Tav and Luke their subjects since they're driving."

Micah stared at the pictures. Both were taken when the men were raw recruits in boot camp. Age-progression photos hinted at the current look. "Are they still in contact with each other?"

"Why?"

"Because they may compare notes. Would be good if we had our stories straight."

"Agreed. We're researching a story on the Magary Chase. Either wanting to know Quinn's history or where Quinn might be."

"Excellent thinking."

Wendy smiled. "I do have a thought every now and then."

"Which is why Quinn keeps you as his intern."

"I didn't think he had a choice."

Micah grinned. "Oh, he does. He has ways of tanking interns he dislikes or doesn't think he can work with. You've been with him for eight months. A long time for Quinn."

Wendy shrugged. "Maybe he's getting soft."

"Quinn? Never. Stop selling yourself short. That's my gig."

"So I've heard."

Micah's eyebrows lifted. "Oh? So he's been talking about us."

"He gave me a brief—very brief—rundown on you three. Tav's the leader, Luke is the confident one, and you're the glue who holds the group together."

Micah shrugged. "We all have our moments."

The train whistled long and loud. Wendy stood. "Our cue to board, I believe."

They climbed into the closest car and found seats. No crowd, so they put a space between them and sat in the same row. The thirty-minute ride chugged by with small talk and smaller strategy. Situational flow seemed the best bet. Go with it.

Micah and Wendy split up to talk to their respective veterans. Micah walked to the home of the first name: Garland Merritt. Age sixty. Navy Corpsman who served contemporaneously with Quinn.

But didn't know or remember him. Strike one. The gentleman was eager to talk about his service. Or his yard. His garden. His neighbors. Garland wanted company, and a stranger off the street worked fine. Micah spent over an hour entertaining and being entertained by the lonely man.

When he finally managed to leave, he took a break at the corner before moving on to the next house. *Lord, I'm happy I could be there for Mr. Merritt. Not sure that was my intention, but we'll call it a "divine appointment" and thank You for it. Hopefully, it made his day a little brighter. It would make mine brighter if I could find out where Quinn is. If it's in Your will, could this next person have information about him? And want to share it? But only according to Your will, Lord. Thanks.*

Micah knocked. The curtain in the door wiggled, then the door opened. The gruff face matched the tone. "What do you want?"

Micah extended his hand. "Mr. James Tilley? I'm Micah Andres. I need to find Quinn Magary. This is a long shot, but you may have served with Quinn back in the day. Is it possible?" Micah showed Quinn's picture to the man.

The man's eyes twinkled as his face drew into a concentrated frown. "Quinn Magary? Quinn Magary?

Navy?"

"Marine, sir."

"Of course. Sorry. It's been how long ago?"

"I think it's been thirty years. I wondered if you remember him."

Tilley nodded. "I remember Quinn. He's not someone you forgot. Disciplined son of a gun."

Which was not the idiom Tilley used, but Micah supplied the translation. "Yes, he still is. I'm wondering if you have been in contact with Mr. Magary?"

Tilley shook his head. He waved Micah into the small living room. It had been neatly furnished with a comfortable nineties "vibe." Floral print couch. Stacked electronic radio tuner/cassette deck/VHS player. Three-foot-tall speakers. Some things hadn't changed in thirty years.

Tilley motioned for Micah to take a seat. "Are you a friend of his?"

Micah waffled. "Yes. As much as Quinn has friends. He's a very private person."

"Yes, he is. Yes, he is indeed. But you consider yourself his friend? You talk to him regularly?" Tilley paused. "I don't want to give out information to someone who doesn't know Quinn. That would be breaking a confidence."

Micah nodded. "I can appreciate your concern. Yes, I know Quinn. He has a Marine tattoo on his right shoulder and an anchor on his left." Information Micah had garnered the last time the group went boating. Ben fell overboard, and Quinn wrapped the boy in his shirt.

In the present, Micah waited for Mr. Tilley to make his decision.

Tilley studied Micah, then stuck out his lower lip and smirked. The gleam in his eye gave Micah pause. What did it mean?

The older man admitted, "I haven't seen Quinn in

probably ten years. Haven't heard from him in five. But I have a message for him if you'll take one to him."

Micah nodded. "Of course."

"Give it to you on the way out." He smiled. "What did you major in?"

Micah tapped the arm of the couch. "I haven't started college yet. I'm planning to go next semester if everything works out."

Tilley laughed. "Trust me, boy. Nothing ever 'works out' on its own. You have to make it work. Get out there, get it done. Make the decision and go for it." Tilley studied Micah for a minute. "I'm surprised Quinn isn't hounding you about it."

Micah huffed. "He is. But I adopted two boys, and one of them is autistic. I've been trying to get all his schooling and counselors set up. I finally got all the details arranged, so now I can focus on getting into school. I'm going to study accounting. I'm already working in tax prep, so it should be a natural carry-over."

Tilley nodded. "Sounds like a definite plan. You like working with numbers?"

Micah grinned. "Yes, I do. It was my strongest subject in school."

They made small talk for another half-hour before Micah felt he could leave without offending Tilley. He stood. "I have enjoyed our talk, Mr. Tilley. But I need to get going. I've got some other people to talk to. I still want to track Quinn."

Tilley stood as well. "When you find him, you be sure to give him the message I give you. Since you're his friend, I need you to relay it verbatim."

Micah bobbed his head. "I will, sir. You can trust me."

Tilley held out his hand. Micah extended his. Tilley grasped it in a vice-grip. He swung fast with his left hand, striking Micah hard in the eye. Before Micah could react, Tilley dropped their hands and punched Micah dead in the gut. Micah doubled over. Tilley hit him again with an uppercut to the jaw.

Micah went to his knees. He gasped and groaned. Tilley stood back, then helped Micah to his feet. His eyes narrowed, and he leered at Micah. "Tell him what I said exactly the way I said it. You got it, boy?"

Micah straightened despite the pain. Blood trickled from his eye, and his vision doubled. Through clenched teeth, he muttered, "I'll tell him." Tilley clapped him gently on the shoulder. "Nice to meet you, Mr. Andres." He held the door open for Micah, guided him through, then closed the door behind him.

Micah steadied against the doorway, then made his way down the front sidewalk to the street. He kept his head down to avoid the glances of passersby. Micah straightened enough to reach the train station, find a bench, and sit. He leaned back against the posts, closed his eyes, and sighed.

* * *

"What happened to you?" Wendy's voice carried disbelief and concern.

Micah didn't bother to open his eyes. "Quinn's old friend had a message he's been dying to send Quinn. I'm the lucky messenger."

"Friend?" Micah sensed Wendy sitting beside him. "No one needs friends like him." She touched his cheek. "I'll get some ice." Wendy paused. "Did you lose consciousness?"

"Not before he hit me. I don't know about after. What time is it?"

"Nearly one."

"Couldn't have been much past noon when I left Tilley's house. Maybe I passed out. I don't know."

Wendy's voice tightened. "I should call an ambulance."

"No. Call Tav. He and Luke can pick us up and take me home. I can sleep it off there."

"Not gonna happen. I'll call Tav, but you can't be left alone."

"I won't be alone. I have kids."

"You want them to find you dead? I don't think so. Neither would you if you were thinking straight."

Micah heard Wendy on the phone. "Yes, Tav? Whatever you and your brother are doing, drop it. Micah got pummeled and refuses medical treatment. We need a ride back home, and now. Then he needs someone to watch him overnight."

Micah opened his eyes and put some energy into his voice. "I do not. I'll be fine."

Tav's voice came back. "Tell him to shut up, and we'll be there in fifteen minutes."

Wendy put her phone away. She studied Micah. "You up to telling me what happened?"

"I talked to Mr. Tilley. He remembered Quinn. Hadn't talked with him in five years but recalled their time together in the service." Micah leaned forward on the bench, determined to pretend he didn't hurt. Ribs protested, as did his head. Changing altitudes was not the best idea. Micah moved past vertical and leaned on his elbows.

"He had a message to deliver, and I got to carry it." He motioned to his battered body. "This is the message."

Wendy's tone narrowed, as did her eyes. "We should call the police."

Micah didn't shake his head. Made no abrupt movements. "No. Quinn wouldn't. I won't. This is obviously a grudge between the two of them. I'm just the lucky herald."

Tav and Luke rushed to the bench. Micah grimaced.

"Hi."

Tav scowled. "Hi yourself. Let's get you home." Luke and Tav each took a side and pulled Micah to his feet. He groaned as he rose but swallowed any further complaints until they deposited him in the backseat of the 4X4. Tav climbed into the driver's seat. Luke waved at Wendy. "You want shotgun?"

"I'll sit in the back and make sure he doesn't die between here and home."

Micah grumbled, "Thanks. I'm fine. Or I will be. Promise."

Tav warned, "If you pass out, we're taking you to the hospital."

"I won't pass out." Micah caught hold of the inside arm of the door. "I'm good, I'm telling you."

Luke shook his head. "You lie."

Micah admitted, "I lie. Marines and Navy. They never forget a grudge."

Wendy climbed in beside him, "So I've heard."

Micah lay his head back on the seat behind him. "Anyone else get anything?"

Tav pulled the car into traffic and headed north on the highway. "I didn't. Lonely sailors. But didn't remember Quinn at all."

Luke agreed. "Yeah, my first guy turned out the same way. I spent too much time with him." He stopped. "Retract that. I spent the time the Lord would want me to listen to his stories and make him feel seen. Then I talked to a man who had actually spoken to Quinn this past week."

Micah sat forward and instantly regretted it. He lay back against the seat again. "What did he have to say?"

"He and Quinn had business. Financial business. Quinn sold a piece of property. Mr. Smalls and Quinn had to wait for the tax office to open, then had to wait for the assessor, then had to wait…you get the idea. Took them three days to get the deal done. But they took the time to catch up and talk about life."

"Did he know where Quinn went after he finished here?"

"Quinn didn't say. Told him he needed to make the hardest decision he's ever had. His life depended on making the right choice. Then he left."

Tav kept his eyes on the road. "Great. Now we know he's in trouble. Deep trouble. We need to find him. And soon."

Micah raised a hand. "You don't need to sit with me."

"Shut up, Andres. You're not getting out of this one." Luke turned to face his brother. "You should stay with the boys at Mick's. I'll keep our punching bag at the apartment."

Tav nodded. "Sounds good." He checked the rearview mirror. "Does someone need to pick the boys up after school?"

"No. BB stayed home to watch Ben. They were taking the bus to the Amazatorium."

Luke smiled. "Ah, I love the place. Maybe they'll want to go again tomorrow."

Micah put heat in his voice. "I will be there for them tomorrow."

Wendy tapped his shoulder. "If you make it through tonight. Concentrate on staying alive, will you, Andres?"

All the bravado seeped into the back bench. Micah sighed. "Yeah. What you said."

* * *

The ride to student housing took less than an hour. Tav passed Wendy his keys, and she opened the doors to let them in. Tav and Luke flanked Micah as the men passed Wendy and took Micah straight to a back room. Wendy remained in the living area. The apartment was open-concept. Kitchen, dining area, and living room all faced each other. Books were piled neatly on two desks at either corner of the common area. Dishes were precisely stacked in the glass-faced cabinets. She'd be hard-pressed to believe two bachelors lived here. Bachelor student brothers.

She wandered around, looking at the pictures on the wall. Four young men sat arm-in-arm on a picnic table. Wendy guessed the photo included the missing Knight, Jeremiah, who had been murdered during the Magary treasure hunt. She stared tight-lipped at the shot. So much promise.

Wendy wandered to the opposite wall and considered a family tree. Tav's name graced the bottom. Taylor Alexander Vaughn. Mrs. Vaughn must have chosen that one.

Wendy cocked her head. There was a familiarity to the branches. She'd seen those names before. Her eyes narrowed, then flared. Those names...all those names.

Wendy took out her phone and snapped several photos of the tree before slipping her camera back into her pocket. No one needed to know. Not until she verified her gut feeling. What were the odds?

Tav walked into the living area with a backpack. He grabbed a stack of books from the desk, a motorcycle helmet, and a jacket from the closet, then nodded to Wendy. "I'll see you in the morning, Ms. Smothers." The man bumped out the door, letting it close behind him.

Luke called from the bedroom, "Have a seat. There're drinks in the fridge if you want one."

Wendy called back, "Thanks." More opportunity to see how "knightly" these men were. She opened the door and stood back.

Two gallon containers of milk sat in the center. Bottles of water graced the door. Absent were the beers and colas and vices of student life Wendy remembered. Okay, so they really were on the "straight and narrow" side. Wendy took a water and returned to the living area. She sat on the couch but remained on alert. It never left her mind there were two men in the room beside her. Knights or not, she would not let down her guard.

Luke came into the living room, closing the bedroom door behind him. "Mick's sleeping. I'm not convinced we shouldn't take him to the ER whether he likes it or not. But I'll give him tonight to get better. If he still has double-vision tomorrow, he's going. Period."

Wendy grinned. "You do watch out for each other, don't you?"

"We try." He jerked his head towards the room. "We don't always succeed."

Wendy nodded. "Understood. I'll call my sister and have her pick me up to get my car from the train station."

Luke slapped his head. "So stupid. I didn't even think about getting you home. Tav can't be too far down the street yet. I'll call him."

Wendy waved him off. "No. I'll get my sister." She smiled.

Luke rolled his eyes. "Except we've got you here. It was for a good cause."

Wendy scoffed. "Lost cause. All my information got Micah beat up."

"No. We know Quinn was in Hanford and concluded his work there. Unless Mr. Smalls lied to me. And I'm usually good at telling fact from fiction."

"Fair enough. So Quinn was there and left. Where did he go? Into trouble from the sound of it. But what and where? Where do we even start looking?"

"I don't know, Ms. Smothers."

"Make it Wendy. Please."

"Wendy. All we can do now is chase anyone who knows him in hopes of someone having something. Otherwise, we've got nothing to go on."

Wendy pulled out her phone and made the call to her sister. A year her senior, Jen agreed to pick her up at the apartment, no questions asked, and no snide comments required. Luke checked on Micah before walking Wendy to the curb and shaking her hand at departure.

Jen waited until Wendy climbed in to acknowledge, "He's cute. Is he single?"

"Yes, and he's got a brother. And a friend. Don't get any ideas."

"Why? You get first pick, right?"

Wendy sneered at her sister. "It's business."

"Then I get first pick."

"Jen! Stop it." Wendy stared out the window, thinking about the family tree. What would a blood family look like? She'd been fostered since birth by Jen and her family. Hers was her *real* family. But a blood family?

Jen interrupted her thoughts. "How well do you know him?"

Wendy admitted, "I know the older friend, Micah, better. The two brothers—Tav and Luke—are in college. Micah hasn't started yet because he took in two younger boys."

"Late bloomers, aren't they?"

"Maybe. They were the ones who won the Magary Chase two years ago."

Jen directed the car around the corner and grinned. "Ooo. Rich bloomers. Pick yours, then I'll go after one of the others."

Wendy slapped her sister on the arm. "Stop that."

Her phone rang. Luke's number showed on the screen. "Hello?"

"Tav was in an accident on the way to Micah's. He's fine, but his bike got totaled. He says he was run off the road by—"

"—a white sedan with no markings and no tags."

Luke's voice sounded angry. "You got it. I can't leave Mick alone here."

Wendy thought fast. "Where's your brother? And is he really okay? Or is he okay like Micah is okay?"

Luke chuckled. "I think he's fine. He's insisting he's well enough to go to Mick's house and stay with BB and Ben."

"But he needs a ride. Right?"

"Yeah. He's at Filmore and Sweet. The cops are still processing the scene."

Jen leaned over and whispered, "We can swing by there on the way to get your car. I'll take him home."

Wendy glared at her sister. She gave the cutthroat hand motion to silence her. "We'll get my car, then I'll pick him up and take him to Micah's." Jen's lower lip stuck out in a mock pout. Wendy swallowed her laughter and continued. "Tell him it'll be about forty minutes."

"Right. Thanks, Wendy."

The line disconnected. Jen shook her head. "That's stupid. We'd have to go across town to get your car, then double back to get your friend. Makes more sense to just swing by and get him, drive him to wherever he needs to be, then take you to the train station."

Wendy frowned. Much as she didn't like to admit it, Jen's plan made more sense than her own. "Fine. But no flirting."

"Why? Is he yours?"

Wendy shook her head. "He doesn't belong to anyone I know of."

"Well, then? I'm not getting any younger."

"You're twenty-three."

"And a half." Jen grinned. "Relax, Wenders. I'm joking." She steered the car through the roundabout. "Mostly."

They reached the crash site in under half an hour. The police were finishing the investigation. Tav's motorcycle sat on the trailer, being hauled away. For recycling from the looks of it.

Tav appeared shaken. Angry and shaken. But he smiled and extended a hand that tremored only slightly. "Nice to meet you. I'd say Wendy has told us all about you, but I'd be lying."

Jen laughed. "She tries to hide the family connections."

Wendy rolled her eyes. She studied Tav. "Are you all right? Honestly?"

"Knights honor. I'm good. Mad about being used for target practice. I'm guessing this is personal."

"Climb in." Wendy eyed the man closely to see how damaged he might be. Tav moved stiffly but without groaning. Excessively. He sat in the back. Wendy asked, "Who would want to kill you?"

"No one I know of. I'm sure I've offended a few people in my day, but none who would want this kind of revenge."

Tav trailed off. He sat forward, his eyes narrowing. After a moment, he sat back, and his features relaxed.

Wendy eyed him. "What was that about?"

"A thought. Easily dismissed."

"Yeah, well, share it anyhow."

Tav frowned. "Luke and I are estranged from our parents. Bitterly. Long story. We have a younger brother. There could be some renewed animosity with Luke and me in school. But I can't imagine it going to murder."

"Bodily harm?"

"Or even that. Addison, our brother, is a first-string

quarterback. I don't see our dad still caring what we do."

Wendy raised her eyebrows. "You'd be surprised."

"Probably not." Tav stared out the window.

Jen jumped into the conversation. "What did you mean 'night's honor'?"

Tav chuckled. "We—my brother, Micah, and I—are the Knights of the Octagon. Octagon because no one had a round table, and Knights of the Oval sounded weird." Tav stopped. Wendy heard the wistful note in his voice. "That was Jeremiah's line." He gathered himself and continued, "We pledged ourselves to honesty, integrity, loyalty, chastity, and sobriety. And each other. Got us through tough times and school. We never saw a reason to stop, so we're still Knights."

Jen smiled in the mirror. "I'm impressed."

"We're works in progress. And human."

Wendy demanded, "Pull over."

Jen did a double take. "What? Why?"

"Do it. I'm driving." Wendy shifted in her seat.

Jen pulled over onto a driveway. "What's wrong with my driving?"

"Nothing. But I don't want to be looking over my shoulder." She switched places with Jen. "In case we're being followed."

Tav sat forward. "You think they'd come after you, too?"

Wendy pulled into traffic. "We're not sure if it's personal about you or concerns Quinn being missing. Since you live a pious life, I have to assume it's about Quinn."

Tav frowned. "I wouldn't call it pious. We're trying to follow Jesus."

Jen asked, "Follow him where?"

"Wherever He takes us. We're trying to live as He did. Love who He loved. Hate who He hated."

Jen's head snapped around. "I thought Jesus loved everyone."

Tav beamed. Wendy saw the mischief in his eyes. "Exactly my point."

Jen rolled her eyes. "I deserved that, I suppose."

Wendy repeated, "If it's about Quinn, then we're all targets. If it's about you, the less the opposition knows about where you are, the better for everyone around you. Especially those kids."

Tav nodded. "Good thinking. But if it is my parents, they won't hurt anyone else."

"You're sure about that? You want to bet those boys' lives on it?"

Tav paused, then frowned straight-lipped. "I would. Unless, in your professional opinion, I shouldn't."

Wendy thought about it. Jen looked from Wendy to Tav. "You'd really take her opinion over your own judgment?"

"Where it comes to BB and Ben's safety, yes. My ego isn't so fragile I'd endanger them. We owe them our lives."

Jen considered Tav, then turned back to Wendy. She put her hand to her cheek to shield Tav from seeing and mouthed, *Wow! Mine.*

Wendy shook her head.

The GPS showed three exits before Micah's turnoff. Wendy took the nearest exit, did a U-turn, slipped back on the freeway going the opposite direction, drove four exits, exited, flipped back around again, drove two, left the freeway, and hopped back on the next entrance. Satisfied she wasn't being followed, she went to Micah's house and parked. Tav gathered his books and pack and slid out the door. "Come on in and meet BB and Ben. Friends of Quinn are friends of theirs, too."

Wendy exchanged looks with Jen. Her sister shrugged.

The women climbed out of the car and followed Tav around the back to the rear entrance.

Loud, happy barking welcomed them at the door. Tav held out his hand sharply. Mialma sat immediately, only the tip of her tail indicating her excitement. Tav raised his brows at Jen. "You okay with big dogs?"

"Labs? Oh, yes."

Tav addressed the dog. "Mialma, no jumping. You may greet Jen, but no jumping."

Mialma collapsed on her side and went belly-up. Jen laughed, knelt to rub the pup's tummy. "Good girl, Mialma."

A tall young man of about fifteen walked into the room. He hugged Tav. "Where's Mick?"

"He got into a fight."

"Lost, huh?"

"Yeah. He's at the apartment so Luke can watch him."

"Concussion?"

"Maybe."

The youngster shook his head. "Mick." He looked up and stuck out his hand. "I'm BB. Ben's brother. Until I think of something else."

Tav introduced the women. "Wendy, who works for Quinn. And her sister Jen." Tav eyed Wendy. "Smothers?"

"Actually, yes. I thought I'd throw the costume on yesterday to see if I could fool anyone. I didn't." She smirked.

Tav nodded. "You didn't."

Jen shook BB's hand. "Nice to meet you. Nice to meet someone not afraid to be associated with their brother."

Mialma disappeared into the depths of the house, then reappeared with a smaller youngster. Maybe eight. He was slight of build, so hard to tell his age. This had to be Ben. Mialma stood between Ben and the women. Ben didn't look at Wendy or Jen directly. He lowered his head, glanced up, glanced down, glanced up. Tav knelt beside him. "Ben, these are new friends. This is Wendy. She works with Quinn." He whispered, "He's her boss, so she can't say bad things about him."

Ben's eyes shone, and he grinned. He nodded one time emphatically. Then he stepped into Wendy's chest. Wendy peeked with confusion at Tav. He motioned for her to hug him. She nodded, hugged the boy, then crouched in front of him. "Hi, Ben. Nice to meet you."

Ben moved in front of Jen. Jen knelt also. "Hello, Ben. I'm Jen. I'm Wendy's sister. Her older sister. And her smarter sister."

Ben peeped from Wendy to Jen back to Wendy. She smiled at him, wrinkling her nose. Ben nodded to Jen, once only. Then he hugged her as well.

BB offered, "Drinks?"

Wendy shook her head. "No. We've still got to pick up my car."

BB turned to Tav. "Where's the bike?"

"Trash heap. I got sideswiped."

Ben grabbed Tav around the middle and held him tight. Tav laid his head on Ben's head. "It's okay, buddy. I'm fine. I wore my helmet and my jacket. Only the bike is hurt."

Ben didn't let go. He whispered sounds only Tav could hear. Tav nodded. "Yeah. The bike is ruined. Which is why I don't let anyone ride with me. I don't want anyone to get hurt if I have an accident."

Ben nodded once. He gazed around the kitchen, then head-butted Tav. Tav chewed the side of his cheek. The man thought a moment, then bent to look directly into the child's eyes. "Mick is over at Luke's. Your dad hit his head while we were in Hanford. He's fine like I am. But we wanted to make sure he stayed safe. So we told him he had to remain with Luke for the night. You can call him later if you want."

Ben stared at the floor. BB picked a burl of wood out of a bowl and handed it to the boy. "Ben, buddy, hold this. Dad is fine. He'll be here tomorrow. Okay? We'll see him tomorrow." Tav indicated the wood. "That came from the Knight's first camping trip together. Quinn used it to calm Ben. Micah kept it for future use. The chip's come in handy more than once. Like now."

BB picked up the diminutive child and carried him to a refrigerator-size calendar on the wall. He set Ben down. "Show me today."

Ben pointed to the day with two boys' faces on it. "Right. Now show me tomorrow."

Ben pointed to the next day. BB handed him a marker. "Draw Dad coming home tomorrow."

Ben did a quick sketch of Micah's face. Wendy's jaw dropped. She stared at Tav. He nodded. "He's incredible. They used his sketches to put the bad guys in prison."

BB took the marker. "Good job. Since Tav will spend the night with us, what should we have for dinner?"

Ben ran to the pantry and grabbed Mac 'n Cheese. Tav crowed. "Yes! And chicken fingers. My favorites."

Ben smiled.

Wendy and Jen made their way out the door. Jen shook her head. "Amazing. All of them. Amazing. I want to be a knight."

Wendy nodded. "I know what you mean. Come on, let's get my car and get home. Then I can tell you about the other two."

Jen grinned. "I'll hold you to that."

* * *

Luke sat at his desk studying. Micah lay on the couch, studying the back of his eyelids. So the man said the last time Luke checked on him. The danger had probably passed. Mick could go home in the morning. At least, that's how Luke read the situation. He'd still wake his friend every two hours to make sure.

His phone pinged. *Know Grace, know peace. No Grace. No peace.*

Luke stared at the message from Chay. Was Grace missing now? He texted back. *How long?*

Twenty-four hours.

Call me.

When can.

Luke groaned. Micah opened his eyes. "Psych really tough?"

"No. Just got a text from Chay. Grace is missing."

Micah sat up abruptly. Luke watched the man jerk forward, then sit back slowly. Still feeling the effects, hmm? Mick paused. "Grace now? What did Chay say?"

"Grace has been gone about twenty-four hours. She's going to call me when she can."

Micah sat up more slowly. "I don't like this. First Quinn, now Grace? And someone after Tav? What's going on?"

Luke shook his head. "I don't know. Sounds like open season on Knights and their friends."

Micah scowled. "I think we should circle the wagons. Get your stuff. We're going to my place."

The man stood slowly. Luke hesitated, then nodded. "Right. The boys will be safer with all of us together."

"Let Tav know. I'll text Wendy. She'll want to be kept in the loop."

Luke sent the message to his brother. Tav texted back. *K.* Luke gathered some necessary items, picked up his books, and followed Micah out the door. He noted the man kept one elbow pressed close to his side. "You crack a rib?"

"I don't know. I could go to the ER. They'd take six

hours to do an X-ray to tell me it's cracked or broken, and they can't do anything about it. I'll live."

"Right." The two friends walked to Luke's 4X4, climbed in, and drove off.

Micah's phone rang. Luke watched him tilt his head, then nod. He held the phone so Luke could hear without putting it on speaker. "Mrs. Vaughn! It's been a long time since I've heard from you."

Luke's mom's voice filled with concern. "It took me forever to find you. But I remembered you used to do taxes, so I played a long shot and looked you up. And there I found your business on the internet." Her tone shifted. "Oh, Micky! I only just heard about Jeremiah being killed! I am so sorry. It's terrible. His poor parents. And those babies…how must they be feeling?"

Micah cringed visibly at the "Micky" but kept his tone civil. "I know, Mrs. Vaughn. We all feel Jeremiah's loss." Even hearing the words stung Luke.

Mrs. Vaughn continued her outburst. "I never got any details. I only heard it from Rachel Farley. She heard it from Mrs. Acosta, Jeremiah's sister-in-law. They are in a new Bible study, and the group discussed losing a family member. That's how Rachel found out about it. Rachel does my hair, and we were talking…"

Micah interrupted the monologue. "It's horrible, I know. We all miss him." He closed his eyes. Luke felt the pain.

"I know how tight you all were. But you weren't as close these last few years, were you? Do you know if Taylor and Lucas know about it?"

"They know." Luke wanted to shout, "We were there when it happened," but didn't. Some things were better left unsaid.

"Are you sure? I'd love to talk to them. Do you know

where they're living now?"

Luke exchanged narrow-eyed looks with Micah. Luke shook his head slowly for emphasis. Micah didn't lie. "I know where they are. But I'm not free to give out the information without talking to them first."

"I'm their mother. You can tell me."

"No, I can't. I'm sorry, Mrs. Vaughn. Tav and Luke have asked I not give out their address without permission."

"Oh, Micky. You know me. You practically lived at our house."

Micah closed his eyes. "I know. But that was a few years ago, and things have changed. Tav and Luke are adults, and I can't betray their confidence. I'll talk to them and see what they say." He did not add any assurances.

The noise of the speaker being covered rustled. After a moment, Mrs. Vaughn came back. "All right, Micky. Tell them...tell them all is forgiven, and we'd...I'd love to talk to them."

"I'll tell them."

The call disconnected. Micah glanced at Luke. "What do you think 'all is forgiven' means?"

"Not a thing. She didn't ask for our phone numbers. Only our address. Maybe that answers the question of who is after Tav."

"Why just Tav? And why after all this time?"

"No. I suspect our father found him first. His looks haven't changed since the last time they saw him."

Luke sported a well-trimmed beard and mustache. He'd also darkened his hair before trying out for the football team. He was far from the blond he'd been when his father beat him and threw him out in high school.

"Maybe he thought Tav was you."

"Could be. Still not sure of the why, unless..." Luke trailed off, then shook his head. "It's been six years. He's got

Addison. Why does it matter what we're doing?" Luke checked the rearview mirror for anyone following. No one.

"I would say we should have Quinn talk to him, but Quinn being gone is our first mystery."

"Followed by Grace disappearing."

"Yeah. We'll know more about her situation after Chay calls."

Micah's phone pinged. Wendy. *Call me.*

When back to my house. Twenty minutes.

K.

Micah sniffed. "Didn't take her long to pick up the lingo."

The drive home went without issue. Micah climbed out stiffly, trying to keep from moving his head. Luke noted. "You sure you're okay, Mick?"

"I was. Then we added you two to the endangered list, and now I'm not."

"There's still the ER."

"Yeah, and you know what you can do with that suggestion." The two men walked up the back steps. Mialma met them at the door, her tail wagging, but her seat on the floor. Micah ruffed her ears. "Good girl, Mialma. No jumps."

Luke patted his chest. "Here, Mialma. You can jump on me."

The lab happily complied and gave Luke a doggy hug. She woofed quietly, then raced to let the rest of the house know the master had come home.

Tav, BB, and Ben met Luke and Mick in the kitchen. Tav hugged his brother. "What's up?"

"Chay says Grace is unaccounted for. We thought we should all stay in one spot."

Mick nodded but carefully. Sort of a Ben "once only" nod. Only with less vigor. "Then I got a call from Mrs.

Vaughn asking for your address."

Tav led the way into the living room. "Oh, really? Must have been an interesting conversation."

"Well, you know." Mick sank into his recliner. Ben climbed on his lap and hugged him. Luke noted the boy treated Mick with extreme caution. Either someone told him Mick had been hurt, or the boy sensed it. Which was par for Ben. A human mood barometer.

Luke waited until everyone sat, then explained, "Mick and I are thinking our father is the one tailing and crashing you, Tav. My guess is he just figured out we're in school with Addison. He wants to put a stop to any possible interference."

Tav's eyes narrowed. "Warning shot across the bow?"

"I don't know. Did the guy who hit you stick around to apologize?"

"No, but he didn't try to run over me once he had me, either." Tav sat back in his chair for emphasis.

BB held up his hand. "Did he know you were still moving?"

Tav tilted his head. "Good point. I didn't exactly jump to my feet."

Luke nodded. "My thought is he—Dad—thinks you were me. He may be afraid I'm going to join the football team."

BB added, "Except you already are on the team."

"As 'E. L. Von.'"

BB shook his head. "It wouldn't take a genius to figure out your identity."

"Except our dad never had eyes for anyone except number one. Addison and I didn't exist while he worked with Tav. When Tav blew out his knee, Dad dropped him and focused on me. Addison was still non-existent. But with me and Tav gone, Addison becomes the single focus."

Tav tapped the table in front of him. "Except Addison isn't number one. He's second string. Correction, he's first string waiting for the other two first-stringers to graduate."

"Or crash and burn." Mick threw in the obvious.

Tav continued, "But you are a starting receiver. Two years now. You're starting to get headlines. Dad won't stand for Addison being upstaged."

"So far, he's not done anything about it. Unless Addison actually gets in a game, it won't matter."

BB held up his hand again. Ben copied BB's gesture. Mick smiled. "You don't have to raise your hand, either of you."

BB shrugged. "I don't want to break protocol."

"No protocol. Just throw out the questions." Luke noted a bit more color in Micah's face. Being home suited the man.

"What does all this have to do with Quinn and Grace?" BB queried the obvious.

"Nothing, and that's the problem. I don't think the two cases are related."

"What does Wendy think?"

"I don't know. When she calls, I'll ask her."

Mialma barked and raced to the backdoor. Luke heard the knock, then the door open. Milama's woofs meant she knew the intruder and was happy.

Heads tilted to see who would come in. Wendy stuck her head around the corner. "Is this conference of Knights open to interruption?"

Mick called, "Come on in."

Tav added, "If you dare. Mia is the only female in residence."

Ben stood, walked to Wendy's side, and hugged the woman. He took her hand and led her to a space on the couch. Then he shifted Tav over and made room for himself and her.

Wendy laughed. "I think Ben trusts me." She hugged the youngest Knight.

BB asked, "Do you trust us?" His eyes twinkled with mischief.

"Wouldn't be here if I didn't." Wendy leaned forward. "I figured if I heard things firsthand, it would save time and maybe confusion."

"You want something to drink while we kick nightmares around?"

"Coffee?"

Luke chuckled. "How strong do you like it? Mick makes a mean cup."

Tav echoed. "A mean cup. And he doesn't let anyone near his coffee pot."

Micah sneered at Tav. "I can share. When needed."

Wendy laughed. "I've been working with Quinn for eight months. I know about strong coffee. He's trained me well."

Micah waved his hand. "Go. Make coffee. Ben can show you where things are."

Ben jumped to his feet, caught Wendy's hand, and dragged her into the kitchen. Luke grinned. "Nice move, Mick. Ben really has come out of his shell."

They waited until Wendy called, "Does anyone else want any?"

"Yes, please." Micah, of course. Luke chuckled. The man's blood type was probably dark roast. A cup would keep Luke awake to study a little more. He called, "I'll take some. But I'll get mine. You don't have to serve me."

He started to rise but stopped as Wendy called, "I'll bring it. Ben pulled out a tray for me to use. Tav?"

"Oh, why not. Sure."

"BB?"

BB glanced at Micah, then shrugged. "I'll take one."

"Anyone need condiments?"

"Micah doesn't allow them." Luke eyed Mick for his response. None. Must be hurting more than he'd admit.

Wendy came in with a tray, five cups of coffee, and one cup of milk. Ben would not be left out of the drinking party. She distributed the beverages, then took her seat beside Ben.

Luke filled in the gaps. "On the way here, Micah got a call from our mom wanting our address. He deflected. But it tells me our dad is likely behind the tailing on Tav and possibly the sideswipe. I'm convinced he thinks it's me he's chasing."

Wendy's eyes narrowed. "What does any of this have to do with Grace being missing?"

"Nothing. That's the point. I think they're not related. Grace and Quinn disappearing are separate from Tav's issue."

"You think Quinn and Grace are connected?"

Luke continued in the lead. "You think an agent and an archeologist both disappearing would be?"

"Ordinarily, no. Except they know one another, and they both disappeared around the same time. Which makes it suspicious. I'm not big on believing in coincidences."

"But you will accept Tav's issue is separate?"

Wendy stared at the floor. She raised her head. "Tav?"

His brother shrugged. "I think the phone call from our mom says my issue is personal with the family. Not connected to Quinn. Until something else proves otherwise."

Wendy nodded. "Fine. Remind me what the problem is with the family that would make a father try to kill his son."

"I don't think he tried to have me killed. Maimed, maybe."

"And how does maiming you make things better?" Wendy's tone was incredulous.

Tav shook his head. "You have to understand the dynamics. Dad wanted an NFL quarterback. He expected me to fill the bill. Luke is two years younger than me and spent his life playing receiver to my arm. We were on track until I blew my knee out my junior year. Spent the next months rehabbing it, only to blow it out again my senior season. Dad discarded me and tried getting Luke to take my place."

Luke added darkly, "Which I wouldn't do. I like being a receiver. I've been catching since I was three. When I refused to step up, Dad beat me and threw me out."

Tav continued, "And pinned his hopes on our youngest brother, Addison. Who's three years behind Luke."

Wendy eyed Tav. "After he threw Luke out, you took on Luke to raise."

"*We* took on Luke. The Knights did. I'd moved out of the house and had a job and a one-bedroom apartment. Luke moved in with me. Dad let Luke keep his 'legal residence' for school, but we paid for everything. Which is old history. The problem now may be we're in school with Addison, and Dad is afraid we'll somehow show him up or ruin his chances at stardom."

"He knows Luke is on the team?"

Wendy sat back and sipped her coffee. Luke decided he'd do the same. He swallowed the first mouthful. His eyes flew wide. It would keep him awake through tomorrow's classes. And practice after. And maybe even tomorrow night's study.

Luke set the cup down. "I'm on the team, but under an alias and in disguise. The coach knows who I am and has agreed to let me stay incognito. I'm trying to get close to Addison to see if I can establish a relationship with him." His voice darkened. "Addison needs someone to help him. He's self-destructing. I know he's drinking. Heavily. I want to be there for him if I can. And if he'll let me."

"How does getting close to Addison help Tav?"

Tav shrugged. "Now I know what's happening, and I can handle it. I can call our mom and fill her in on our plans. None of which will involve showing up Addison. Maybe it helps."

"If it doesn't?"

"I'll deal with it then."

Micah lifted his coffee in salute to Wendy. "You have learned well, Grasshopper. That's good coffee."

"Thank you, Sensei." Wendy smiled. She lost the expression quickly. "What of Quinn and Grace?"

Luke's phone pinged. "It's Chay." He answered it. "Chay, I'm putting you on speaker. We have the Knights plus Quinn's intern here."

Chay's voice was tense. "Mom disappeared yesterday. She's been working on a site in the Santa Clara mountains. Her assistant said she had vanished. Poof. Gone. No notice, no warning, just gone. I've been trying to call her, but her phone is off. I need help."

Luke assured her, "We'll get someone there. Have you called the police?"

"She's an adult. She has a right to disappear. They'll put out a 'Be on the lookout for' BOLO. I talked to some of the students she's working with, and they gave me mixed messages about how she left. Not exactly 'poof.' It's all messed up. The police are still trying to decide if there's a case or not."

"Where are you?

"I'm at school. I've got finals, or I'd be in the mountains looking."

"Right."

Micah offered, "I can be there tomorrow."

Three voices voted him down. "No!"

He amended the statement. "Give me three days. I'll be there." He glared around the room.

Luke knew better than to argue. At least now. "We'll find her, Chay."

"I have to go. Love you all."

Chay disconnected the call. Luke put his phone away. Wendy eyed him. "Does Grace have a habit of disappearing?"

"No. She's very dependable. And she keeps in contact with Chay. They're very close."

Tav added, "Now. Since Magary."

"Lots of changes since Magary," Luke agreed.

Wendy eyed Micah. "How do you think you're going to find Grace?"

"I don't. I think I'm going to go and ask questions. Nose around. Someone should know something. No one 'poof' disappears. Someone knows. I'll find out who."

"And who stays with the boys?"

Micah's tone became aggravated. "Look, Luke and Tav have school. They can't just cut out and go. They can both stay here, which keeps them safe from the attackers. I'm the only one who can come and go. I'm self-employed. No commitments."

Tav drawled, "Shouldn't you ask BB about it? Or maybe Luke and me?"

Micah closed his eyes. Luke leaned forward. "Mick. You're not thinking straight. Give yourself a day or two. We'll work this out, trust me. The world doesn't rest on you alone. Go get some rest. We'll call it a night, and we can talk again in the morning."

Mick nodded. "Okay. Agreed. Meeting tabled until the morning."

Wendy finished her coffee, then stood. "I'll check back with you tomorrow. In the meantime, I'll see what I can find. Maybe I can pull some records about the dig site."

Luke pushed his coffee aside. "Thanks for coming, Wendy." He walked her to the back door.

The woman lowered her voice. "You think Micah is okay? Really okay?"

Luke nodded. "Yeah. Mick's tough. He'll be better in the morning. Call him in the afternoon, and he should be coherent." He grinned. "He can warm the leftover coffee and be just fine. It should cure anything." Including sleep for the next twelve hours. He didn't add the comment.

Wendy ducked her head. "Thanks. I'm getting to like you guys. I don't want anything to happen to any of you." She smiled and walked out and away.

Mialma woofed softly. Luke patted her head. "I agree. She's a good one. A little old for me, but hey...we'll keep her."

Mialma woofed again and followed Luke back to the living room.

* * *

MONDAY

Micah watched a young man in blue jeans and a biker jacket climb out of a car in front of Micah's house. The man wore a ballcap with a ponytail sticking out behind. He had his right arm in a sling. Micah noticed a serious bruise on the right side of the man's face. Dark glasses covered his eyes. Micah waited at the door until the man reached the porch, then opened to him. "Can I help you, man?"

"I'm looking for Micah Andres." He motioned with his head toward the wounded arm and held up his left hand.

Micah smiled. "Come in, Wendy. Sorry, Wendell. Nice disguise. You're getting better."

Wendy walked into the house. "I didn't think I'd fool you. But maybe someone who hasn't seen me before?"

Micah shut the door. "Yeah. The sling is a nice touch."

"Keeps me from having to shake hands. And the bruise draws the focus away from the eyes."

"It looks very realistic." Micah gave her the side eye. "That is make-up, right?"

Wendy smirked. "Of course. I'm not into self-mutilation."

"Me neither."

Tav strode into the living room from the back of the house. "No, you let other people do it to you." He studied

Wendy a moment. "Nice. Very nice. You've made yourself taller."

"Lifts in the shoes." She motioned outside. "And I brought a seat for the car so when I ride along, I look the same size as the driver."

Micah grinned. "A booster seat."

"Watch it, mister." Wendy scowled at Micah.

He held up both hands. "I apologize." He tilted his head toward the street. "We should get going. It's a three-hour drive. If we want to talk to anyone, we need to get there before they all scatter."

"Right." She waved at Tav. "See you this evening."

"Drive safe."

Micah looked out the front door. A car pulled up and parked. He groaned. "Ms. Phelps."

Tav's head jerked sharply. "This early?"

"Must want to catch the boys before they go to school."

Wendy eyed Micah. "Does she do this often? It feels like harassment."

"Feels like it to me, too. But they're 'only looking out for the children.'" Grr. Micah put on his best face. "Good morning, Ms. Phelps."

She tilted her head to the side to look at his face. "Good morning? What happened to you?"

Micah waved her in. "You remember Mr. Smothers."

Wendell raised his one good hand. "Ms. Phelps."

Her eyes narrowed. "Mr. Smothers. Did you and Mr. Andres have a disagreement?"

Micah answered for the agent. "No. I...ran into a friend of the friend we're missing. He wanted me to deliver a message." Truth. Then you don't have to remember what you lied about and in what order. "Old Navy-Marine friends."

Ms. Phelps raised her eyebrows but said only, "I see." What she saw remained unspoken. She cleared her throat. "I wanted to catch the boys before they left." She nodded. "Just checking on things."

Micah nodded. "I know you are." He went to the back and knocked on BB's door. BB came out dressed for school. "What's up, Mick?"

"Ms. Phelps is here checking on our family life. Probably wants to make sure you're getting a balanced breakfast."

"So, no ice cream?"

"Please."

BB smiled. "Gotcha. You want me to get the little guy?"

"I'll get him. Why don't you show the woman what you have available for breakfast."

"Will do."

BB went to the front of the house. Micah tapped on Ben's door. "Buddy? You up and moving?"

The door opened. Ben stood dressed in jeans and an inside-out button-up shirt he had managed to button. Must have put it on over his head. What a kid.

Micah rubbed the boy's head. "Morning, Ben. How are you this morning?"

Ben hugged Micah. The boy stepped back, held his arms out, and did a full circle for Micah to see he was dressed and ready for anything. Micah grinned. "Good job. Now, we have a visitor. Ms. Phelps is here to see you get a good breakfast before you go to school. Can we show her you know how to choose healthy foods?"

Ben nodded once. He lifted his head and marched to the kitchen.

Ms. Phelps gagged on a cup of coffee. Micah swallowed his smirk. "We like our coffee strong."

For once, she broke character. "That stuff will kill you!"

She eyed BB. "You don't drink this, do you?"

BB shook his head. "Never. Ever."

He lied, but Micah would let it pass. Just this once, of course. Honesty. Integrity. Self-preservation. One for all and all for…

Ben went to the refrigerator and pulled out the milk. The white milk. He opened the pantry to show Ms. Phelps the variety of cereals available: Raisin Bran, granola, and whole-wheat flakes. No sugar here. He made his selection, took it to the table, and sat. Micah set the table for him. Bowl, spoon, napkin. Ben poured his own cereal (a healthy portion) and milk. He took his first spoonful, then looked at Ms. Phelps. He smiled with his mouth full.

Ms. Phelps laughed in return. "Nice choices, Ben. You're eating healthy this morning." She eyed him. "Do you eat like this every morning?"

Micah instructed, "Chew and swallow. Then you can answer."

Ben exaggerated chewing and swallowing. Once he finished, he jumped and went to the pantry. He pulled out a waffle maker and showed it to Ms. Phelps. He put it back, pulled out a panini maker, put it back, pulled out a frying pan.

Ms. Phelps nodded. "I see. Lots of different kinds of breakfast. Very good. What's your favorite?"

The waffle maker made a repeat appearance. Ms. Phelps laughed. "I agree. Waffles are wonderful. Do you eat anything else with your waffles?"

Ben dug into the refrigerator and pulled out the bacon. He held it up, put it away, and pulled out the eggs. He carefully held one to show the CPS agent. She laughed. "May I come over the next time you have waffles?"

Ben placed the egg back gingerly, closed the fridge, then walked over and hugged the woman. Ms. Phelps hugged him in return. She eyed Micah and whispered, "He's a great kid." She cleared her throat. "I see you're doing a great job teaching your young men about proper nutrition. Thanks for allowing me to visit this morning."

Micah walked her to the door. "I appreciate you caring for BB and Ben. I only want the best for both of them. They saved my life, and I want to spend the rest of it giving back to them."

Ms. Phelps smiled. "One of these days, I'd like to hear the full story." She pointed to his face. "Take care of yourself, Mr. Andres."

She walked to her car, climbed in, and drove off. Micah sighed. He waited until the car disappeared around the corner, then led Wendy out the door to Luke's 4X4 and slid into the driver's seat. Swapping cars was as natural as swapping houses. It made sense to take the all-terrain vehicle to the mountains. Better than the van. Micah waited until Wendy settled in with her booster seat, then nosed the vehicle into traffic.

Wendy chuckled. "Between your bruises and mine, we look like someone did a number on us."

"Tell them to imagine what the other guys must look like." Micah checked to make sure no one followed them. Just in case they had their assumptions wrong about the cases. And who had done what to who.

"Better than us."

"Truth, but we don't need to say that."

Wendy sneered.

They drove the three hours to Mount Diablo State Park, where Dr. Grace Painter had been last seen. She taught newbies the fine art of archeological sciences in real time. On the last group camping trip, she told Micah and the Knights how she loved the excitement new students demonstrated when they made their first find.

Maybe one of them would lead Micah and Wendy to find Grace. He could hope. Micah located the name of the assistant at the project, Rand Leisch. He'd worked with Grace for the past two years. Micah parked the car and headed to the site manager's tent.

According to his name tag, Rand Leisch looked up from a dust and dirt-covered folding table. "Can I help you?"

Micah extended his hand. "Micah Andres. I'm looking for Dr. Grace Painter. I understand she's working here."

Leisch shrugged. "She was. She left a day or so ago."

"Left? To where?"

"I don't know. She didn't say. She packed her things, told me goodbye, and took off."

Wendell pointed to a grimy sedan. "That's her car, isn't it?"

Leisch frowned. "Yeah. She left with someone else."

"Who?"

"Don't know. I didn't see them."

"'Them?' As in multiple people?" Micah leaned forward over the table.

"As in, I don't know who she left with. I wasn't there to see it." Leisch ignored Micah.

"You said she told you goodbye." Wendell pointed out the discrepancy in his story.

Leisch's face darkened. "Are you police?"

Micah raised an eyebrow. "Do we need to be? We're looking for a friend. Is there a problem?"

Leisch shook his head. "No. No. I've got fifteen students to supervise. I can't do it and answer questions all morning."

Wendell motioned to the dig area. "This is all for practice anyhow, right? Summer school camp training. There's no chance of finding anything earth-shattering, correct?"

Leisch shrugged. "No. But we still want to maintain a professional air." He led Wendell and Micah to where students had cordoned off four-by-four sections of earth. Many dutifully scraped at layers of dirt, sand, and rock. Others recorded what they found. Still others cleaned the finds. The site appeared to be an authentic dig.

Micah asked, "Has this area been salted with these artifacts? Specifically, so students have pieces to find?"

"Yes. This area has been excavated many times before. We only use it for practice."

A teen, maybe fifteen or so, looked up. His face beamed with excitement. "The bottle we found, though. You said it was unexpected."

Leisch all but patted the boy on his head. "Yes, Peter. That was new. We still haven't verified its origins. But it was interesting."

Wendell asked, "Did you find the bottle before or after Dr. Painter disappeared?"

Leisch scowled. "She didn't disappear. She left. Of her own accord."

"Right. Of course." Wendell raised his eyebrows at Micah behind Leisch's back. Micah raised his in return.

Micah cleared his throat. "We'll let you get back to supervising. Thank you for your time, Mr. Leisch."

They walked back to the car. Wendell kicked the tire. "He's lying. He knows more."

"Of course he does. But why hide it?" Micah laid his hand on the door handle.

"I don't know. I'd like to poke around and talk to some of the students before we leave."

"Who said we're leaving?" Micah motioned for Wendell to climb in. Wendell's eyes narrowed, but he complied. Micah drove the 4X4 to the far side of the site, away from the students. Then he parked. The two climbed out. Micah eased the door closed. Wendell followed suit. Ducking low, they walked back toward the site, approaching it from the rear. Micah checked the tents for signage, looking for names to identify whose tent was whose. At last, he located the one marked "Dr. Grace Painter."

Micah and Wendell slipped in. Stifling heat met them. A cot, blankets, suitcases, and duffle bags littered the area. When Grace disappeared, she left everything behind. Micah and Wendell exchanged glances. Grace's computer sat on a makeshift desk. Wendell turned it on. He tapped the keys, then whispered, "Guess a password."

"Knights."

Wendell shook his head. "Guess again. And not octagon, either."

Micah thought hard. "Mercy."

Wendell typed. "Bingo. Good guess." He gave him a quizzical look.

"Easy guess." Micah shrugged.

Wendell went back to the computer for information. "Her last sign-on was Wednesday."

"The day before she disappeared."

"No notes or Word documents to detail anything. No suspicious emails."

Wendell worked a few more minutes. Micah searched for a camera or other recording device that could shed light on the disappearance. Nothing. Wendell completed his survey. "Spreadsheets all look innocuous."

An excited shout sounded from the site. Wendell's eyes flared. "That's not a chip of pottery."

Micah and Wendell slipped out of the tent and wove around to see what caused the excitement. A student chattered, "A bone! It's a bone!"

Leisch ran to join the crowd and shouted curt orders. "Back! Everyone out of the hole. Now!"

The student pointed with the trowel. "There. Right there. And I didn't move it, either."

Someone in the crowd muttered, "No one said there'd be bones."

Leisch examined the area the student indicated. "You're right. It's a bone. Okay, everyone, back up. We're shutting down."

More mutters, not all of them happy. "Why? What's going on? Wasn't the bone planted there?"

Leisch pulled out his phone. "We'll need to call in a professional team. We can't have students disturbing possible human remains." The man spoke into his phone. "We need a forensic team at the Diablo site. Right. Bone. Maybe human. Soon as you can. We'll cover the area with a tarp for now."

Wendell nudged Micah. He kept his voice at a whisper. "He didn't put it on speaker. And Leisch didn't actually punch in any numbers. He just pulled it out. He didn't make a call."

A chill ran through Micah. He shook it off. The ground was too hard for Grace to be buried there. This had to be something else. Something Leisch wasn't expecting.

Leisch waved to the group. "I'm sorry, people. That's a wrap. We'll arrange to bring you back another time to finish the camp. But for now, go pack your stuff. This dig is done."

"Why?" "Why can't we continue?" "Can't we stay and watch?"

"Because we will have professionals here who'll need your space. We'll require all the tents. Go pack."

Fifteen students grumbled and complied with the edict. Wendell and Micah stole between the tents and back to the car. "We need to get a safe distance away, then come back after the others leave."

Wendell nodded. "First a bottle, now a bone. This is off

here. Way off."

"Call Tav and let him know we'll be late."

Wendell tapped in the number. "Tav. We've found some loose ends. Not sure what they mean, but we're staying to check it out. How are things there?"

Tav came back. "All good here. We're having pizza tonight. You want me to save you some?"

Micah leaned over and spoke into the phone. "With BB, there are never any leftovers. Don't worry about it."

"Good enough. Stay safe."

Wendell finished the call. "Out."

Micah grinned. "That was very Quinn of you."

Wendell chuckled. "Guess it was."

They waited until the cars thinned out and stopped leaving, then stole back to the dig site. Two cars remained. One belonged to Grace. The other, Micah assumed, belonged to Leisch. Micah hid his vehicle as best he could, coasting in behind rocks and trees. He and Wendell crept through the tents and moved silently to position themselves for a view of the exposed area.

Leisch worked alone. He scraped, dug, and tipped around the bone, exposing more and more remains. A hand emerged. The man continued digging, carefully uncovering the arm, the shoulder, and finally, a skull. He lifted it and crowed. "Gotcha. I knew it. You'll pay now."

Wendell stepped out of his hiding spot. "Who'll pay? And for what?"

Leisch dropped the skull and spun around to face his accuser. "What are you doing here?"

"Who will pay for what? Why didn't you call the forensic team?" Wendell moved closer. "You expected to find this body, didn't you? Friend of yours?"

Leisch stood. "I don't have to answer to you. You're not the police."

"Never said I was." Wendell pointed to the skeletal remains. "You didn't bury him here. But you were looking for him. From the advanced decay, he's been here for at least six months. Given the compacted condition of the soil, I'd say it's been several years."

Wendell turned to Micah. "Can you think of any cold cases in this area in the last five years or more?"

Micah shrugged. "Not that I can remember." He closed in to be near Wendell. Just in case.

Wendell smiled without mirth. "What did you need the students for? Cover more territory? Get more eyes looking? You must have known the general area, though. Maybe you were in on it but lost the body?"

Leisch stepped out of the cordoned area and put his hands in his pockets. Micah stepped to the side and slightly in front of Wendell. If his instincts were right... Leisch pulled a gun and trained it on Wendell. "You ask too many questions."

Micah glanced at Wendell. The man dropped his hand to his side and waved Micah off. No heroics. Fine. Go with it.

Leisch motioned for Micah and Wendell to walk ahead of him. "Go. Keep moving." A darkened space lay ahead in the rocks. Cave? Tunnel? Micah didn't know. They were about to find out.

Wendell hesitated, but Leisch waved the gun. "Stop right there." He pointed to Micah. "Empty your pockets. Slowly."

Micah pulled out his keys and phone. He dropped them on the ground in front of him.

Leisch ordered, "Kick them here. And no stunts."

Micah flipped the phone with his foot, then the keys. Both landed near Leisch. The man kept the gun pointed at Wendell's middle as he knelt and picked them up. He pitched the phone, then the keys as far as he could throw them down the hillside.

Leisch motioned to Wendell. "Now yours." Wendell complied, emptying his jeans and jacket pockets of their contents. With his arm in the sling, it took longer to get to all of them. Keys and cell phone. Leisch disposed of them as he had Micah's. Then he pointed into the dark. "Move. Go." Micah edged into the blackness. Leisch turned on his phone's flashlight. "Keep going."

Wendell ran his left hand along the side of the tunnel. "Gunshots will really echo in here. Could probably hear them all the way to the fire tower."

Leisch sneered. "I'm willing to take the chance." He pointed the light deeper into the gloom, past several openings. Micah counted *Two left. One right. One left. Two...center? Right?* It was hopeless. He prayed Wendell had a better memory for a way out.

Praying. That's what he needed to do. *Lord, I know You're there. The darkness is as light to You. Help us. Keep us alive if it pleases You. It would please me, Father. Being with You would be best, I know. Your will, Lord.*

They walked for fifteen minutes or more. They walked, Micah prayed. And the darkness grew more stifling.

Leisch called, "Ten more steps. Go."

Wendell called out, "One. Two. Three." He walked forward, Micah behind him. At ten, he turned to face Leisch. "Is this far enough? Can you shoot us now?"

Two flashes of light exploded as Leisch fired his pistol. He swept around a corner. Then the blackness descended to envelop everything. A darkness so deep it could be felt. Micah closed his eyes.

Wendell whispered, "Listen."

Nothing. They couldn't hear anything. Once around the bend, Leisch could light his way, but Micah and Wendell would never see it.

Micah reached out and felt until he touched Wendell's arm. "Are you hit?"

"Grazed my middle. I'll be fine."

"How bad are you bleeding?" Wendell would have to tell by feel. The same as Micah.

"I said he grazed it. It's a cut. Not deep. It's fine. What about you?"

"He caught my thigh. It's not bleeding too bad."

Wendy demanded, "Give me your shirt."

Micah complied but grumbled, "Why is it always my shirt?"

"You want me to take off mine?"

"No. No." Even in the dark, it was a bad idea. Wendy worked to wrap a makeshift bandage around Micah's thigh, leaving him to position it. He tied it off himself, then reached out and gripped Wendy's arm. "We have to stay together."

Wendy snapped, "Why? So we can die together?"

"Versus dying alone? Yeah." Micah slid his hand to grasp Wendy's hand. "At least to my mind."

A chuckle. "If I were a guy, would you hold my hand, too?"

Micah nodded, then said, "Yep. Here and now, yep."

They sank against the wall.

Wendy asked, "Any suggestions?"

"Wait until the moon comes up. Maybe it shows us an exit."

"That's what you got? Wait for the moon?" Wendy sounded aghast.

Micah shrugged. "What do you have?"

"Follow the wall to the first break."

"Then what?"

"Guess."

Micah mirrored her tone. "That's what you've got?"

"No dumber than your idea." Her voice snapped.

"Tell you what. We'll follow your plan until we find moonlight. Which won't be for another few hours. Until then, I'll hope for something more tangible."

"You do that, Andres."

"I will, Smothers."

They held hands and slid along the wall together.

* * *

Luke watched his teammates throw each other in the swimming pool. Spray each other with sodas. Knock each other around. Generally, be the football jerks they were at a party. He ducked and dodged to avoid the jocularity, which could devolve into injury, while keeping his eyes on Addison Vaughn.

Two of the female members of the cheer squad passed him. "Hey, E.L., how's it going?"

He saluted them with his soda. "Going fine."

The short redhead, uh, Rena, smiled at him. "Are you ever going to tell us what E. L. stands for?"

"Extremely Lucky to be here." Luke deflected the attention. He slipped closer to his brother. He'd seen the flask Addison had hidden. And how often the younger man went to the contents. Addison was drunk. Or would be. Luke needed to intervene and soon.

He moved over to stand in his brother's orbit. Addison regaled a squad member with tales of his athletic prowess. The girl fawned over him. "That's incredible. Why don't we leave this party and find one of our own?"

Luke took the girl by the arm. "Addison isn't going anywhere but home. He'll catch up with you tomorrow."

She glared at Luke, but he pointed. "Coach is looking for you."

The girl spun her head, and Luke caught Addison's shoulder. "Come on, man, I need to get you out of here before Coach sees you."

Addison slurred, "Why? Afraid he'll tell my dad? Cut me from the team? Who cares?"

"Don't care about the team. Don't care about your dad. Only care about you not screwing up your life. Let's go."

Addison stared at Luke. "You're…you're…"

"E.L. Von. Receiver. Let's get you out of here."

Addison shook his head. "You look like someone I should know."

"I have that kind of face. Come on, man. Let's go."

Addison let himself be led outside and into Micah's van. *Good thing he's not a mean drunk.*

Addison snuck another few sips while they drove away from the party. "Where are we going?"

"Somewhere you can sleep it off, and no one sees you." Luke checked in the rearview mirror for anyone following him. Paranoia. Of course, Luke wouldn't put it past his dad to be shadowing Addison. And mistake Luke's concern for malfeasance.

But where to take him? Too many mementos at the apartment. And Tav was at Micah's. Most everyone Luke knew was on the team, and rumors would spread. Luke called Tav. "Hate to do this, brother, but can you go home? I've got Addison, and he needs a place to crash."

Silence on the other end. "Why?"

"Guess."

"Gotcha. Sure. I'll take my stuff and scram. I leave it to you to explain to Ben about Addison."

Luke noted headlights in his mirror. He changed lanes. So did they. "Thanks, brother." Explaining Addison to Ben would be the least of his worries.

Addison slurred, "You got a brother? I got two of 'em."

"Yeah? Who?"

"Taylor. I used to call him Tav, but Mom gets upset and demands we all call him Taylor." Addison snorted. "Dad doesn't like him. Dad doesn't like anyone."

Luke turned a corner. So did the lights. He turned again. Followed. "Your dad likes you, though. Right?"

Again the snort. "As long as I'm playing football. He can't wait until I'm the starter. I've heard him talking about knocking off Henri and Blake."

The two starters. That would be about right. "No one would do that. He was joking, right?"

"He gets…mean." Addison sipped his courage. "He hit Mom once. I told him if he did it again, I'd call the police. Then he hit me. But as long as he's not hitting Mom, it doesn't matter."

Luke scowled. "It matters, Addison. No one has a right to hit someone else."

"He's Dad. It gives him the right. So he says, anyhow. Says he owns me. He could have tossed me aside like he did my brothers. But he knew he could make a quarterback out of me. I owe him."

Luke doubled back, caught the freeway, and accelerated. The headlights dropped back but continued on the same path as Luke. "That's how you want to play, huh?"

Addison looked at him. "What? Play what?"

"There's someone following us. He wants to play games."

Addison turned to look behind him. "Following us? Who? Why?" He jerked his head around to stare wide-eyed at Luke. "You think it's my dad?"

Luke didn't answer. He exited the freeway, slipped under the overpass, and waited with his lights off.

Addison stared hard out the window to watch. The tail passed them and drove on down the highway. Luke kept his lights off and jumped back on the freeway. He hit his lights as soon as he reached highway speed.

Addison glanced at him. "Why do you know how to do that?"

"Practice." Luke decided to change the subject. "I'm gonna take you to a friend's house so you can sleep it off. His name is Micah, but he's not home. His kids are, though, so try to keep the noise down."

Addison leaned back against the seat. "I know a guy named Micah. He was a friend of my brother. My oldest brother." He closed his eyes and mumbled. "A good guy. Called him Mick. He let me hang around with him. So did my brothers." The mumbles got softer. "I love my brothers. I did. Wish I knew where they were."

Luke whispered, "I'll bet they miss you, too."

Addison snored. Luke shook his head and checked his mirror. Nothing. He drove to Mick's.

Tav hadn't left yet. He met Luke at the car. "Figured you might need some help getting him in the house."

"Figured right." Together they lifted Addison out of the car, and with one on each side of him, they half-carried, half-dragged the younger man into the house and into the bedroom at the rear of the house. They dumped him on the bed, took off his shoes, then threw a blanket over him. Luke and Tav slipped out, closing the door behind them.

"Thanks, Tav. What word from Mick?"

"None, and I'm getting worried. Nothing from Wendy, either."

"Not good." Luke scowled.

"His 'FindMyBuds' app was still moving last time I checked. We'll give it 'til the morning, then we can panic. Get some rest. You've got a test in the morning." All the Knights had it on their phones. It was a way to keep track of each other. But only in an emergency. Knights's rules:

Emergencies only. No snooping.

They hugged briefly, then Tav left the house, riding home on his new, used motorcycle. Luke debated whether to knock on BB's door or wait until the morning to tell the teen what had happened. He regarded his phone. Eleven p.m. He'd wait. BB was probably still awake, but Luke would give him his privacy. And his sleep. After all, Tav and Luke were interchangeable as guardians. It didn't matter which of them stayed with the boys so long as someone did.

Luke stretched out on the couch and kicked off his shoes. Mialma jumped up beside him and snuggled her way close to his chest. He grinned. "Sure, pup. Make yourself at home. Since it is your home. I'm the intruder." He looked at her. "Nice bark, by the way, when we came in."

Mialma gave the lightest of "woofs" and nudged Luke with her muzzle. Luke laughed. "Right. You know me. No sense playing guard when I'm a regular here." He roughed her ears. "Good night, girl." Luke put his arm over his eyes and slept.

* * *

In the caverns, Micah took the lead. He and Wendy skimmed the wall until they reached the first opening. They had to bend to enter. The arch felt wide enough to go through side-by-side. But still no light.

"Which way?"

Wendy cleared her throat. "Keep following the wall. If we run in circles, we're no worse off."

Micah led to the right. He slipped his foot ahead and followed with his hand. Foot. Hand. Foot. Hand. Foot.

He'd counted a thousand feet when his foot clinked. He stopped. "Did you hear the noise?"

"I heard it. Sounds like glass."

So as not to lose contact with one another, they knelt

together. Micah felt around until his hand encountered a solid article. Solid and round and flat on the bottom. It tapered to the top. "A bottle. It's a bottle."

"Wonder if it matches the one they found at the dig site?"

"What do we do with it? If we leave it here, we'll never find it again. If we take it, we've contaminated a crime scene."

"Except we don't know if there has been a crime. Could have been kids with beer. Could have been adults with beer. We don't know."

"In this dark, we'll never know. What do we do, Wendell?" Micah appealed to Wendy's official persona.

"Take it with you. Try not to wipe off any prints."

"How do you suggest I do that?"

"Give it to me. I'll carry it in the sling. I forgot my arm isn't really hurt." Wendy took the bottle. Micah heard her rustling around until she said, "Okay. Let's keep going."

They walked another thousand feet. Clink. Another bottle. It joined Wendy's stash. Micah moved forward a hundred feet and hit another unknown object. It gave way as he tapped it. "Stop. I don't think this one's a bottle. It's more solid but moveable."

"And down..." Wendy knew the drill. They knelt. Micah reached out with his hand and felt in front of him. He muddled around until he could identify the object. "It's a boot."

"What?"

"A boot. Like a biker's boot. Large, from the feel of it."

"Pass it to me."

Micah grabbed hold of it. The top seemed stuck, but he yanked the footwear, which came free. He passed the item to Wendy. "Here."

"I need both hands."

Micah slid his foot so he could feel hers. There was no way he would lose direct connection.

Wendy maneuvered next to him, bumping his thigh. The bullet wound burned. Micah groaned through gritted teeth. Wendy muttered, "Sorry."

"Forget it."

A long silence ensued.

"Mick." Wendy's voice sounded terse.

"What is it?"

"There's a bone in this boot."

Micah nearly jerked away from her. "What?"

"There's a bone in this boot. A leg bone from the feel of it."

Silence.

"Mick? Did you hear me?"

"Oh."

"That's it? That's all you got is 'Oh'?"

"That's all that's coming out. Wendy, what are we doing here?"

"Solving murders, apparently. Or deaths, anyhow."

"No. No. We're here looking for Grace. We are not looking for dead bodies."

"Well, we got 'em. And I need suggestions of what to do next." She stopped. Her voice became fierce. "I am not carrying a bone around."

"I wouldn't suggest it."

"Feel around the ground and see what else you can find."

"I'm not feeling around for bones! What if I find them? Then what?" Panic rose in his voice.

"Calm down, Mick. I thought you wanted to be a pirate. Pirates do this all the time."

"Which is why we're Knights and not pirates. Wendy, I can't feel around for bones. I can't. What if..."

Micah drew in a deep breath. "Hang on to my foot. Don't let go." Micah stretched out on his stomach and began feeling along the opening.

Yes, there were bones. Lots of them. *The leg bone connected to the knee bone. Knee bone connected to the thigh bone...* Micah shuddered. He felt shreds of material. A metal medallion around the skeleton's neck. A skull. With hair. Short, wavy hair.

Micah jerked his hand back and cupped it at his waist. He shook both hands off, trying to rid himself of the sensation.

Wendy demanded, "What's going on? What did you find?"

"The skull. He's all here. The whole skeleton." Micah rubbed his hands in the dirt and sat back next to Wendy. "Okay, boss. Now what?" He shuddered.

"We have to mark this somehow. We have to. We can't leave him and never find him again."

"What do you suggest?"

Wendy's voice echoed defeat. "I don't know. I don't."

"He is wearing a medallion. You want to take it?"

"Yes. No. Leave it. We'll get it when we come back."

Micah and Wendy sat side-by-side in the dark. How long they sat, he didn't know. He guessed that it had to be getting dark outside. Maybe matching the darkness in the tunnels. Their only hope was light from above. That there would be cracks in the ceiling or roof or whatever the "up top" was. He prayed it so, anyhow.

Eventually, the darkness went from black to gray to pale. Light beamed enough to get a bearing. Together Micah and Wendy stood. Wendy laid the boot with its owner. In the dimness, she patted the footwear and promised, "We're coming back. We are."

Micah asked, "Which way do you want to go?"

"Left."

Lord? You provided the light. Which way is out of here?

Go right. Follow your right hand.

Micah shook his head. "Right. The Lord says go right."

"'The Lord said.' An invisible, imaginary deity said go right, so you want to go right?"

"He's not imaginary. He is Lord of my life, and yes, I trust Him. He gave us the light, and He'll lead us out. We need to go right."

"And that's the guess you're betting our lives—yours and mine—on?"

"Yes." No hesitation. "What are you betting your guess on?"

Wendy paused. "Intuition."

"So you are God."

"No. Yes. That's not…I mean…I don't know what I mean." Wendy blustered.

Micah played his ace. He hoped. "If I told you I wanted to play a hunch, you'd go with me, right? But because I said God told me, you want to kick against me."

Wendy remained silent. "Okay, fine. We'll go right. And see where it leads."

"And see where God leads." He packed all the conviction he had into the words.

"We'll see."

Your lead, Lord.

They walked, led by Micah's right hand. He counted steps carefully. Memorized each turn. Their skeletal friend deserved Micah's utmost attention. And Micah would give it to him.

Time passed, and the light dimmed and went out. Micah continued to lead, feeling along the wall. Wendy didn't fight him. Yet. Scripture in Isaiah filled his mind. *The man who has to walk in darkness, who has nothing to light his way, let him trust in the Name of the Lord. Let him rely entirely on his God. Even in the dark.*

I'm trusting You, Lord.

Another few minutes and the light reappeared. Except this time, as they came around a bend in the corridor, it came full force. A spotlight of whiteness bloomed from the ceiling, illuminating the area.

Micah guffawed. *Do not gloat...oh, go ahead. This once.* Micah pointed to the large channel in the roof. "See? The Lord did tell me. That's our way out."

Wendy didn't refute him. She considered the opening, then made a jump. "Too high."

"Not if I give you a boost."

"Fine. I'm out, and how do you escape?"

Micah reached into his shoe and pulled out a car key. "We always carry a spare for whatever car we're driving. Make your way back to the 4X4 and drive it here."

"You're assuming Leisch left the 4X4, I can find it, and I can somehow drive it all the way to this spot."

Micah rethought his plan. He nodded. "Yeah. Exactly what I'm thinking."

"How does that help you?"

"There should be rope in the back. I can climb out."

"Uh-huh. What does your God have to say about it?"

"He thinks it's as good a plan as any, and you should quit arguing and do it."

Wendy stared at him. Even in the shadows, he could read the incredulity. "He said all that, did He?"

"Not in those words. Look, get up there. We're wasting time."

He braced himself to lift her and let her crawl to his shoulders. She had to step on his bad leg, but he said nothing. Escape mattered. Discomfort didn't. He could heal when they got back to civilization.

While Wendy ran for the 4X4, Micah planned their next move. Police? Let Wendell handle it in his "official capacity?" It would advance the situation here, but how did it help find Grace? Was it not about Grace but about solving some cold cases? Is that why they'd ended here?

Micah bowed his head. "I don't know what You intended with us being here. Maybe for the cold cases. Maybe so Wendy could hear about You. Maybe both those things, but what it wasn't was about finding Grace. Even less about finding Quinn. Unless one of them's going to pop up in the next few minutes." Micah grinned. "Which would be amazing. And not beyond You. Still, thank You for all You have done. For life. For getting us out of the caverns and keeping us alive. Help me use the life You've given me to bring You glory. In Jesus's name, amen."

He sat and hummed praise choruses until he heard a car engine surging and faltering as if it crawled over hillocks and boulders. Micah heard metal grinding as the undercarriage scraped along the bumps. Occasional crunching sounds meant a bush or shrub had met its demise. But eventually, light shone across the hole, dimming the moonlight and throwing the cave into almost darkness. He stood and waited for Wendy to appear.

She scrutinized the pit. "You down there?"

"Yeah. You expected someone else?"

"I forgot to mark the hole. I nearly forgot which one I came out of."

Micah instructed, "Get the rope out of the back. Tie it to the axle, not the bumper. Those things come off if you look at them wrong."

After a moment, Wendy called, "There's no rope."

"Look under the pad. There's a compartment…"

"There's no rope, Mick. I'm telling you."

Micah thought hard. Luke had a rope. Luke always had

a cable or something. Why not now?

Wendy came back to the mouth of the hole. "Take off your jeans."

"What?"

"I'll tie mine and yours together to make a rope. Give me the rest of your shirt, too. It should all be long enough."

"Are you sure about this?"

"It's dark. You'll be on one side of the car, and I'll be on the other. I think your God will forgive you."

Micah grumbled but tossed his jeans to Wendy's waiting arms. He threw the remains of his shirt as well. "There better not be one word of this to anyone. Right?"

"Not one word." She snickered.

Micah amended the sentence. "Not any words, Wendy. Especially not to Quinn or the guys."

"Do you want to get out of this hole or not?"

Micah sighed. "Yes."

"Then quit complaining."

After a moment, a pant leg extended into the hole. It dangled just beyond his reach. Another moment, and it slipped closer to him. Micah grabbed the makeshift rope and tried to climb. His thigh protested in pain, refusing to make the ascent. Micah dropped back. "I can't make it, Wendy. I can't climb."

"Can you wrap the pants under your shoulders and hang on? I'll pull you with the car."

"Will it hold?"

"Ask your God." Sarcasm laced her voice.

Though Micah knew Wendy meant it to harass him, it sounded like good advice. "Lord?"

Trust in the Lord with all your heart and mind and strength.

"It'll hold. Give me a moment." Micah wrapped as much of the jeans as he could under his arms, held on tight, and called, "Go for it." He would rise or fall spectacularly.

The engine gunned. Micah's feet came off the floor. He rose a foot…two feet…three feet…he cleared the top of the hole.

But here proved the downfall of their plan. To get above the lip, he had to reach with his arms. But to reach meant letting go of the rope…and falling back. He pulled his knees up as high as he could and pushed away from the edge, trying to get some clearance.

Wendy gunned the engine again, and the makeshift rope jerked forward. Micah's face ground into the dirt. He kicked with his knees. His shoulders cleared the hole. She dragged him another few feet until all of him came above the cavern. He heard the sound of fabric ripping, and his salvation went limp. Face in the dirt, Micah laughed. He rolled over and breathed, above ground and alive.

The engine stopped. The driver's door opened, and Wendy called, "Can you untie the pants?"

Micah sat. "In a minute."

"I don't have a minute. It's cold."

The air above three thousand feet dropped low at night. Micah struggled with the tightened knots but finally got them untangled. The fabric ripping he'd heard had been his shirt. Or what remained of it. Micah slid his jeans on while still lying on the ground, then tossed Wendy's to her.

He waited until she came around the front of the car. She slumped beside him. They tapped knuckles. Micah sighed. "Nice rescue."

"Happy to oblige." She leaned against the bumper. "Now what?"

Micah hesitated. "Is there anything you can do in your 'official capacity'? Or are you out of your jurisdiction?"

"I have jurisdiction everywhere." Wendy shrugged. "Whether I can use it or not is another story."

"Meaning?"

"If this is a local case, a county, a state case…it all matters."

"What if it's murder?" Micah's voice darkened.

"There's no proof of murder. Not even suspicion. All we have is bones. Until forensics comes and determines age and cause of death, we've got nothing."

"What do you suggest?"

"We make sure a forensic team gets here."

"We do that how?"

"Find our phones and call."

Micah snorted. "Sure. In the dark?"

Wendy pulled up her pant leg, revealing a leg holster. "Always carry a spare."

Micah looked at her sideways. "Why didn't you use it in the caves to get us out?"

"This is an old flip phone. Very limited battery life. If we'd used it in the caves, it might have died before we needed it to call for help. Phones don't work well underground if you haven't noticed."

"I haven't."

"They don't. And they don't work well in the mountains. With this, considering where Leisch threw the phones, we should be able to find them and maybe the keys, too. Beyond that, we're on our own."

They drove back to the entrance to the caverns, where Leisch had taken their phones. With the light from the car and the flip phone, Micah and Wendy were able to locate their phones. Then it was back up the hill to the car. Micah scanned the area. "Which way?"

"Leisch won't be at the camp. Let's go have a look at Grace's tent again. I want to see what else she left behind."

The campsite was vacant. Leisch had indeed gone for the night. Obviously, he expected Micah and Wendy to die in the caves. And their bones to be left to rot. Like their friend, the skeleton. And the bones in the ground.

A search of Grace's tent revealed she'd taken her backpack. But she left her clothes, laptop, files, and several personal items. Wendy shook her head. "She intends to come back. Wherever she went, she planned on returning."

Micah asked, "If you wanted to make it look like someone had left, wouldn't you hide all this?"

"Certainly."

"Then either Leisch isn't very smart, or he didn't have anything do to with her going missing."

"I vote for both." Wendy nudged a bench. "I think Grace expected to leave. If she could take her backpack, some thought would be involved. Some planning. I don't know what, but I don't think she left against her will."

"But then, why leave her laptop? Why not contact Chay? Why leave the details a secret?"

"Maybe where she went, she wouldn't need the laptop. Maybe she didn't expect to be gone long. Maybe it was a secret rendezvous. I don't know. But I don't believe the part about saying she wasn't coming back. I believe she intended or intends to return. I think Leisch said it to cover his tracks. Pity we didn't get to talk to any of the students before they left."

Micah began searching the papers on Grace's desk. "I bet she's got a roster with phone numbers."

While he dug through the paper files, Wendy went back to the computer. After a moment, she crowed, "Got it."

Micah gazed over Wendy's shoulder and saw the neatly designated "Fall Session" spreadsheet. Names, addresses, phone numbers, emails...

Wendy pulled out her phone and took a photo of the spreadsheet.

Micah considered the time. "It's too late to call tonight. What do you suggest?"

"Long way to drive home, only to turn around and return in the morning. I say we call the forensic specialists tonight to have them assemble here tomorrow morning. We spend the night here and be prepared for Leisch when he comes back."

Micah nodded. "Sounds like a plan."

Wendy grinned at him. "And we can stay in separate tents, too. Leisch thinks we have to be dead or dying. He won't come looking for us."

"I like that plan even better."

Wendy took a seat behind the desk. She folded her hands in her lap. "Is it your god who keeps you so tight on the straight and narrow? Why do you follow him?"

Micah pulled up a camp chair and sat as well. "He's not all about rules and regulations and do this, don't do that. He's about life and what it takes to live it."

"How do you know?" It wasn't a challenge as much as an inquiry.

"Because He saved mine."

"How? When?"

"I was fourteen. I had decided to end it. Tried to end it by hanging myself. Then changed my mind and asked someone, anyone, to help me. I'd follow Them anywhere if They did. Tav came by, pulled me down, introduced me to Jesus, and I've been following Him ever since."

"Couldn't have been a coincidence Tav walked by, could it?"

"What did you tell me about coincidences?"

"I don't believe in them."

"There's your answer."

"But there could be. I could be wrong."

"So could I. But I've spent ten years following Him and

never regretted it. I think I'd regret a coincidence somewhere in that time."

"I've never had that kind of coincidence."

"When you're ready, you will."

Wendy rocked back in the chair. "Let's get ready for Leisch."

"Heard." Micah left the tent and found an empty one to stretch out in. And prayed, "All You, Lord. Your will, Your time. Thank You."

He slept.

* * *

TUESDAY

Morning at the Andres's home. Luke fixed breakfast. BB drank a protein shake and packed his bag for the day. Ben sat on the floor discussing the day's activities with Mia in their private way. Luke heard footsteps in the living room.

Addison walked into the kitchen, confusion and consternation on his face. Ben took one look at Addison and rolled to his feet. The boy ducked behind Luke, who smiled. "Nice to see you up. Welcome to Micah's home. This is BB, Micah's oldest son."

BB shook hands with Addison. "When are you going to get into a game, man? I've been watching you since you started college."

Addison rubbed his hand over his face. "Uh, good morning?"

Luke laughed. "BB gets right to the point, as he's going right out the door." Luke waved at the teen. "One of us will see you tonight."

BB sighed but bumped chests with Luke. "Later, brother."

Addison sat at the coffee bar and gazed around. "Coffee?"

Luke nodded. "Strong enough to guard the line. I'll get you some."

While Luke moved to pour coffee, Ben shadowed him, staying out of Addison's line of sight. Or trying to. Luke introduced the boy, "Addison, this is Ben. He's my friend's youngest." He held Addison's eyes. "Ben isn't much for conversation. But he does get his points across when he wants to."

Addison waved. "Hi, Ben."

Ben nodded once. He looked at Luke, then looked at Addison. Then he looked at Luke and looked at Addison again. Finally, he walked over and bowed deeply to Addison.

Addison asked, "What does he mean?"

"It means he accepts you." Luke asked, "Are you ready for school, Ben?"

The boy ran to his room, followed by a barking Mia.

Luke grinned. "He's a great kid. Like his older brother. Micah's lucky to have them."

Addison shook his head. "The Micah I knew shouldn't be old enough to adopt grown kids."

Luke shrugged. "I'll drop you off at the gym after we take Ben to school."

Addison swallowed some of the coffee Luke handed him. He spluttered and coughed. "Are you trying to kill me?"

"It will wake you up." Luke swallowed his own cup. "It's how coffee is served in this house. I told you, strong enough to guard the line."

"I thought you were joking." Addison set his cup down, thought better of it, picked it up, and swallowed a long pull.

Ben came into the kitchen with his backpack and lunch box. Luke packed a lunch for him, stuffed it into the top of the bag, and asked, "Did you get all your homework in there?"

The youngster nodded once. Emphatically.

"You have all your lesson books in there?"

Another emphatic nod.

Luke gave Ben a side-eye. "You have anything in there that's not supposed to be?"

Ben started to nod but stopped. He hung his head. Luke eyed him. "Show me."

Ben pulled out a long coil of rope. Luke stared at it. "Did this come out of my car?" Ben nodded once. "Does your dad know you took it?" Ben hung his head. Again. No.

Luke shook his head. "I hope he doesn't need it. Okay, buddy. You can take the rope as long as you promise me you will not try to tie someone up. Got it?"

Ben nodded with a single happy dip of his chin. He raced to the van with his bag. Luke shook his head. "That kid."

Addison followed Luke to the van. "What does he need the rope for?"

"Maybe nothing. Maybe show and tell. Maybe he just wants something to hold. It's hard to know with Ben. And you don't always get good 'why' answers."

Addison nodded. "I can see that."

The two men rode in silence to Ben's school. Luke got out and walked Ben to the sidewalk. His teacher waited to escort Ben into class. Ben hugged Luke hard, then raced back to the van and stood by Addison's door. Addison stared at the small boy, opened the door, and stepped out. Ben hugged Addison, then reached up and whispered words in the man's ear. Addison tilted his head to stare after Ben as the child raced back to his teacher and gave her his hand.

Luke and Addison climbed back into the car. "What'd he say?"

"'Brothers. Secret.'"

Luke raised his chin. "Ah. I see."

"What did he mean?"

"Maybe he means now you and he are brothers. Ben tends to adopt others."

"But secret brothers?"

Luke tipped his hand back and forth. "It's hard with Ben. Sometimes we don't know what he's thinking."

Addison stared at the floor. Luke watched him out of the corner of his eye. Did he read more into it than Luke wanted him to? Yet?

They drove to campus. As they arrived at the gym, Addison muttered, "Uh, oh. Dad's there."

Luke pulled over short of Mr. Vaughn's presence. Didn't matter. The man raced to the car, jerked the door open, and yanked Addison out. He slapped the young man and shouted at him, "Where have you been? Where did you go? I followed you from that party last night. Until you gave me the slip." He went to slap him a second time, but Luke stepped between them and blocked the shot.

"Enough. Leave him alone."

Mr. Vaughn turned to swing at Luke, but Luke dodged the hit. Yells from students drew attention to the fight. Luke demanded, "That's enough."

Vaughn cursed at Luke, then cursed at Addison. "Is this how you repay your mother and me? Disappearing? Going off where no one can find you? I searched all night for you. You never came back to the dorm. What were you doing? With who? You ungrateful…"

Vaughn faced Luke. "Who are you? What's your name? You think you can ride my son's coattails to the NFL? You're a nobody."

Before he could continue, Coach Wiggins hustled in and demanded, "What's going on here?"

"Having a discussion with my son. So stay out of it," Vaughn shot back.

Wiggins muscled into Vaughn's face. "We've had this discussion before, Mr. Vaughn. When these boys are on campus, they're my boys. You'll treat them with respect, or I'll have you banned, you hear me? Leave."

Vaughn glared at Wiggins, glared at Luke, and pointed at him. "I'll find out who you are. I will. You think you can—"

"I said leave, Mr. Vaughn, before I call security." Wiggins raised his hand.

Vaughn backed off and left, but not before mouthing some threat Luke chose to ignore. Coach Wiggins asked, "What's all this about? Where have you been? The headcount in the dorm last night came up short. And with more than just you, Vaughn. You know we keep track of the freshmen on the team. As long as you're in my program, you'll be where I can find you."

Luke nodded. "I wasn't comfortable at the party last night. You know me, Coach. I mentioned to Addison I have a friend with an autistic son. Ben loves football players. Addison said he'd come over and meet him. It got late, so we spent the night there. Micah Andres. You can call him."

"I know Andres. He tutors some of the freshmen in math. Good man. I've met his son, too. Ben, isn't it? Thank you for your consideration. Good job, both of you." Wiggins smiled. Like an alligator smiles. "The party you left last night? Someone brought in alcohol. There's a few of your teammates running hot laps this morning." He chuckled. "You'll probably see them later. They'll be running laps before practice this afternoon as well." Coach Wiggins moved off.

Addison breathed an exaggerated sigh of relief. "Thank you. And thanks for defending me from Dad. He won't really bother you. He talks a lot, but he never follows through."

Luke shrugged. "Whatever. I've got to get to class. I've

got a psychology test. I'll catch you at practice." He waved, got back in the car, and headed out. As soon as he got to a parking spot, he called Tav. "Watch your back. Dad went after Addison this morning. I stepped in. He's fired up."

"You watch yours."

"He doesn't know me. Didn't recognize me. But I'll be careful."

"Do that."

"Hear from Mick?"

"Yeah. He and Wendy are alive but still up north. Nothing on Quinn. They're hoping to be finished there by this afternoon. He and Wendy should be back before the boys get out of school."

"Ben will appreciate Mick getting home." Ben had patted the wall calendar when he woke up. Probably to remind himself his dad was coming home. Ben loved his dad. Ben loved everyone.

"I'm sure. See you later. Stay safe."

"You, too."

* * *

Luke came out of psychology with his head down, trying to recall the questions he might have missed on the test and what the answers should have been. A voice called, "Hey!"

Luke caught sight of his dad standing on the curb. The man held his hands up in a sign of submission. Luke swallowed, slid on his tinted glasses, then crossed to stand before him. "Can I help you?"

"I wanted to apologize for the misunderstanding this morning. I didn't realize you saved Addison's bacon last night."

Bacon wasn't the word used, but it was as close as Luke chose to translate. "We saved each other. The party seemed like it would get out of hand, so he suggested we leave, and I suggested the place."

Dad reacted in surprise. "Addison suggested you leave?"

"Yeah. Your son is a good kid, Mr. Vaughn. He's smart, and he's trying to...be the best team player he can be." Luke almost said, "...trying to make you proud," but remembered he shouldn't know that. He kept the tone of his voice low. He'd still been a tenor when he left home. Knowing Dad never really paid attention to anyone but Tav might still shield him from recognition. That and the hair color. And beard and mustache.

Dad nodded. "He's working hard, I know. Compensating for the ones who weren't."

Luke didn't bother to follow the rabbit trail. "Well, he's doing fine. He'll be the starter once Henri and Blake graduate."

"Sooner, if one of them drops out."

Luke laughed. "Yeah, I don't see that happening. They're both too good."

"Accidents happen every year." Dad kicked the ground in front of him.

Luke decided to change the subject. "Is there anything I can help you with?"

"No, just wanted to apologize. And invite you to dinner. Get the chance to meet the missus, you know."

Luke shrugged. "That's not necessary, Mr. Vaughn."

"You can't pass up a home-cooked meal, even if it is from my wife. Come on, Von. We're practically family. What do you say?" He held out his hand to shake Luke's.

This is what I wanted. But now? Luke hesitated. "Let me know when works for you, and I'll check my school schedule."

"How about tonight?" Dad fairly beamed.

"I'm usually in a study group, but I can miss one night. Have to keep the grades to stay on the team."

"What? Basket weaving?" The man chuckled.

Luke smiled. "No, sir. I'm taking pre-med." He laughed. "In case the NFL doesn't work out, you know."

Dad shook his head. "That's bad thinking, there, Von. You always focus on the primary target. Nothing else matters."

Luke continued to deflect. "I don't have your son's skill, Mr. Vaughn."

"Chris. What does the E.L. stand for?"

"Extremely Lucky." Luke paused. *Forgive me, Lord.*

"Extremely Lucky, huh? Then call me Chris."

Luke deflected. "I can't. The best I can do is 'sir.' It's how I was trained."

"Then someone trained you well. Where are your folks?" Dad put his hands in his pockets.

Luke shook his head. "I'd love to talk, sir, but I need to get to my next class across campus."

"Addison will let you know about dinner."

"Thank you, sir. Have a good day." Luke hiked away from the man as fast as possible without being rude. *Whew. This is going to get complicated. Can I even keep it up?*

Should he? *Lord? I wanted to get close to Dad, to try for reconciliation. I don't know if it's even possible. His attitude...but maybe this is for Addison and not Dad. Maybe not the outcome I wanted, but it is an outcome. And it could be a good one. Direct my steps and my words, Father. In Jesus's Name, amen.*

* * *

TUESDAY

SANTA CLARA MOUNTAINS

Wendell and Micah met at the intake tent to wait for Leisch. Daylight showed the grave remained undisturbed. The forensic team was on their way and should arrive by nine. Micah had scrounged a shirt from Grace's tent. She had several overshirts that worked for him. At least he had some covering. Having Micah around unclothed, even partially, created a tingling the Wendy persona hated to admit. Wendell had retrieved his service revolver from his backpack the night before and kept it low.

Micah's stomach growled as they waited. Wendell laughed. "You need to do something to quiet the noise, or you'll blow the stake-out."

"I'm sorry. Unless you have anything edible in your pack, you'll have to listen to my complaints."

"Sorry, no. I didn't think we'd be out here this long." Wendell stretched carefully. He winced as he pulled the bullet wound.

Micah nodded to Wendell's side. "How's the middle?"

"Probably like your thigh. It stings."

A car labored up the hill, whining on the switchbacks. Wendell narrowed his eyes to see the car better. "We taking bets?"

"It's not a caravan, so I'm guessing Leisch. How do you

want to play this?" Micah studied the approaching car.

"I want you to stay in the tent. Let me take the lead, the rear, and everything in between. I want you to stay out of it." The younger man smiled tight-lipped. "Not because you would get in the way. But Leisch proved he's capable of murder. I don't want him using one of us against the other."

Micah nodded. "Makes sense. But why not let me—"

"Because I'm trained for this, and you have kids. Think of Ben."

Micah scowled. "That's low."

"As long as it gets the point across." Wendell shifted in his seat. "Here he comes."

Micah moved positions to be out of sight of Leisch yet still see what would happen. Which meant he took a place behind the tent flap with a view of the table. Wendell slipped out of the tent and behind the opposite flap.

Leisch parked and climbed out of his car, walking purposefully towards the dig site. He bypassed the tent and headed straight to the excavation. Within minutes he had uncovered the skeleton and the skull he had dug out the night before. He twisted the skull around and around, examining it. Looking for bullet holes? Cracks? What did he hope to find?

Wendell stepped out from behind the tent. "'Alas, poor Yorick.' Did you know him well?"

Leisch spun to face Wendell. Wendell displayed the firearm. "Put it down. Slowly. Carefully."

Leisch laid the skull with the rest of its body. He stated the obvious. "You're supposed to be dead."

"Surprise." Wendell gave an alligator smile.

"What about your partner? Is he around?"

"What partner?" He raised his eyebrows, then he motioned with his chin. "Have a seat on the ground. There'll be a forensic team here soon. They'll figure out this poor soul's history and identity eventually. You want to save them some time and yourself some years on a prison sentence?"

Leisch shrugged. "Why? Maybe they need the practice."

Wendell took a seat a safe distance from Leisch. He kept his eyes on the man's hands. Sifting through the sand. Always sifting…

"You expected to find him. Which was what the students were for, weren't they?"

Leisch nodded. "Peter should get an 'A' for his efforts. He really was the overachiever in the bunch."

"Tell me again about Dr. Painter. Where did she go? I know those bones aren't hers. But what did you do with her?" Wendell fished for answers.

Leisch shook his head. And sifted sand. "I had nothing to do with her leaving. And she did leave. One of the students said some guy came to the site. She seemed upset, crying. Said she had to go and would be back. That's all I know."

"Why'd you tell us she wasn't coming back?"

"I was in a hurry. I don't need extra bodies poking around." Still sifting. Was he looking for something?

Smooth stones.

Wendell ducked just as Leisch found his rock and flung it, missing the agent by a handsbreadth. Wendell rolled, Leisch pounced. Leisch grabbed for the gun. Wendell refused to give it up. Both hands locked on the weapon. Leisch slammed Wendell's hand against the ground. The gun went off. Wendell cringed inwardly but kept fighting for the firearm. He caught Leisch with a knee in his middle, doubling the older man over. Leisch groaned and released Wendell's hand. Wendell doubled his fists and smashed Leisch's head, knocking the man to the ground. He then kicked Leisch in the skull, knocking him out. Wendell yelled, "Mick! You okay?"

Micah looked out around the tent. "Are you done shooting?"

"Are you hit?"

"Grazed the flap above me. I'm fine. Sort of." The man's voice shook.

Wendy walked over and sat beside Micah. "Next time I tell you to hide someplace...don't do it. Stay in plain sight." She hugged him.

Micah leaned against Wendy and hugged her as well. "Next time." He put an arm around her shoulders. "Is this okay?"

"It is with me. What does your God have to say about it?"

"He's a God of dispensations. He forgives."

"Nice to know."

"Yes, yes He is."

Wendy decided to shift the subject. "You heard what Leisch said about Grace leaving in tears?"

"And some man picking her up." Micah's eyes darkened. "This is all wrong."

"We still have our list of students to contact. We'll start on those when we get home and see if we can track down whoever actually saw her leave." Wendy regarded Leisch. "Sure be nice to have a rope to tie him with."

"I'm not giving you the shirt." Micah scootched away from her as if she would take the garment forcibly.

Wendy laughed. "No, I prefer you fully clothed." *I don't, but...*

Wendy Smothers!

Wendy stood and moved to guard Leisch. And made sure there were no more stones in the near vicinity.

* * *

TUESDAY NOON

Tav tapped in the phone number Wendy sent him. He waited, then when the female voice answered, asked, "Jen? This is Tav Vaughn. Wendy asked me to give you a message."

The inflections did a roller coaster. "Oh?" *Up.* "Oh." *Down.* Tav swallowed his grin. Jen continued, "Did she say where she is?"

"She said to tell you she'll be home this afternoon. All is well, and there's only a little blood this time." He'd promised to relay the message as she gave it. At least he could relay it over the phone. Unlike Mick. How he would pass his message on to Quinn was a question with no answer. But they still had to find the man. If they could.

Jen's voice became dry. "That sounds like Wendy. Okay, I'll wait to see her before I grill her."

Tav chuckled. "Yeah, Mick's message was about the same." He scribbled on the notepad.

Now the tone mirrored surprise. "She's with Micah? She didn't tell me that part."

Tav nodded, then realized the woman couldn't see a nod, so he explained, "Yes, they went together to look for a friend of ours who's missing." Two friends, actually.

"You people lead exciting lives for college students." There was sarcasm to her tone.

Tav laughed. "We live boring lives with periods of intensity in between."

"Like winning the Magary Chase? I'd love to hear about that someday."

Someday? Today was someday. Maybe... Tav scanned his clock. "What are you doing for lunch?"

"Peanut butter and jelly unless I get a better offer."

"How about Super Wednesday at one?"

He heard the smile. "I'll be there."

"See you then." Tav hung up. "Why not? She said yes. And she's Wendy's sister. That has to count for something." He lifted a defense. "It's lunch, Lord. Not a lifetime commitment. Lunch with a friend. Not a yoke." *I won't make it one, either. I know better. But if she wants to know about Magary, I can certainly tell her all that You had to do with it. She will hear the Gospel. I promise.*

* * *

Tav arrived at the restaurant fifteen minutes early. Super Wednesday could be busy or dead, depending on the day of the week and the activities at the campus. Today was a "we'll get a seat, no problem" day. The server at the check-in desk took his name. "We'll seat you when your whole party arrives."

Tav rehearsed what Jen looked like. Tall, dark hair, hazel eyes. Unlike Wendy's blue. Slender. Attractive. *Attractive, yes. But it's her personality I'm drawn to. She didn't hesitate to bail me out when I crashed. I don't know if I ever properly thanked her for taking me to Mick's. We just sort of dragged her into the house and the confusion. I'm surprised she is even speaking to me.* By all rights, she should be running in the other direction.

The woman of memory walked to the front door. Tav grinned. She wore black slacks, a pullover jersey, and a scarf that tied back her shoulder-length hair. Yeah, she was attractive.

Tav held the door open for her. "Welcome. I'm glad you could make it."

"I'm glad you asked," Jen demurred.

Tav motioned to the server, who took them to a booth

near the back. After a soft-drink order had been placed, the server left to allow them time to peruse the menu.

Jen laid the list of options down. "I'll have the French dip. It's my favorite."

Tav nodded. "Good choice. I like the hot chicken salad."

Jen groaned. "Now you're going to shame me for eating food other than a salad?"

"No. But the salads are so big I can take half home for Luke after he gets done with his study group." *Why did I say that? She'll think we're joined at the hip. We are, but she doesn't need to know that.*

Jen's eyes sparked. "Wendy said you and your brother are close. That you helped raise him?"

"It was a joint effort with Jeremiah, Mick, and I trying to keep him out of trouble and get him through school. Trust me, God's grace, not our skills, saw him graduate."

The server returned, took their order, then left. Tav changed the focus of the discussion. "I owe you a thank you for taking me home after the accident. I don't think I ever said it. But thank you. I'm grateful."

"Did they catch the guy who hit you?"

"No, they're still looking." He glanced into her eyes. "What do you do for fun?"

"Besides badger Wendy about her career choice?" Jen laughed. "I work downtown in a law office. I'm a paralegal."

"Studying to be a lawyer?"

"Never. I like what I do, and that's enough. I don't want to have to make the hard choices." She shook her head. "There are enough tough decisions of my own without trying to make them for someone else." Her eyes deepened.

Tav pressed, "Like?"

"Like live at home and care for an ailing parent, or move out and establish my own life. Care for younger foster siblings, or have my own family. Play violin or oboe. Paper or plastic. You know, all the deep questions of life."

Tav nodded. "I understand. Are both your parents living?" *She's got quite the wit. I like that.*

"Mom has early onset Alzheimer's. Dad tries, but men can be useless when it comes to caregiving." She sighed. "Forgive the generalization." She took a deep breath. "Sorry. It's been a tough morning." She sat straight and smiled. "All better."

Tav touched her hand. "Honesty is the first value of the Knights of the Octagon. I appreciate yours." Sparks tingled in his fingers.

"Yeah?" Jen eyed him sideways. "What other values do you hold? And why?"

Tav drew his hand back. "Honesty. Integrity. Faithfulness. Loyalty. Sobriety." He grinned. "Which Micah will add is not the same as abstinence. And chastity. At least until marriage. Those are the morals we choose to live by." He decided to go for it. "Then there's the God-qualities of love, joy, peace, patience, gentleness, goodness, faith, kindness, and self-control. That about sums it up."

"And when you fail?"

The food runner brought the meals. An older couple shuffled in, both with walkers. They sat in the booth across the floor. A group of two women and six children assembled at a table in the center aisle. The children all appeared to be under the age of five. Hands full, and the quiet would definitely be interrupted.

Tav scowled at Jen. "Excommunicated. Banished. Shunned." He laughed. "Forgiven. Loved back into the fold. We wanted to grow together into men our parents would be proud of." He shrugged. "We did. They weren't. It's complicated." He shuffled the chicken around in the salad.

The server came. "Does everything look all right?"

Tav studied Jen. She nodded. Tav addressed the server. "Everything is fine." The server disappeared.

Jen laughed. "Why do they ask that when you haven't had time to eat it yet? Everything looks fine…but what it tastes like is another story. Or might be."

Tav tasted his chicken. Perfect. He waited until Jen had swallowed her first bite. "And how is it?"

She nodded. "Delightful."

They suspended the talk until both had consumed a good portion of the food. Then Jen asked, "Why Knights?"

"We couldn't be pirates. So we went the romantic route and became knights."

"But who's the king?"

There it is. "Our King is Jesus. We wanted to be His best warriors."

"How old were you when you started all this?"

"Maybe twelve. In junior high school."

"Isn't that kind of young to make a religious decision?"

"It wasn't religious. It's about a relationship with a Man. Jesus saved each of us. Different times, different ways. But at the core of our beings, we knew we owed Him our lives. And we wanted to follow Him. Wanted to follow hard after Him. So we pledged it all, and we're trying to live it all." He shrugged. "Some days, we're more successful than others. But the bottom line is we try."

"And you're never tempted to quit?"

Honesty. "Every day. It's not a 'one and done' decision. It's an every morning, every hour decision to live like Jesus."

Jen nodded. "I can see that. I admire your resolve."

Tav smiled. "I admire you're still sitting here. Some people would say we're crazy and run away."

"I don't think you're crazy." Jen's eyes softened. "It must be wonderful to have a team of friends who hold you up."

Tav laughed. "We're not saints by any means. We can fight like brothers."

Jen grinned. "Or sisters. Wendy and I have our share of disagreements. Even not being blood, we still fight like it."

Tav cocked his head. "She's not your blood sister?"

"No. My parents fostered both of us when we were infants. After three years, they made it permanent."

A busser walked quickly past the booth. So quickly that he bumped into the table with the elderly couple. He did not apologize or look back but headed straight out the front door.

An outcry from the kitchen caught Tav's attention. An explosion rent the air. Shards of burning metal, oil, and wood erupted, setting the dining room ablaze. Screams from the diners added to the confusion. Another blast destroyed the wall. The force of the detonation knocked over chairs and tables.

Tav grabbed Jen and shoved her toward the front. "Get out, now!" He heard the older couple calling for help. The group with the children screamed and cried. Tav hesitated only a moment, then forced his way to the booth, and the man and woman trapped there. He dragged the man out, then pulled the woman free. Neither would be able to walk. Tav picked up the woman and yelled to her partner, "Crawl! As far as you can."

The knight staggered with the woman's weight but managed to stumble to the front and the clear area. He set her down, looked back, and saw Jen assisting the women with the children. He dashed back in to grab a screaming child, pull another out of the highchair, dragging it with him as he raced to get them to safety.

Smoke and chaos descended, leaving Tav coughing and blind. He dropped to the floor and made his way out on his knees. As soon as he saw daylight, he deposited the children in the arms of someone on the outside. Then he turned back to save someone else…anyone else. He could hear screams and cries from inside.

A firefighter grabbed him. "Enough. Stay out. We'll get them."

Tav spun around, looking for Jen. He heard a call, "Over here. Tav, I'm over here." He saw his date leaning against a parked car, still comforting the young mothers. He fought to his feet and joined them, coughing. He cleared his lungs and breathed. "I take you to all the hot places, don't I?"

Jen groaned. She reached out and hugged him. Tav hugged her back.

Thank You, Lord. Save the rest, please, Father. Amen.

✳ ✳ ✳

TUESDAY LATE AFTERNOON

"Whoever it might have been, they weren't after me. It wasn't Dad. He might have come after me on the bike. I wouldn't put it past him. He wouldn't try to blow up an entire restaurant with who knows how many people just to get to me. He wouldn't." Tav sat back in his chair, his eyes and face fierce.

The living room at Micah's served as the debriefing room for the day. And the night before. And the day before that. Micah and Wendy gave the rundown of their time in the mountains. Two deaths, neither of them Quinn or Grace. And no closer to finding out where they might be.

Wendy waved her hand. "I believe you, Tav. I'm only saying that coincidences are getting harder to ignore."

Micah sat with Ben on his lap. Yes, the thigh hurt. Yes, having Ben snuggled on top of him made it worse. But for the boy's sake, Micah would endure any pain. "It wasn't a coincidence Tav and Jen were there. God used it to save people. I agree with Tav, though. His dad had nothing to do with it."

Jen looked at her sister. "It wasn't a coincidence you had him call me. It wasn't a coincidence I had the afternoon off." She eyed Wendy sideways. "Unless you did it deliberately?"

"Not in the middle of a situation where you could be put in danger." Wendy's comeback carried some heat.

Jen dipped her head. "Fair enough." She stretched. "I think we're all strung out."

Luke sniffed. "I'm about to be. I've been 'ordered' to appear for dinner at Addison's. This should be very interesting."

Tav shot forward in his seat. "What?"

"Yeah. No matter how often I said it, Dad wouldn't take no for an answer. So I'm going over. Can you believe he really doesn't recognize his own son?" He examined the clock. "And I need to head out." He eyed Tav. "You sure you're okay?"

"Yeah, I'm fine. You watch yourself."

"As long as we talk about Addison, everything will be fine. Dad'll never even see me."

Micah saw the pain in Luke's eyes. Mirrored by the pain in Tav's. *Did you ever stop wanting your parent's approval?* Micah had to mention the elephant in the room. "What about your mom?"

"She won't say anything to upset Dad. She might approach me later, but I doubt it."

Luke stood. He bumped fists with Micah, Tav, and BB. He reached down and kissed Ben on the head. "See you later, little man."

Ben sat and hugged Luke, then went back to snuggling with Micah. Luke nodded to Wendy and Jen. "Ladies. Take care of yourselves." He grinned. "Stay away from these two, and you'll probably have a better chance at it."

The corner of Jen's eyes wrinkled. She tossed her head. "I'm not worried."

Wendy muttered, "You should be."

Luke looked out the front window. "Are you expecting company?"

Micah glanced where Luke indicated and groaned. "Ms. Phelps."

Wendy lowered her head and laughed. "You look worse every time she visits. How do you explain this one?"

Micah shook his head. "I don't. I'm not saying a word."

He walked to the front door and opened it before the CPS agent could knock. "Good evening, Ms. Phelps. Yes, I look like I've been run over. No, this is not my everyday lifestyle. I've hit a bad stretch. What can I help you with?"

Ms. Phelps eyed him sideways. "May I come in?"

"Of course." Micah waved her in.

She walked into the living room. Micah rehearsed what she would see. Tav and Jen's burns. Wendy...actually Wendy. Her bruises and cuts. His own scrapes and bruises. Only BB and Ben were unscathed. Well, and Luke.

Ms. Phelps eyed the room. She tilted her head at Wendy. Wendy took the bait. "DHS. Agent Smothers. We've met before. This is my sister Jen."

The CPS agent's eyes widened. She turned to Micah. "A bad stretch, you say?"

Tav held out his hand. "All very explainable. He's still looking for our missing friend. We"—he indicated Jen and himself—"got caught in the downtown restaurant explosion. Jen is a hero for rescuing several children, by the way."

Ms. Phelps raised her eyebrows at BB. "You vouch for this crowd?"

"Absolutely. They protect me with their lives. They try to protect others, too, and it gets them in trouble. But they're great people. I wouldn't want to be with anyone else."

She didn't look satisfied. "They don't drag you into their rescues, do they?"

BB shook his head. "Nah. Mick leads a very boring life most of the time. Like he said, they've hit a bad patch."

Micah waved his hand. "Have a seat, Ms. Phelps. We can always use another partner in our world."

She shook her head. "I think not." She smiled ever so slightly. "I came by to give BB his deliberation form." She focused on BB. "You can decide if you want Micah as your guardian or if you want to be adopted as his son. Mr. Andres has indicated he is willing to adopt you as his legal son if you choose."

BB nodded. "Yeah, we've talked about it. Feels weird to have a dad who's only a few years older than me. But being someone's son is cool, too. So I don't know."

"Well, you have two weeks to decide." She tapped her clipboard. "He can always adopt you later. We have adults adopt adults all the time. Mostly as a way to determine an heir or possession of an inheritance. But it can be done any time."

BB nodded. "I'll think some more about it."

"Very well." She handed some papers to BB. "And I hope you think long and hard. This can change your life."

BB glanced at Micah. "Mick and these guys already have."

She motioned to Ben. "Because Ben of Ben's age and disability, we can't be sure he understands the difference between guardianship and adoption. We believe adoption is the best avenue for his future." She dipped her head to the side. "We can't ask him and be certain of his answer. So we believe it is in his best interests that you, Mr. Andres, be his father."

Micah nodded. "Though I think you can ask Ben, and he will give you a definitive answer."

Ben climbed off Micah's lap. He stood in front of Ms. Phelps. He signed the word "Father." Then he stood in front of Luke and shook his head. Hugged him but shook his head. He did the same for Tav. He hesitated in front of Wendy, then shook his head. Hugged her. Repeat with Jen. Finally, he went over to Micah. He signed, "Father." Hugged him and climbed in his lap. Hugged him again. Signed, "Father." He faced Ms. Phelps and gave a single emphatic nod.

Micah raised his eyebrows at the CPS agent. "Does that look convincing?"

She laughed. "Yes, it does." She tilted her head. "If it weren't for the physical condition I keep finding you in, I'd have no qualms about signing off on this arrangement. As it is, I still feel you are a good match." She smiled. "Do try to stay out of trouble between now and the next time I see you, will you?"

Micah nodded. "I always try. Trust me, I don't do this for the fun of it."

Luke escorted Ms. Phelps out the door.

Wendy stretched and addressed her sister. "Maybe we should head out, too. I'll take you back to the restaurant, and you can pick up your car. Or we can ride home together, and you can get it tomorrow."

"That. I'll drive. And stop at the ER. For you. Paramedics at least examined my wounds."

"You'll walk." Wendy scowled at her sister. "I've gone all this time without a doctor's visit. I'm not starting now."

Jen pointed at her sister. "Gotcha. I know better."

Wendy rolled her eyes. Micah grinned at the exchange. So much like Tav and Luke.

Tav cleared his throat. "Jen, I'm sorry—"

"—Don't. Do not apologize. I'm glad I could be there to help those people." She touched his arm. "And I'm glad you invited me. We'll do it again without the drama if the Lord allows."

Tav stood and walked the women out. Micah waited until his friend returned. "Did you hug Wendy for me?"

"Hugged her for me. Next time, get up."

Micah motioned to Ben. "My lap was occupied."

"I hear you."

BB offered, "You want me to take the little guy and entertain him until bedtime?"

"You have your homework done?"

"Did it in school." BB smirked. He leaned against the doorjamb.

Micah sighed. "You did Math in English, and English in Science."

"And Science in History. You know how it goes." BB shrugged.

Tav laughed. "Yes, he does." Tav stretched, then winced.

Micah eyed him. "You want to spend the night here?"

"No. I want to be home when Luke gets there, so I can interrogate him about how his evening went."

"So you can process your next moves?"

"Something like that." Tav stood. "Appreciate the clean clothes." He grimaced. "And the burn salve."

BB picked up Ben and shook his head. "You guys are walking accidents. Except you don't wait for them to happen. You go out and find them."

Tav shoved the younger man lightly. "Faster that way."

Ben clung to BB's neck, kissed Tav, and the two disappeared to the back of the house. Micah didn't get up but tapped fists with Tav. "Get some rest, man."

"You, too. We still have to find Quinn and Grace."

Micah sat forward. It hurt. "What do you think it means? They both left under uncertain circumstances."

"I don't know. I don't like it. We'll all take some of the student names tomorrow. Maybe we can track the one who actually saw Grace leave. Get a description of the guy who picked her up."

"That would be a start."

"Yeah. See you tomorrow."

"Stay out of trouble."

"Plan on it." Tav walked out the back door.

Micah sighed and slipped back in his chair. Maybe he'd sleep here tonight. Maybe.

* * *

TUESDAY EVENING

Addison met Luke at the door. The younger man kept his voice low. "I'm sorry to put you through this. But I appreciate you coming. Takes the pressure off me."

Luke chest-bumped Addison. "No worries. It's fine."

Dad called from the living room. "Get in here! Dinner's almost on the table."

Addison and Luke ambled into the area. Luke eyed the room. Nothing had changed in the six years since Dad threw him out at age fifteen. The chairs, sofa, tables, pictures on the wall...everything exactly where it had been. Mom used to rearrange every year or so to "mix it up." But not now. Not since the blow-up. What did it mean? Dad stepped in and forbade the change? Mom got too tired to move things? No one cared anymore? Hard to know.

Dad waved to the furniture. "Have a seat. May will call us when it's on the table."

Luke hesitated. "Does she need some help?"

"Help? Not my woman. She can do it all, and all by herself. It's her job."

Luke sat on the couch, staying on the left side. The right cushion had a drop in the middle from prolonged use. Unless Mom had replaced it, the left side had always been more comfortable.

Addison observed Luke, a quizzical smirk on his face.

Luke didn't ask. Not in front of Dad. Let the youngster have his secrets.

"Secret. Brother." Did Addison suspect the truth? Luke shifted on the couch, suddenly uncomfortable. Would he say something? Would the evening blow up?

Mom called from the kitchen, "Dinner is ready."

Dad stood. "Let's go, boys. Whatever it is, we'll eat it."

Luke scowled at his dad's back. Always with the insults. Mom had been a good cook back in the day. He couldn't imagine she'd changed so much.

Dad took his place at the head of the table. Mom sat beside him. A half-full wine glass marked her place. A can of beer sat beside Dad's plate. Mom smiled at Luke. "Welcome, E.L. Addison has told us so much about you."

Dad motioned to the refrigerator. "There's beer in there if you want. Help yourself."

Luke shook his head. "Um, no drinking for me. Coach made it clear we're not to drink while we're in season."

Addison retrieved two sodas and tossed one to Luke. "Right. We don't drink during football season." He smirked only slightly.

Dad shrugged. "I can't see how a beer at home can hurt you."

Luke ducked his head. "I prefer not, sir."

"Call me Chris."

Luke cleared his throat. "My folks taught me to call people older than myself by their full names. Mr. Vaughn." He placed his napkin in his lap.

"My house, my rules. Your folks aren't here. So call me Chris."

"Chris." How awkward could this get?

Addison sat across from Luke. Luke deliberately took what had been Tav's seat next to Chris. No sense in adding to the reveal. Mom sat beside Addison. She used to sit at the far end of the table. It had always been Dad, the empty chair, Addison, Mom, Luke, Tav, then back to Dad. Now the places were mixed. Cozier? Luke gave a silent sigh.

Mom served all three men fried chicken, scalloped potatoes, and green beans. She sat beside her husband, then looked at Luke. "What are you studying?"

"Pre-med. Heavy on biology and physiology and science right now."

Addison kicked Luke under the table. Luke barely nodded to Addison, then asked Mom, "What do you do to stay busy?" He glanced at Addison. What did he need?

Addison had sliced into his chicken. The center was pink. Deep pink. The chicken had been undercooked. Luke lowered his head again slightly and began dissecting cooked pieces from the raw. Would anyone say anything? Would Mom recognize the error?

Dad carved his pieces and chewed away, oblivious to the danger. "Good chicken, May. Excellent." He laughed at Luke. "Bet you don't get meals like this on campus, do you?"

"No, sir...Chris...we don't."

Addison divided his chicken into salvageable and un. He buried the raw meat under some potatoes he separated from the main mass. Luke did the same. He tasted the scalloped potatoes and nearly gagged. The salt content was ten times what he expected. Luke picked up his soda and quickly washed the mouthful down.

Addison caught Luke's eyes. Luke tried to read the message there but could only guess what his brother meant. Addison took another bite of salt, washed it down, then repeated the action. So. No one would mention the quality of the food. Pretend it was fine.

The green beans had been layered with Italian seasoning, but at least they were edible. Luke chewed, then swallowed and ducked his head to Mom. "Delicious. Thank you for the meal. I appreciate the invitation." *I appreciate the invitation. Not necessarily the meal. But the invite is good.*

Dad motioned, and Mom supplied him with another beer. Mom finished her wine and poured a second glass. She lifted it to Luke. "To friends."

Luke and Addison saluted her in return. Luke busied himself, pushing the food around the plate, making it look like he'd eaten. He repeated his question. "What do you do to stay busy besides cook meals for hungry football players?"

Mom's eyes lost focus. "Oh, managing the house is work enough. Keeping up with our son and his schedule fills my days." She came back and added, "I used to be busier, but now it's just Addison. He's enough. I know he lives in the dorm, but he's home after school and on weekends when there's no football. It's almost like having him here all the time." She reached over and laid her hand on Addison's.

Addison kicked Luke under the table. Hard this time. No chance Luke would mention any other siblings. Luke tapped Addison on the foot to let him know they agreed. He needed to teach Addison to sign. Much better than playing footsie under the table and trying to decipher what being kicked meant. He asked, "Are your parents in the area? Do you have brothers or sisters close?"

Dad laughed, harshly. "Yes, we put up with her brother and his wife living across town. Freeloader. I'm surprised he's not here tonight. Anytime we have a meal, he shows up out of nowhere." Dad added a few words which were less than complimentary. Luke filtered them through the Holy Spirit.

Dad's answer surprised Luke. He hadn't known Mom's brother moved to the area. Who else was living here? "What about you...Chris? Is your family near?"

"I have three brothers, all living north of here. The oldest is an engineer. He makes my life miserable, giving advice about how to run my family." Dad swallowed his beer and went for a third. "My middle brothers are working slobs like me. They come for the games. Or they did until Coach made it clear Addison wouldn't be starting this year. Unless something happens to Blake or Henri." Dad chugged half the beer. "I can always hope."

Addison coughed. "Good joke, Dad. You know those guys are solid."

"You never know what can happen. Car accidents happen all the time. Places catch fire. Who knows what kind of disaster might happen?"

He chugged more of the beer. "Did you two hear about the restaurant fire today? At Super Wednesday? I'd bet money it started in the kitchen. And they'll find out it was insurance fraud. Kitchens always burn for fraud." He set the can of beer down as if punctuating the proclamation.

Luke scowled. "Fraud would be bad. All those innocent people inside? What if someone got killed?"

Dad nodded. "Yeah, what if some star quarterback got killed? Wouldn't that be a shame?" he crowed.

Addison's tone sharpened. "It's not funny, Dad. You don't wish bad stuff on anyone." He glared at Dad.

Dad shrugged. "It's just a thought. I can have thoughts." Mom quietly poured a third glass of wine. Luke decided since everyone had finished eating, he would break up the party. "Let me clear the table."

Dad waved him off. "No, no. It's the wife's job. She doesn't have anything else to do, anyhow. Taking care of Addison is nothing. Now my middle brother's wife. She has four boys to care for. She's a busy woman."

Luke looked across the table at Addison. The younger man's eyes teared, and he blinked the moisture away. "I'll help, Mom. E.L., you sit. Won't take a moment."

Addison jumped to his feet and helped Mom clear the table. She stacked the dishes on the counter, then grabbed a covered cake plate. She set it on the table. "I made this just for tonight. I hope you boys enjoy it."

She pulled the cover off the saddest-looking chocolate cake Luke had seen. One side leaned heavily to the right. Frosting dripped down the far side and puddled on the plate. She handed the knife to Luke and said, "You get the first piece."

Luke didn't know whether to decline or not. Addison's face said he should cut the cake and take a piece. He smiled. "Here goes nothing." He stuck the knife into the center and sawed a line toward the outer edge. A gooey mass clung to the blade. He wiped it on the plate and went in for a second cut. He lifted out a wobbly mass and dropped it onto a small dessert plate. He handed the plate to Addison, who passed it to Dad. Luke repeated the performance until everyone had a semblance of a piece of cake in front of them. Luke forked a mouthful, determined to swallow whatever it might be.

Pathetic as it appeared, it tasted great. Nuts and chocolate chips and coconut and shaved almonds... He grinned at Mom. "This is wonderful. Thank you for making it."

She wagged her head back and forth. "You're welcome. I'll let you take some back to the dorm with you. You can share it with the team." Her face beamed with the approval.

Addison laughed. "First lineman through the door would swallow it whole."

Luke motioned to the cake. "I'll take a piece with me and smuggle it in for a midnight snack." *Tav will love it.*

Dad stood. "Let's go in the other room while May cleans. We men can talk." He opened the fridge. "You sure you don't want a beer?"

Luke shook his head. "No, thank you. I don't drink."

Dad addressed Addison. "Son? I know you drink. I taught you early."

Addison stared at Luke, and his eyes widened. Luke held his gaze but gave no answer to the question. Addison would have to do this on his own.

The younger man shook his head. "No, Dad. Not during the season. After. Then we can tie one on together." He led Luke to the living room.

Dad laughed. "I'll hold you to it." He took out another beer. "Nothing says I can't have one." The man popped the top and took a long swig before leaving Mom alone in the kitchen.

Once the three men were seated, Dad began the interrogation. "What about you, E.L. You got family around here? Where do your folks live? What's your dad do for a living?"

Luke started to answer, but Dad interrupted him. "Tell me what E.L. stands for again? Who names a kid E.L.?"

Luke chuckled. "It stands for Extremely Lucky. Mom always said I was extremely lucky to have made it out alive, so it sort of stuck."

"What about the rest of your family?"

"I'm...in the middle, you'd say. I've got two older brothers, three younger ones."

"How old is the youngest?"

Luke paused. Let them think he tried to remember. *Lord, Ben is my brother. As much as Micah is. I'm not lying. Stretching the truth, but forgive me.* "Uh, he's nine."

"And how old is the oldest?"

"Twenty-four."

"How many are boys?"

"All of us." *We'll leave Chay out of this for the time*

being. Besides, I don't want her as a sister. Except in the Lord. I've got other hopes.

"He's quite a man." Dad swallowed more of his beer. "I admire anyone who keeps his woman busy. What's he do when he's not making sons?"

"He's in sales. Management. The folks don't live in this area."

"Out of town?"

"Out of state." Luke cringed as the lies flowed. Too easily. Way too easily.

"Which—"

A crash from the kitchen interrupted the questions. Luke and Addison jumped to their feet and raced to the kitchen.

Mom sat on the floor, her left arm and hand covered in blood. A broken wine glass lay on the floor beside her. Her eyes were out of focus, and she wobbled side to side.

Luke ordered, "Call 9-1-1." He grabbed a towel and covered the cut on her wrist, applying pressure to the wound.

Dad yelled, "No, you don't. She doesn't need a doctor." He walked into the room and took charge. "Get the first aid kit and some bandages. She doesn't need anything else. I'm not having my wife 5150'd for a cut." Addison disappeared into the back.

5150, a mental hold for people presenting a danger to themselves or others. Why would Dad jump to such a conclusion? Luke looked at Mom's right hand. White-line scars crisscrossed the wrist. Luke glared at his dad. "She's—"

Dad cut him off. "She's fine. She'll be fine. She has these accidents all the time. They bandage her and send her home. She loses her balance and falls. We've replaced a whole dinner set by now." Dad finished his beer, set the can down, and knelt beside Mom. "Here, May. Let's get you on your feet."

The woman leaned heavily on her husband but rose to her feet and sat in the chair. Luke maintained pressure on the cut. He took a quick look at it. "She'll need stitches."

"Nah, I don't think so. It's not too deep, is it, May? It's fine."

Addison returned with the first-aid kit and bandaged the wound tightly. He tied the dressing off. "The bandages should hold til you get to the ER."

"She's not going to the ER." Dad's voice hardened. "She's fine. I said so. End of the discussion."

Luke opened his mouth. Dad cut him off again. "I think you've overstayed your welcome, boy. Time for you to leave."

Addison objected. "You can't throw him out because he—"

"That's enough of you, too, boy. Go back to campus now. Or you won't be enrolled tomorrow. You hear me?"

Mom nodded. "Go, boys. I'm fine. Really. I will be. It's a little cut. Go back to your dorms. We'll talk tomorrow." She stopped, "Oh, E.L., you didn't get your cake."

Luke glared at the back of Dad's head but addressed Mom. "It's fine, May. I'll get it another time. Thank you for dinner." He stalked out the door. Addison walked with him.

Luke headed to his 4X4. Addison caught his arm. "We need to talk. Meet me at JoeJoe's."

Luke raised his head. "I'll be there." He climbed into his car and headed to campus.

* * *

Luke got a booth at the coffee house. Tables were packed with late-night study groups. Lighting was minimal. Servers whispered to take orders. Murmurs and mutters droned around.

Addison walked in, dropped his backpack on the floor, and sat opposite Luke. Luke ordered black coffee. Addison ordered a latte. He viewed Luke's order. "How are you going to sleep tonight?"

"I'm not. This is an excuse."

Addison stared at the table. "I didn't know Mom had gotten so bad. I swear I didn't."

"When did it start?" Luke took a long swallow from the cup and wished desperately for some of Micah's coffee. He'd need three cups of this to do what one of Mick's would do.

"What? Cutting herself on broken dishes?"

"The drinking. And the 'accidents.'"

"After my brothers left." Addison shifted in his seat. "We all started then."

"I think your dad started long before your brothers left."

"Probably. But it got worse. Mom's wine addiction really took a turn then."

"What made you start?"

Addison stared hard at Luke. "Having to fill in for my brothers. They moved out, and Dad made me take their place. Plus, he wanted a drinking buddy. Made him feel like we were 'bonding' or some garbage. Didn't matter that I was only thirteen."

"You ever tell him no?"

"Did you?" Addison's anger flared.

"Yeah, I did. Which is why I'm here and you're there." Luke twisted his hands around his cup. He gazed at the table. "You weren't home the night we got thrown out. I told him I wouldn't replace Tav. He said I would and beat the snot out of me to prove it. Tav came home from work and found me bloody on the floor. Picked me up and walked me out. We were told never to come back. We never have."

Luke held his brother's eyes. "We never wanted you to have to fill in for us. But I wouldn't replace Tav, and Dad wouldn't let go of his dream. We tried to contact you, but Dad kept too close an eye on you. He wasn't taking chances we'd corrupt you from being the player he wanted."

Luke swallowed a draught of his coffee. "Only reason I can talk to you now is the disguise. Dad can't see through it. Can't believe I'd be so bold as try to get close to you." He looked at his brother. "When did you figure it out?"

"When you sat on the couch. Like you knew where the bad spot was. Then I saw you look at the table before you sat. The natural spot would have been to sit where you normally did, next to Mom. But you deliberately took Tav's seat next to Dad to throw us off. Except that give it away to me." He motioned to Luke's hair. "Nice disguise, by the way. You should keep it. It suits you." He dropped his eyes to the table. "Where is Tav?"

"Living on campus. Hiding from Dad."

Addison's head jerked. "What? Why?"

"He's been followed. The same person who followed him ran him off the road and totaled the motorcycle. It was three days ago. Today, the restaurant where he had lunch blew up."

Addison shook his head. "No. Dad wouldn't try to kill Tav. He's all talk." Addison emptied his drink and waved to the server for a refill.

Luke took more as well. No sleep tonight. "I've got scars that say he isn't." Luke lowered his head. "I don't want to believe Dad would try to kill Tav. But he's determined we won't ever replace you. Or show you up in any way."

Addison threw his hands in the air. "I'm not even in the game!"

"You heard him. Accidents happen. If he could figure a

way to put one of the other two quarterbacks out, he'd do it."

"He's not a monster. He's not. Maybe—"

"Don't tell me what he is." Luke couldn't keep the heat from his tone. "He's either willfully destroying his family, or he's sick in the head. He got you drinking, and I know how far you've taken that. How much you're drinking and when. Team talks, brother. Coach knows. He hasn't caught you, but if he does, you're done."

Addison slapped the table. "Then tell him. Let's get this sham over with. Maybe I can find a life of my own."

"Stand up to Dad. Tell him you don't want to be a quarterback. You have dreams of your own."

"Stand up like you did?" Addison sneered. "Worked well for you, didn't it? You're still both hiding from him. And then what? Who's there for Mom?"

"Who's there for Mom now?" Luke let the accusation sink in as he let his anger die. He tapped the table. "You can't save her when you're not even there." He backed off. "No one can help her if she won't help herself. Mom has to want to get better."

"What if we all three went to her?" Addison's face bore hope Luke had long since lost.

"Are you ready to stand up to Dad?" Did his brother know what the consequences would be?

"I'll lose my support. Have to drop out of school." Addison stared into the distance. Moments went by. Luke knew his brother's struggle. Was it worth it? Was he ready? What if...

Finally, Addison nodded. "Yeah. This isn't a life." He turned back to face Luke. "I want to see my brother first. I want to see Tav."

"Let's go, then. I'm sure he's waiting."

Addison grinned. "He waits for you?" His eyes crinkled.

"Only tonight. He wanted to know how the dinner went." Luke stood and tossed money on the table. "Follow me."

"Give me the address."

A cold feeling ran through Luke's gut. He swallowed it. "245 Belling. Apartment 25. I'll meet you there."

Addison grabbed his pack and followed Luke out. They hugged quickly, then split up. Luke muttered, "Lord, if I'm wrong, don't let this fall on Tav. My fault, my consequence, please. Jesus, help me."

He climbed into his car and drove.

* * *

TUESDAY LATE EVENING

Wendy sat at her desk and studied emails. Every email Quinn had written in the past month sat before her. And none of them gave her a clue. "Where are you, boss? What happened to you?"

A knock sounded at the door. "Enter."

Jen walked in and dropped onto the bed. "Hey. You had something you wanted to show me."

"Yeah. Let me get out of here." Wendy closed her computer. She dug into her closet for a lockbox, unlocked and opened it. She pulled out a crinkled piece of paper and handed it to Jen.

Jen stared at it. "What's the date stamp?" She turned the paper over back and front.

"The official record of when and where and who found this." Jen read off the date and place. Wendy nodded. "An infant—a baby girl—was dropped in a safe box. Doctors think she might have been only a few days old. The only thing with her was the blanket her parents wrapped her in and this sheet of paper."

Jen peered closer. "It's a family tree."

"Uh-huh. Keep looking." Wendy waited for her sister to notice the details.

Jen fell silent, then said, "All the surnames are crossed off. It's just the first names."

"Right. What else?"

"The father's name has been crossed off."

"Crossed off?"

Jen looked. "Scribbled and crossed and x'd and every other way you can obliterate a name. Someone must have been upset with the man."

"I think that puts it mildly. This came in the box with the baby girl. Because it was a safe box, the police didn't try to track the parents. Safe boxes are, by nature, a place to put an unwanted child, and no one asks questions."

Jen handed the sheet back to Wendy. "And?"

"And so the little girl ended up in foster care. But a family who was fostering one little girl decided to foster her as well. After three years, they decided to adopt them both. And she's been happily living with them ever since."

"And the authorities gave the paper to the foster parents?"

"Who gave it to the child when she turned sixteen. And she's kept the paper but never tried to do anything with the information." Wendy sighed. "But she, being an inquisitive child, memorized the names and their positions on the tree. In case she should ever come across them, you know?"

Jen pulled her knees on the bed and curled her hands around her feet. "Where did she come across the names?"

"Strangest thing. A friend of a friend of a co-worker had an accident. When the woman was at their house, she saw the family tree. And she photographed it. Because you know...what were the odds?"

Jen rocked back and forth. "Which all means what?"

"Well, for one thing, my sister may just have been on a date with my brother."

Jen's eyes widened. She grabbed a pillow and threw it at Wendy with force. "No!"

Wendy nodded and laughed. "Yeah. Oh, you're fine. There's no bloodline involved. But it gets more convoluted. Micah considers Tav his brother, too, so I've been out with my brother's brother."

Jen buried her head in her hands. "This is unreal."

Wendy half-smiled. "Yeah. I've been thinking about this all evening. When I'm not looking for Quinn." She threw her head back and groaned. "Oh, Jen. Quinn thinks of these boys as his sons. Which would make Quinn my father?"

Jen shook her head. "Maybe a step too far, even for this story. Bring it back to earth. Right now, you've got a possibility Tav's mom is your mother. What are you going to do about it?"

"I'm going to ask Tav for DNA."

"What about the father being crossed off? How are you going to explain his mother may have had an affair?"

"I thought about that." Wendy pointed to the paper again. "But the parents' and grandparents' names are still there. Only the father's name is gone. Like she had been mad at him. But still accepted the rest of the family. I don't know. Maybe I should try to sneak it?"

"Which would hardly be keeping with the code of the Knights, you know."

Wendy cocked her head to look at her sister. "And what do you know about the code of the Knights?"

"I know it's honesty and integrity." Jen closed her eyes. Her face scrunched. "Faithfulness. Loyalty. Chastity. Sobriety." She opened her eyes. "I think those were all of them. Besides the God-nature ones of love, joy, peace, and

I can't remember the others." She rocked again. "I've never been with someone as straight and narrow as Tav. He gives the credit to Jesus. If Jesus is where all this goodness comes from, I think I want to meet Him."

Wendy laughed. "Yeah, I know. Micah does the same thing. I don't know if they've been brainwashed into some cult. If they have, more people should sign up."

"Including you?"

"I'll look into it."

"Tav says it's a lifetime commitment." Jen examined a fingernail.

"So did Mick."

The women fell silent. Finally, Jen sighed, "Ah, well. We'll see where it goes."

"Right. Now get out of here."

Jen stood, kissed her sister, and left. Wendy pulled out her laptop and began looking at emails again. "Where are you, Quinn? What kind of trouble are you in?" She resumed her search.

∗ ∗ ∗

WEDNESDAY

Tav called a war council of the Knights at Micah's the next day. Wendy and Jen were invited as they both were involved. Addison Vaughn participated in his first conclave. Ben and BB were at school, so the adults had the room.

He took the lead. "Item one: Quinn is missing. Item two: Grace is missing. Item three: I've been followed and run off the road. Item four: you two found a dead body."

Wendy interrupted. "Two dead bodies."

Tav adjusted his agenda. "Two dead bodies. Item five: the restaurant Jen and I were at blew up. Item six: welcome to the family, brother."

Addison chuckled. "Is it always like this? Maybe I'd rather not be part of it."

"Too late." Micah shook his head. "You're in. Hang on tight."

A knock at the door interrupted the meeting. Micah rose to answer. Chay Painter waited and smiled. "Am I late?"

Micah waved her in. "Never. Well, maybe sometimes. But we've just started. You missed the first four points on Tav's PowerPoint...without the power. But we'll catch you up."

He motioned her into the front room. "Everyone who doesn't know, this is Chay Painter. Grace's daughter."

Luke rose first and greeted her warmly. Very warmly. Tav cleared his throat to end the reunion. "Break and breathe."

Luke did but glared at his brother. "I haven't seen her in two months."

Chay waved around. "Hi."

Micah pointed out the participants. "Wendy and Jen Smothers. Wendy is helping look for your mom. Jen got roped into a lunch with Tav that blew up, literally. So she's helping us with the combined cases to see what fits and what doesn't."

Chay took an available seat beside Luke. "You don't know what this means to me. Mom doesn't disappear without telling me first. She does disappear, but never without letting me know she will be incommunicado."

Wendy agreed. "Same with Quinn. He goes, but he always tells me where."

Tav reiterated his points. "So you don't feel left out, and I'll let Luke fill in the details, item one: Quinn is missing. Item two: Grace is missing. Item three: I've been followed, then run off the road. Item four: Wendy and Micah found two dead bodies." He added quickly, "Neither of them, your mom."

Chay's face went from pale to relieved in two seconds flat. Tav continued. "Wendy has a roster with the names of all the students at Grace's archeology camp. We'll call them and see who knows anything about her leaving."

Wendy leaned forward from her seat on the couch next to Jen. She passed out names and phone numbers from her roster. "Everyone has three people to contact." She motioned to Addison. "You're excused, as this is your first meeting. But take good notes." She wrinkled her eyes at him in jest. She dipped her head at Chay. "I know this is your mom, but we already had the split done before I knew you were coming. It shouldn't take long." She looked at the others. "Do you want to go into separate rooms? Or pretend we're a call center and all talk at once?"

Tav pointed to the kitchen. "I'll go in there."

Jen indicated the front porch. Micah walked to the back room. Luke pointed to the floor. Wendy sneered at him. "Fine. I'll go to the back porch."

Tav laughed. "I'll take the porch. You can have the kitchen." Wendy bowed her head. They walked together, then Tav moved on outside.

It was quiet. Mick had picked a great neighborhood for his first home. Houses close enough to be safe, far enough to be private. Kids and dogs sufficient for Ben to have friends, but not so many as to create a major cacophony. Mature trees, streetlights...all the joys that made home.

On to business. Tav dialed his first contact. "I'm trying to locate Gemma Tinder."

"This is her." The voice sounded young.

"Gemma, I'm a friend of Grace Painter. Were you at the archeology camp when she left on Sunday?"

"Yes, I was there."

"Did you see her leave?"

"No, I didn't." Tav crossed the name off. "But you should talk to Mona. Mona Pullis. She told me she saw her leave, and she was crying when she did."

"Mona cried?"

"No, stupid. Dr. Painter cried."

Tav adjusted his thoughts. "Did Mona say why Dr. Painter might be crying?"

"No. She said some guy drove up. Dr. Painter leaned in the window like she was talking to someone in the passenger seat, then turned around, went to her tent, came out with her backpack and bag, and just got in the car and left. She had tears all over her face."

"I'll contact Mona, thanks. Did Mona get a look at the guy in the passenger seat?"

"She didn't say. I didn't ask. Dr. Painter told me I interrupted class too many times to ask personal questions, so I didn't think I should ask anymore," the young woman snipped.

Tav swallowed his chuckle. "I understand. Thank you for the information."

"Do you know anything about when they will reschedule the class? I want to go to Vegas with my friends, but Mom says I can't during camp. Do you think you could talk them into waiting until after the first of the month? Like, maybe over Thanksgiving break? Then I could miss going to Grandmom's house and having to sit with my cousins."

Tav hated himself for asking but had to know. "What's wrong with sitting with your cousins?"

"They're all guys, and they're all ten and eleven, and they talk nonstop about sports and stuff I have no interest in. If I had girl cousins, it would be different, but I don't. Trevor should have been a girl, but the ultrasound got screwed up, and he came out a boy. His parents were really disappointed. Not as disappointed as I was, I can tell you."

Yeah, Tav hated himself for asking. He interrupted the tirade. "Thank you for the information, Ms. Tinder. If I get word on when the camp will be scheduled, I'll be sure to let you know."

He disconnected the call. And looked at the names. No Mona. Drat. Maybe he should trade for her. Maybe not. Ah, go for it.

In the kitchen, Wendy had no Mona. He waved off her tilted head. He glanced over Luke's shoulder at his list. No Mona. He gave his brother's inquisitive look a thumb's up and went to the backroom for Micah's list.

No Mona. Must be Jen, then. He also gave Micah a thumb's up then went to the front porch.

Jen dipped her head side to side and said, "Uh-huh. Uh-huh. That's fascinating. Yes, I'm sure it was. Oh, really? Wow. Okay, then, I need to get...are you certain? Must have been a shock to everyone." Jen held the paper with her finger on the name "Katrina." Tav pulled the paper from her and bingo. Paydirt. Mona. 555-3469. Tav ripped the name off the paper, held it in the air, and waved it. He grinned and used his hand to indicate, "Talk, talk, talk." Jen made as if to hit him but continued on the phone. "Wow. Bigger than your fist?"

He slipped down the porch and circled around to the back again. He dialed. "Mona Pullis?"

"Can I help you?"

"I'm trying to reach Mona Pullis. She's a student at the archeology camp at Mt. Diablo Park last week. May I speak to her, please?"

"This is Mona. Who is this?"

"My name is Tav Vaughn. I'm a friend of Dr. Painter's. We're trying to locate her. I understand you saw her leave the camp?"

"Did Gemma Tinder tell you what I said?"

"Um, yes, she did."

Mona sighed. "What exactly did she tell you?"

Tav debated, but after the last conversation, he decided all the details mattered. "She said you saw Dr. Painter talk to a man in the car that pulled into the camp. She was happy, then she spoke to the man in the passenger's seat, cried, got her stuff and climbed into the car, and left. Can you give me your view of what happened?"

"A car pulled in. Dr. Painter leaned in to talk to the man in the *driver's* seat. There was no one in the passenger seat.

I think she leaned in to kiss him, but I don't know it for a fact."

"Gemma said she cried?"

"She did, but it looked like happy tears. She looked scared and happy, if you know what I mean." The girl's voice became fierce. "You can be both at the same time, you know."

"I know. I agree. So you think she might have been happy?"

"And scared. She definitely knew the man in the car. I'm sorry I can't give you a description of him, though."

"Did you speak to her before she left?"

"I called to her and asked her where she was going. She said she didn't know, but she'd be back soon."

Which made things clear as mud. Tav turned to the side but said, "Thank you for the information, Ms. Pullis. I appreciate your help."

"I hope she comes back soon. I really enjoyed the camp. Until we found the bone. That was creepy. I forgot archeology sometimes digs up people's graves. I'm not sure I like the idea. What if a couple hundred years from now, they go digging up our graves to study us?"

Tav chuckled. "I agree it would feel weird. Well, it wouldn't feel anything, but the idea is weird."

Gentle laughter responded. "I know what you mean."

"Again, thank you."

Tav hung up. Now, did he tell the others to disregard calling the remainder of the students? Or did he wait for them to finish their lists and maybe get additional information? Did he finish his list? Give one name to Jen since he took one of hers?

Decisions, decisions. Tav walked into the kitchen to see how Wendy was doing. He waited until she finished her current call. She eyed him. "Yes?"

"I've got a student who saw Grace leave. You want to wait for all the others?"

Wendy scratched her cheek. "Let's see how many calls they've made. We only thought there were a couple who'd actually seen her." They walked into the living room. Luke sat on the couch with Chay, throwing his wadded-up list into the air.

Tav asked, "You done?"

"Does it look like it?"

"Depends. You either completed the list, or you quit."

"No one saw anything."

"Fine. Good work. I think." Luke threw the wad at Tav. Missed. Which proved why he played receiver and not quarterback.

Tav popped his head into the back room with Micah. Mick still talked on the phone. Tav signed, *Anything?*

Nothing.

Done after this.

Micah nodded. Tav moved out to the front porch. Jen still talked—listened—on the phone. Tav gave her the neck-cutting sign. He grinned.

Jen gave a silent sigh of relief and addressed the phone. "Oh, I'm sorry. I have to go. Bye."

Tav chuckled. "Same caller?"

Jen lowered her head and shook it. "Some people. I know there are people who can talk all day long... I've never been one of them." She looked at him. "What have you got?"

"Pay dirt. Come on in. We can wrap this part."

"Good thing. I think I wore a path on Micah's porch."

The group reconvened in the living room. Tav reported what Mona had observed. Chay shook her head. Angrily. "No. Not Mom. She doesn't kiss men on the spur of the moment. She hasn't been with anyone in years." She stopped. "She's seen Quinn a few times, but seeing Quinn and *seeing* Quinn are two different things."

Micah held up his hand. "For those of us in the back row, explain the difference."

Chay scowled. "She's seen Quinn. They met at some soiree for a new collection of artifacts. And Quinn took her to lunch one afternoon. But they had hot dogs and fries, nothing serious. They've been together a couple of other times. But none of it is serious stuff. Certainly not serious enough for her to kiss him." She shook her head. "Your Mona was wrong. If she saw Mom crying, Mom had to be upset. Scared, I'll buy. But not happy scared."

No one tried to correct Chay's observation. And it matched the original description of when Grace left.

Tav assured her, "We're still looking. Let us know if you can suggest anything, anyone, or anywhere to look. Otherwise, I'll yield the floor to Wendy."

Wendy viewed her notes. "I have nothing new on Quinn or Grace. I have a receipt I'm trying to track. Until I get something solid, it's like everything else. Bits and pieces but no substance."

Tav noted, "The DMV still has nothing on the car that hit me."

Wendy looked at her phone. "The dead body in the dig site proved to be from a cold case six years ago. Leisch had a couple of business associates. They were peddling native artifacts. One of the associates came up missing. They blackmailed Leisch into silence by threatening to implicate him in the murder. Since they were the only ones who knew where the body was, Leisch kept quiet. Once Leisch found his cohort, he could cross the double-crossers. Or so he thought. The County officials are happy to have a resolution and appreciate our help."

Micah added, "The skeleton in the cavern turned out

to be a missing person from three years ago. No foul play. From what they found in the area, drugs and alcohol may have been involved."

"We can cross the dead bodies off the list, then?"

"Yeah. No further action required."

Jen directed her attention to Tav. "I've been trying to recall the busser who left just before the fire started. Seems to me he left in a big hurry."

Tav put a hand to his chin. "I remember. Let's both write a description and see what we come up with. Maybe it helps the police solve the fire. Maybe it's nothing."

Addison tapped his fist on the arm of his chair. "I can't see Dad having any part in trying to hurt you, Tav. I can't. He talks big. But it's the alcohol talking, not him. He'd never actually do something so evil."

"Would he pay someone to run me off the road?"

Addison fell silent. Tav hoped his youngest brother would seriously consider the question.

Micah stated the obvious. "We're still at the 'what do we do about all this?' phase." He pointed at Addison. "And you're item six and seven. What do we do about your dad knowing Tav and Luke are back in your life?"

Addison chewed his cheek. "I was all set last night to blast in and tell him. Now, I'm not so sure." He shrugged. "Coward."

"No one facing a raging bull is a coward, brother." Luke leaned forward in his chair to meet his brother's eyes. "We know. We've been there. The real problem is Mom. What do we do to protect her? Can we?"

"Mom will be ecstatic to have all her children under one roof. It's Dad who will be the issue."

"No." Tav rested back in his chair. "We know how he will react. He'll be furious. He'll come out swinging. Mom will either support him, have a meltdown, or both."

Luke added darkly, "She'll support him, then meltdown after we leave."

Chay suggested, "Leave with her. Take her when you go."

"If she'll come." Luke remained dubious.

Tav shook his head. "We can argue all day about what Mom will do. The fastest way to find out is for us to show at the door. Dad will see we're not on the team to outshine Addison, and maybe, just maybe, he'll get over thinking I'm Luke and trying to kill me."

Micah held up a hand. "Wait. Wait a moment. There's a flaw in there that just occurred to me."

"Just now? Took you long enough to think of it."

"None of you have. You say your dad thinks Tav is Luke. And you're on the team to hurt him. Except you're riding a motorcycle. No one on the team is allowed to ride a bike. Too much chance of being injured. So he can't think you're on the team or even trying to be."

Tav stared at Micah. He felt his jaw drop. *Why didn't I think about the prohibition on bikes?* He dropped his eyes to the floor and studied the carpet. Dog hair tufted under the table. Mialma. Labs shed.

He frowned at Micah. "Point made. So...he knows who I am. And he is trying to hurt me because...why?"

"Because you exist. And didn't fulfill his dream."

Tav exploded. "That was six years ago!"

Addison's tone came out flat. "And he's never gotten over it. Even with me as a quarterback, he still curses you for defying him."

"I did not defy him. I tore my knee. Twice. I couldn't be who he wanted."

Addison ignored his protest. "Then you stole Luke away. So he got stuck with me. Third-string quarterback. Third-string son."

Luke closed his eyes. "You're not third-string anything." He opened his eyes and held Tav's gaze. "Let Addison and me go to the house. I'll shave and strip the hair color. He'll know it's me as soon as I walk up. We can see how he reacts. If all truly is forgiven, we'll call you in. Otherwise, we'll leave and know we tried. Mom will come or not."

Tav glared at the floor. He didn't like it. But it made sense. As much as anything did. He glanced around the room. "Discussion?"

No one added anything. "All in." Tav explained to Addison, "We vote. Fists in. Silent count of four. Thumbs up, we go with the plan. Thumbs down, we come with a different plan."

Micah said, "This is between the three of you. We're not a party to this."

"But you can tell if it's a good plan or not. The more voices, the better."

Chay, Wendy, Micah, and Jen all put their fists into the circle. Tav, Luke, and Addison did as well.

Silent count. Seven thumbs went up. Tav ducked his head. "Carried. You two go. I'll hang back. If you give me the sign, I'll come in. Otherwise, I'll know."

Addison said, "Dad gets home around five."

Luke suggested, "We should be there before he gets home. Maybe before he starts drinking. If we go at four-thirty, we can talk to Mom. Maybe she'll help. Maybe she'll throw me out. We'll have to play it by ear."

Tav huffed. "This whole caper is a 'by ear' production. We need to pray God intervenes and is part of this."

Micah added, "He goes before you. He walks with you. He follows after. All to make sure you arrive safely."

Tav nodded. "Right." He stood. "But I want to pray." He looked around the room for dissenters. No one raised a hand in opposition. Tav closed his eyes. "God, we can't succeed if You're not in this. We need You. Show us Your way, Your truth. If this is Your plan for us to pull Mom out, then show us how. Most of all, keep us in Your will. In Jesus's Name, amen."

He gazed around the room. "I know we didn't deal with Quinn and Grace. Wendy, you keep tracing the receipts, and we'll see what we can do."

Jen spoke. "Let's not forget the busser. We should write out our descriptions and then call the police."

"Right." He smiled at her. "Good reminder."

She smiled back. "I'm good for something."

Wendy shoved her. "Stop that. You're good at plenty. You really are great to have around." She stopped. "But don't tell Mom I said you're good. She thinks we're always at odds with each other. I'd like to foster the misinformation. Keeps her guessing."

Jen tapped fists lightly with Wendy. "Solid."

* * *

WEDNESDAY AFTERNOON

Addison and Luke sat in the car. Addison watched the clock turn to four-thirty. "Time to go, bro."

"Yeah, but only if you're sure about this." Luke's knee bounced.

"Not, but we have to try sometime." Addison gritted his teeth. And tried to loosen the knots in his gut.

"Yeah, I know. Let's do this."

They climbed out of the car and walked up the front path. Addison opened the door and called, "Mom. I'm home. You'll never guess who I met."

Mom called from the kitchen. "Hang on. I'll be right

there." She stepped in from the kitchen, wiping her hands on her slacks. She noticed Luke, did a double take, then stared hard. Her face went slack.

Luke kept his tone even and light. "Hi, Mom."

Mom's eyes flew open wide. She covered her mouth with both hands. Tears flooded her cheeks. She held out her hands and wagged her fingers. "Come here. Come here."

Luke crossed the room, and Mom buried him in kisses and hugs. Luke came up for air at some point. "Mom. It's okay."

Addison lowered his head. She'd never made over him that way. But he'd never been gone six years, either. Give Luke some slack.

Luke repeated, "Mom, it's okay. I'm here now. We're back together again."

Mom held him by the shoulders. "You haven't changed. I'd recognize you anywhere. Any time. My son." She crushed him back to her chest.

Luke glanced over her shoulder and gave Addison the 'not a word' warning. Addison understood. Let her have her delusion. What did it matter?

She led Luke to the couch and sat beside him. "How?" She caught Addison's eyes. "How did you find him?" She turned to Luke. "Where have you been?" Then she shook her head. "It doesn't matter. You're here now, and that's what counts. Oh, your father will be so excited and happy to see you."

Addison drawled, "You really think so?"

Mom nodded quickly. "Of course, he will. He misses Luke as much as I have. He'll be thrilled to see him. He will." She focused back on Luke. "Tell me. Where have you been? What have you been doing? Why haven't you come back before now?"

Luke's tone stayed even. "Dad told me not to set foot

in this house again."

Mom waved it off. "Your father didn't mean it. He didn't. He was upset, but he didn't mean it." She put her arms on Luke's shoulders again. "Look at you. You're all grown. You're a man."

Luke bowed his head. "Mom, Tav—"

She cut him off. "Let's talk about you. Tell me where you're living? Who are you seeing? Do you have a girlfriend? Are you in school? Where do you work?"

Addison suggested, "Dad will be home in half an hour. Maybe all the explanations can wait until he gets home, so they can tell you everything all at once?"

Mom's face carried confusion. "They? Who are they?"

"Tav and Luke."

She shook her head. "No, I want to hear all about Lucas now. He can tell the story again when Dad gets home." She smiled. "I won't get tired of hearing it."

Luke eyed Addison. Addison shrugged. "Yeah, go on."

Luke shrugged. "There's not much to tell. I'm in school, studying pre-med."

Mom clapped her hands together. "My son, the doctor."

Luke laughed. "Only if I make it through the classes. They're tougher than I thought they'd be."

"But if anyone can tackle them, you can. I believe in you, Lucas. I always have." She patted his arm, then squeezed it.

Not the general attitude Addison heard about his brothers, but hey. Revisionist history at its finest, he guessed.

Luke continued. "I have a steady friend. She's studying archeology up north, where her mom teaches. Her name is Chay Painter."

Mom beamed. "Oh, how lovely. How long have you

known her?"

"I met her two years ago. We've been corresponding since then."

"'Corresponding?' Is that a fancy way of dating? Or are you not serious?"

Luke shrugged a shoulder. "It's complicated. Neither of us is ready for a commitment until we finish school. But we are serious about staying in touch."

"This is wonderful. This is all wonderful. And where are you living?"

"On campus. In student housing with Tav."

"Oh." Addison wondered if Luke heard the change in tone. "Well, I suppose that's good. Are you working? It must be terribly hard to stay in school and hold a job, too. Wouldn't it be easier to move home?"

Luke laughed. Addison noted it was a careful laugh. Luke had caught the inflection. "We're fine where we are. I'm not working except at trying to get through my classes."

"How are you paying for school? Oh, you must be on a scholarship. Of course, you'd be. You're too smart not to be." Mom sat back as if having settled the matter, whether true or not. In her mind, a scholarship was an established fact.

How *were* Luke and Tav paying for school? Addison hadn't really had time to ask. Too much catching up on the past to deal with the present. But he would ask. Maybe he could get in on the deal. Unless they were dealing...nah. Not his brothers. Knights of the Octagon, right? Ever and always. Had to be something else.

Luke breathed slowly but said nothing more about finances. "We're doing fine, Mom. Really. Tav—"

She cut him off again. "I want to know about you, not your brother. He can talk for himself. Tell me, how did you and Addison find each other?"

Luke hummed slightly. "I think I'd rather tell the story after Dad gets home. Get it out all at once."

"Well, keep your secrets then." Mom laughed. "Come in the kitchen and get a snack to eat. You're staying for dinner, of course."

"Maybe."

"Maybe? Why wouldn't you?"

Luke exchanged glances with Addison. Addison's eyes widened, then returned to normal. Expose the elephant in the room. Or the one who would be home soon. Addison explained, "Because we don't know how Dad will react. He might not be as happy to see Luke and Tav as you are."

Again, Mom waved off the concern. "He'll be beside himself with joy at seeing you again, Lucas. He will be. I know him. I know how much he has missed you. He'll be happy, you'll see."

Luke stood. "Then I should tell Tav he can come in?"

"Why? Is he outside?" Resentment marked the tone. Mom's eyes narrowed. Luke couldn't miss the change, could he?

"He's waiting down the block. We didn't think it smart to both show at the same time."

"So he threw you to the wolves?" She laughed but shrilly. "That sounds like your brother. He always let you do the hard work. He could stand in one spot and throw the ball, and you had to run all over the field."

Luke corrected. "No, Mom. I'm the one who suggested I come in first. Dad had the most problem with me, so I figured I would be the first to face him."

"Your dad never had a problem with you, Lucas. Never."

Luke's face drew sober. "I remember a night when he did."

"No, no. No. His problem wasn't with you. You

misunderstood him. He wanted the best for you. He still does. Always."

Addison watched his brother's face for expression. The man kept it together and said quietly, "I felt it different. But six years have passed. I've forgiven him. If he's forgiven me, then we can move forward."

Addison noted Luke said nothing about forgiving his mom. Maybe because he hadn't? Or she might bridle at the thought she'd committed anything needing forgiveness? Or for a reason Addison didn't know? In any event, Luke didn't mention it.

Mom, however, couldn't let it go. "There's nothing to forgive, Lucas. Your dad wanted only the best for you. You misunderstood his meaning. It's all water under the bridge now."

Luke's voice softened. "I'm sure Tav will be happy to hear it as well. I'll go get him."

Mom shook her head. "I think it would be better if you saw your dad alone first. You said it yourself, you wanted to meet with him. You should see him, then we'll call your brother. If everything is okay, of course."

Luke eyed his mom. "You said it would be."

"I said it would be with you and your father. He may still have issues with Taylor they need to resolve. But it's not your concern. The two of them can work their problems out. Come to the kitchen. I'll get you drinks."

Luke and Addison took a seat in the kitchen. Addison dropped his hands below the table and texted Tav. *Wait.*

His phone buzzed. The text had been received. Addison tapped Luke on the foot. Luke tapped him back.

Mom brought out beers and held them. Addison's mouth watered, but he shook his head. "Water. With ice, please."

Luke added, "Same. I can get it, Mom."

"Sit. I won't have my sons waiting on themselves when I'm capable of serving them."

A car pulled into the driveway. Addison's gut tightened. He forced his hands to relax from their fists. It would be fine. It would. Everything would be great.

The engine stopped. The car door slammed. The kitchen door opened. Luke and Addison stood.

Dad raised his eyes from his phone. His eyes narrowed. He stopped his approach. Mom sing-songed happily, "Look who's here! Lucas came back to us. Isn't it wonderful?"

Dad threw his phone on the table, dropped his briefcase, and grabbed a beer from the refrigerator. "What do you want?" He stared hard. "It was you last night. It was. I knew it. I knew it."

Luke kept his tone even. "Hello, Dad."

Mom snaked her arm around Luke's shoulders. "He's home, Chris. Our son is finally home. Can't you tell him how happy you are?"

Dad drank a long swig from the can. "I asked you what you wanted."

Luke didn't change tone. "To be a family again."

Dad sniffed. "Why now?"

"Why not now?"

"Your brother is the starting quarterback. You want in on his action, right?"

Mom tried again. "Chris, your son came to see you. He wants to make things right between you. Can't you say hello?"

"You want to make things right, huh?" Dad took a chair and sat, facing Luke.

Luke didn't sit. "Yes, sir. I want to know if we can be a family again."

"Yeah? And what do you suppose family would look like? The four of us all living together in this happy little house?"

Luke shook his head. "No, sir. We're five people. Tav and I have our own place. Addison lives on campus. But we would come to visit and be welcome."

"And all the heartache you put your mother through the past six years, it just goes away? Never happened?"

Luke's voice strained slightly. "Only if you let it."

"Let it?" Dad raised his eyebrows. "Let it." He glared at Mom. "Do we let the past six years disappear like they didn't exist? All the nights you cried and carried on because your son walked away from you? All the days you spent moping and doing nothing because you were too upset to clean house? Or cook? Or do anything at all? Do we just let it go?"

Mom agreed. "Yes. Of course." Her tone became frantic. "It doesn't matter now. He's home. That's what counts. We're together, and it's how it should be."

Luke lowered his head, then said, "There's still Tav."

Dad swigged his beer. "Of course there is. Where is the little coward? I mean, my oldest son? Hiding?"

Addison took the focus off Luke. "He's up the street. Waiting to see if he's welcome or not." Addison's fists tightened.

"Call him in. The more, the merrier. Let's get this all out in the open."

Luke glared at Addison. Addison shook his head. He addressed his dad. "I'm not bringing him in here if you're going to tear into him like you have Luke. We'll just leave now."

"What do you mean 'we?' Where are you going?" Dad faced him, his eyes narrowing dangerously.

"With my brothers. If they're not welcome, neither am I."

"They'll be welcome when they apologize for the pain

they've caused your mother and pay back the money they owe me." Dad sat back in his chair and gloated at Luke.

Luke's head came up. "Money? What money? We never spent a dime of your money after we left. What money are you talking about?"

"I'm talking about all the travel sports, all the coaching, all the lessons I paid so your brother could become a star quarterback. Then there's six years of your mother's drinking. I figure one bottle of wine a day, ten bucks a bottle, times six years?" He paused. His eyes darted back and forth as he did the math. "I figure twenty-two thousand right there. Then there's my drinking on top of that."

Luke snapped. "Give me a figure. What do we owe you?"

"More than you can pay, I know." The gloat continued. "Name the price."

Dad thought a moment. "A hundred thousand dollars."

Luke's eyes narrowed. "And what does it get us?"

"You could never pay me a hundred thousand." Dad rocked forward, eyeing Luke. Unsure.

Mom stepped forward. "Stop this. Stop. Lucas is home. Nothing else matters. Why can't you be happy?" She hugged Luke around the shoulder, reached out to include Addison. She begged Dad, "They're here. Together. Please. Stop this. For me?"

"What does a hundred thousand buy us? Forgiveness? Happy ever after? Never mentioning the past again?"

Dad laughed. "You'll never know."

Luke slammed the table. "Tell me what it buys us. You named the figure." Even Addison jumped. He'd never seen his brother so angry.

"Nothing. It buys you nothing." Dad snarled. "There's not a price high enough for the grief you caused."

Mom grabbed hold of Dad. "Stop! He's our son. We

love him."

He pushed her away. "You love him. I don't want anything to do with him. Or his...brother." Dad added several derogatory descriptions. He pointed. "There's the door. Leave."

Mom begged, "Darling, please. Please. For me? For my sanity. Please."

Dad sneered, "You lost your sanity when your sons walked out the first time. Them coming back won't change anything." Another beer joined the empties.

Addison glowered at Dad. "Don't be cold. Don't attack Mom."

"You shut your mouth, or you'll be out of school tomorrow. You're not on scholarship. Your brothers robbed you of your money. I never had time to showcase your talents like I did Taylor's. Luke here didn't want what I could make of him, so he missed it. I'm paying for your education, and you will do as I say."

Luke laid his hand on Mom's arm. "Come with us." His tone softened.

"Where?" She was lost. Totally lost.

"Away from here. We can still be family. Tav, Addison, you, and me."

Dad chugged his beer and went for another. "And live where? And do what? You two never held jobs. You're useless. You'll be on the street tomorrow."

Luke ignored Dad. "Mom, please. Walk away from this hate."

She stared at Dad, then gazed at Luke again. "You and me and Addison? We could be family?"

"And Tav, yeah."

"Not him." Mom hardened her tone in anger. "He stole you away from me. He tore this family apart. I don't want to have anything to do with him." She put her arm around

Luke. "But we could be together again." She fawned over him.

Addison pleaded, "Mom, Tav—"

Mom screamed, "His name is Taylor! I gave him that name. He's been ashamed of his name and hated me for giving it to him. Well, I'll never forgive him for stealing you away from me. No, I won't be family with him again."

Luke lowered his head. "We're done." He lifted his eyes to Addison. "I'm done. I'll see you at the car." He walked to the door, then stopped. He turned and faced Dad. "I have to know. Are you the one trying to kill Tav?"

Dad's head jerked. "Kill him? And jeopardize my freedom? I'd never be so stupid." He swilled more of the beer. "Though I salute anyone who does try. No, I'm not after my..."

Again with the nastiness. Addison caught the guilt in his mom's eyes. Haunted. What did the expression mean? Was she after Tav? Mom? Never.

Luke walked out the door. Addison headed to his room, grabbed his duffle, and shoved as much as possible into the depths. Sentimental stuff. Personal stuff. Irreplaceable stuff. Mom raced after him. "What are you doing? Why are you packing?" She pawed at him, trying to get him to stop.

"I'm leaving. Going with Luke." Addison kept packing.

"No, no, no, no. You can't go. You can't. You're all I have left." She sank on the bed.

"You could have had all three of us." Addison stopped and shook his head.

From the kitchen, Dad shouted, "Let him go! I'm canceling his tuition. He'll be on the street in no time. His brothers want to ride his coattails. They'll dump him when they see he's out of school. You watch."

Addison walked past Mom. She continued to paw at him, trying to stop him from leaving. Addison walked out the door. An empty beer can flew past him and slammed against the metal trash can. Dad never could throw. Addison tossed his duffle in the back seat of the 4X4, slid into the shotgun position, and shook his head. "I'm sorry."

Luke started the engine. "We had to try. Tell Tav we'll meet at Micah's. We can make plans from there."

Addison stared at the floorboard. "Not much to plan. I'll be out of school by the end of the term."

Luke pulled into traffic. "You're staying in school. We've got you covered, Addison."

"You two become independently wealthy since leaving home?"

"You could say that. Ever hear of the Magary Treasure Hunt?"

"The crazy dude who said he buried a million bucks? And no one's ever found it? That hunt?"

"Magary wasn't crazy, he did bury the money, and someone did find it."

Addison stared sideways at his brother. "Yeah? Who?"

Luke grinned. "The Knights of the Octagon, brother. The Knights of the Octagon." He lost his smile. "We lost Jeremiah. But we found the treasure. With some help. But yeah, Tav and I have enough to put you and us through school. Because we love you. And you deserve it."

Addison sat back in the seat. He could think of nothing to say. Nothing. Except, "Wow."

* * *

Tav received the text. *Meet at Micah's. No joy.*

So their plans were a bust. He dropped his head. "Okay, Father. This wasn't Your way. We'll follow You. And keep praying for Mom and Dad to forgive."

He started the bike and headed off down the road.

He saw a car pull out into the lane in his rearview

mirror. Tav kept his speed legal. He also kept his eyes on the car behind him. It didn't close the distance between them but didn't vary in the interval either. His shadow stayed with him.

Tav looped around a block or two. The car remained with him.

Tav sped. The car matched his speed.

He slowed. The shadow slowed as well. Was he only interested in Tav's destination? Trying to follow him to Micah's? But anyone could find Micah. He was on the Internet. If the person shadowing Tav knew him at all, he would know where Micah lived.

Unless he didn't know Tav? And could simply be a psycho stalker? What were the odds?

Tav entered the traffic circle at the proscribed twenty-five mph.

The car behind leaped to full speed. As Tav looped around the drive, the vehicle cut across two lanes to attack him. Tav dodged at the last moment. The motorcycle's wheels lost traction and skidded out from under him. The bike toppled over onto his leg, pinning him.

The car accelerated and blasted out of the area. No plates. No tags. Only darkness.

Tav waited until his breathing slowed to normal, then wriggled out from under the bike. He set it upright, started it, mounted it, then headed to Micah's. He rode the distance watching his rearview mirror more than what preceded him. But he saw nothing. Whoever had crashed him had done his work for the evening. And unsettled him again. He needed the Knights to help him figure it out. What did the attacker want? Why Tav? Why now? Why wouldn't God answer why?

Trust in the Lord with all your heart, and don't lean on your own understanding...

I hear You, Lord.

Tav drove the rest of the way to Micah's.

* * *

WEDNESDAY LATE EVENING

Micah poured coffee for Jen, Wendy, and Chay. "The guys will be here soon. We can get a full report from them about what happened at the house. And after."

Wendy accepted the beverage, tasted it, and saluted Micah. "I've got a proposal I need to run by everyone."

Jen glanced across the room at her sister. "Oh? You didn't mention anything to me about a proposal."

"Thought I'd do a one-and-done. Then I don't have to be turned down multiple times for the same offense."

"Smart."

Mialma barked excitedly. Ben ran in from his room and raced to the back door. Micah heard the backdoor open and an "oof… Hey, Ben" from Tav. Guess he came first in the door.

Luke's "Hey, Buddy" followed. Then a "Do you remember Addison? Your secret brother? But he's no secret anymore. He's all our brother."

In his mind, Micah saw the solemn nod and the hug. The "Thank you, Ben" confirmed his thoughts.

The three Vaughn brothers, united at last, walked into the living room. Micah greeted each one with a hug. Wendy and Jen saluted with hand waves. Chay moved to sit beside Luke. She held his hand. From the look on Luke's face, he probably needed a hand to hold.

BB came in from the back, his earphones around his neck. "Did I hear company arrive?"

Another round of welcomes and salutes passed the

group. Followed by drinks all around. At last, everyone was seated, drinked, and ready for the meeting.

Micah asked, "Who has the lead?"

Tav and Addison pointed to Luke. Luke lowered his head. "First, I need to confess losing my temper. Kept my mouth but lost my temper."

Micah held up a hand. "Absolved. Forgiven. Go on."

Luke detailed the meeting with their parents. Addison supplied the moments after Luke left, and Tav described his escape from being roadkill once again.

Once everyone came up to speed on the events of the evening, Ben went from Vaughn brother to Vaughn brother to Vaughn brother with quieting hugs. Tav rubbed the little guy's head. "Thanks, Ben. Your love helps."

Luke's voice choked. "It heals. Love you, bud."

Addison merely hugged Ben. Long hug. The youngest Vaughn's eyes glistened when he released the boy.

Ben took his place back between Wendy and Jen. Best seat in the house, of course. BB could be jealous. But Micah knew he had enough sense not to be. Micah gazed around the room. "Family. I want to propose a trade, Tav. Let me ride the bike for the next week. You can drive my car."

"Why? You can't take the boys to school on the bike."

"No. But I want to see if whoever is after you is really after you or the bike. Is this just someone who can't see a motorcycle? Someone who hates motorcycles? Hates the color black? I don't know. But I want to change the variables and see what happens. I'll drive your routes. We're different enough in size they won't mistake me for you. And my helmet and jacket are from a separate manufacturer. If they come after me, we know it's not personal."

Luke growled, "Unless they're after all the Knights."

"Possible. Not likely. Tav?"

"What about school?"

BB raised his eyebrows. "We're out a few days for teacher conferences. No school." Ben crossed his arms and pouted deeply. BB laughed. "We'll do some fun stuff, trust me." Ben dropped the pout. But not his arms. BB would have to prove his statement.

Tav stared at the ground. Micah looked at him sideways. "Do we need to put it to a vote?"

"No. I don't like it. It makes sense, but I don't like it."

"So?"

"So fine. One day. I'll give you tomorrow, and that's it."

"I'll take it." Micah gave Tav the thumbs-up sign. Tav grimaced but reciprocated.

Micah moved on. "Next subject. What to do about Mrs. Vaughn."

Wendy held up a hand. "I have some insight on how to help but need to clarify a detail first."

Micah cocked his head. "Clarify what?"

"Nothing critical, so you can drop the defensive posture. All of you." She glanced around the room and smiled.

Micah felt the group exhale more than heard it. "All right. What is it?"

"You've all done your family DNA, right? Have you accessed your records lately?"

Micah eyed Tav. Tav nodded, then shook his head. Micah did the same. "Yes, we've done them. No, we haven't checked them lately. Why?"

"Jen and I are both adopted. Since there is some question of future relationships here, I'd like to ensure none of us are connected."

Tav shook his head and chuckled. "So whenever you go on a date, you ask to see the DNA profile first?"

Wendy and Jen chuckled. Jen raised her eyebrows at Tav. "You should know the answer to that. No."

Wendy added, "Not on the first date, anyhow." Micah noted the general laughter. His stomach tweaked. Was there a chance? *Lord, forbid I'm related to Wendy. Please.*

Wendy continued. "I'd like to compare notes. Just for fun, if nothing else. May we, please?" She smiled at BB. "And yes, I'm including you and Ben as well. I could have younger brothers I know nothing about." She motioned over at Chay. "Or a sister."

Micah checked the room. All assents. Mostly chuckles. But variations of "Yeah, why not?" came back.

Wendy signed on to Micah's computer. After a few moments, she pulled her DNA registry. She had a hit. Micah asked, "Did you know about the possible link?"

"I'd seen it. I just haven't checked it out yet."

Wendy moved away from the screen. "Jen, why don't you do yours first? See if we come up with anything new."

Jen accessed her registry. No new hits. Micah saw Tav relax. Good news for him. Would it be as good for Micah?

Wendy went to her profile. The link. She pulled it up.

Brothers. Parents. A name. A record. Micah peered over her shoulder. His mouth dropped open. He turned to Tav. "You have to see this." He moved aside to let Tav view the computer.

Tav walked over. "What?" Then, "Luke…Addison." His voice shook.

Luke joined his brother behind Wendy's shoulder. He stared at the results. He whispered, "Houston, we have a problem."

Wendy bit her lower lip. She raised a hand and waved weakly. "Hi."

No one spoke. Addison knelt beside Wendy. He asked, "May I?"

She backed away from the computer and let Addison type. The younger man clicked at the keys. He enlarged a copy of a document. His birth certificate. At the bottom, it read, "Four of four live births."

Tav stared from Wendy to Micah. Then to Wendy. Then to Micah. "Wendy is my sister."

Luke added, "Wendy is all our sister." Chay put her arm in Luke's and laughed.

"How? How is this even possible?" Tav eyed Wendy. "You expected this. Tell us how."

Wendy related the facts of her birth, her family tree, and her suspicions. When she was done, Tav's face mirrored horror. "This can't be. It can't."

Luke laughed. "Stranger things. It's weird, but—"

Tav cut him off. "You don't see it. Wendy is our sister. Micah is dating our sister."

Wendy chuckled. "And my brother is dating my sister."

Tav shook his head. "Nah, this can't happen. No way. Huh-uh." He turned away from Wendy.

Wendy's eyes widened. "You mean I'm not good—"

Tav cut her off. "I mean, Micah isn't good enough for you. My sister deserves a college man. Not some slouch who only offers excuses. This...this...this can't happen. No. No way."

Micah laughed. "Cute, Tav. Real cute." He was joking, right? Right?

Tav held Micah's eyes. "Do you see humor in my eyes? I'm serious, dude. You get enrolled in college, and then we'll talk about you dating my sister. But not until then. You hear me, Knight?"

This might be worse than being distantly related to Wendy. This might be...

Worth every insult. He valued her above anything Tav could throw at him. Granted, they weren't "a couple" yet. But they would be if he had anything to say about it. And he would say plenty.

"I'll be at the registrar's office tomorrow morning."

Jen bumped Wendy's side. "You gonna let this go on? Your brother telling you who you can date and who you can't?"

Wendy grinned. "This time. This one time." She raised her eyebrows at Tav. "You hear me, big brother?"

Tav hugged Wendy around the neck. "I hear you, little sister."

Luke and Addison embraced Wendy as well. Then Luke asked, "You said you had an idea about Mom. How does this help?"

Wendy lowered her eyes. "I have no illusions your father will want to have anything to do with me." She raised her head. "The story of how I came to be abandoned made that clear in the first place. But there's a chance your mother might want a relationship. Might. Which is a big 'maybe.' But it allows me to approach her." She turned to Addison. "Can I use a copy of your birth certificate?"

Luke leaned forward. "You can use mine."

"Addison was the last. The 'four of four' is telling. And she is still most closely connected to you." She motioned to her youngest brother. "Please?"

"Yeah. You can copy it."

"Thanks, Addison."

Micah shook his head. "We're going through all this, and we still don't have any clues about where Quinn and Grace are."

Tav groaned. "One crisis at a time. And I know Quinn being missing is the catalyst for all this. But we've got immediate problems to deal with. We'll get back to finding Quinn. I swear we will."

Micah instructed, "Fists in." Addison tipped his head to the side. Micah explained, "Fists in. Silent four count. Thumbs up, we go with the plan. Thumbs down, we stay for more discussion."

Addison nodded. "Got it."

Nine fists went in. Micah called, "Go."

Four count.

Nine thumbs went up.

"Carried." Micah pointed to Addison. "You're welcome to stay here or with your brothers. I've got more room, but you might want to do some catching up."

"Absolutely."

Wendy stood. "Jen, we'll be going, too. I've got work in the morning."

Jen snipped, "And I don't?"

"Then we're both leaving."

"Not without saying goodbye."

Wendy grinned. "Of course."

Tav took Jen's hand. "I've got the front porch."

Micah took Wendy's. "Back stairs."

Luke grinned. "So Chay and I have the living room?"

Micah agreed. "Yeah. With Ben and BB and Addison."

Luke groaned. "Not fair."

Tav ordered, "It keeps you honest."

Micah and Wendy moseyed to the back steps. Micah lowered his eyes. "I will get registered in college tomorrow." He stopped. "Wendy, um…I'm not good at this."

Wendy smiled. Her eyes twinkled. "I think that's commendable. It means you haven't had a lot of practice."

Micah shrugged. "None, to be exact." He held her eyes. "I want to get to know you. The 'off-the-clock' Wendy. We've been through some strange and intense experiences. But it doesn't mean I know you. And I don't even know what I'm saying right now."

Wendy touched the side of his face. "Then don't talk." She reached and kissed him.

Micah took her in his arms—

Luke slammed the door open. "Addison just got a text. Half the team came down with food poisoning. We've got to get back to campus and the dorm." He disappeared back into the house.

Micah groaned. Wendy laughed. "I'll talk to you tomorrow, Mick. Good night."

"Good night, Wendy." She walked around the back of the house to meet with Jen. Micah sighed deeply. Luke came out with his backpack. Addison followed him. Chay followed Addison. Luke patted Micah on the back. "Sorry, dude. God protects us, even when we may not want it."

"Yeah, I hear you." Micah tapped knuckles with Luke and Addison. He hugged Chay, then watched them drive off. He went back into the house. Tav tossed Micah the keys to the motorcycle. "Be careful, bro."

"You know me. Caution is my middle name."

"Keep it that way." Tav picked up Micah's keys. He hugged Ben. Ben waited until Tav stepped away, then made little kissing noises. Tav whirled around and stared at Ben. "You did not just make that noise. You weren't mocking Jen and me, were you?"

Ben sat upright on the couch but would not look at Tav. He sat stone-still and stared at the wall.

Tav glared at BB and Micah. "Who taught him that?"

Micah laughed. "No one. No one here, anyhow."

Tav pointed at Ben. "I better not hear those noises when Jen is here. Got it?"

Ben nodded one time. Tav grinned at him. "Smart guy. No more funny business." He hugged Ben again. "Love you, Ben."

Ben hugged him in return. Tav left. Micah sat beside Ben. "I know we think it's funny, but we shouldn't make fun of anyone except each other. Jen might be hurt by what you did. Or it would make her feel uncomfortable. So if it's just us, making a little joke is okay. But not when there are other people around. Not until we know them well. Got it?"

Ben nodded once more. He threw his arms around Micah's middle. Micah hugged the boy. "Okay, go get ready for bed."

Ben ran off. BB lowered his head and chortled. Micah joined him. They pulled it together, then BB asked, "How can half the team come down with food poisoning?"

"Half had chicken? I don't know. It will be interesting to see which quarterback got hit."

"Or if both did."

All the levity drained out. Micah stared at BB. "This could have been deliberate?"

"I hope not. That's all I can say."

"Yeah. Let's wait and see what Luke reports."

"Agreed." BB eyed him. "You sure about riding the bike?"

"I'm sure I will be the slowest, most careful motorcycle rider on the road tomorrow. I'll be fine."

"You better be. I'm just getting you broke in as my guardian."

"Yeah, I know. Good night, BB."

"Night, Mick."

Micah headed to the back to tuck Ben in.

* * *

THURSDAY

The boys went to visit friends for the morning while Micah worked. He was busy with his tax business when Wendy called. "I found an address. 255 S Harcourt. Do you recognize it?"

Micah looked at his phone. "No. No one I know. You want me to check it out?"

Wendy's voice was flat with sarcasm. "No, I do not want you to check it out. That's my job. I wanted to know if you recognized it, that's all. If it meant anything to you from your time with Quinn."

"No, I don't. I can go there if it will help."

"Don't you think you've been beaten enough? Why don't you sit one out for a change and let me do what I'm trained to do."

"Because Quinn always says don't go alone. If you tell me honestly that someone is going with you, I'll let it go. But not unless you do."

"Fine. I'll call you back."

Micah hung up and returned to working on the tax files before him. They didn't have the same appeal they had before Wendy called. Filing extensions for companies that could afford to pay the taxes, but filed late on principle, irked him. It was the game, he knew. But not a game he liked anymore. Maybe he should think of a different career.

Like being a spy?

Uh, no. He had sons to think of. And maybe a wife...one day. Being a spy took too much energy. Not that Quinn was a spy.

Truth was, no one knew exactly what Quinn was. Or did. Even Wendy avoided the subject, which might make sense for her, but still... Quinn could give them a hint.

He did. Often. He repeatedly told them, "You see nothing. You know nothing." Nothing is what Quinn did.

Okay, so Wendy had an address. No law said Micah couldn't Google it and see where it was. Maybe they'd been there under cover of darkness. Maybe Quinn had driven them past it. Maybe...

Micah pulled up the map. Hmm. Not in the best part of town. Which wasn't in itself a problem. Who decided what was the good part, anyhow? So scratch that. In the industrial part of town. A residence. No company name, anyhow.

Micah went in and changed out of his slacks into his blue jeans. Hung up his white accountant shirt and pulled on a Henley jersey. Put on the sneakers. Better for running. Then waited for Wendy to call. He still had Tav's motorcycle, so he could meet her on the way downtown. Quieter in a car than on the bike. Less showy. Less conspicuous.

He went back to his office and sat at the desk. He could work while he waited. He should work while he waited. Wendy might be a long time calling...

Half an hour later, his phone rang. He smiled. "Andres Tax Service. How can I help you?"

Wendy sneered, "Like you didn't know it was me. Okay, I can't get anyone here to back me up on short notice." She paused. "Honesty, right? I'm not expected to take Quinn's cases while he's gone. The supervisors keep telling me to wait. To give him time. He still has those thirty days. Well, I don't like it, and I'm going looking. Meet me at Larry's Pinball on Seventh. Does forty-five minutes give you enough time?"

"I'll be there in thirty."

Wendy fell quiet a moment. "You don't have to do this, Mick. I keep getting you hurt."

"No, people keep hurting me. Not your fault. You have yet to order someone to hold me down and punch me. So I'll see you at Larry's." He hung up. "After I find out where he is."

Micah mapped the address, took his helmet and jacket, and set out. Okay, so it still wasn't a date with Wendy. But he'd take the contact. Any way he could get it. There was something special there. And he would find out what.

∗ ∗ ∗

Larry's Pinballs was a repair shop for video machines. Maybe in its heyday it had sold pinball machines. Not now. He parked the bike around the back, being sure to fill the parking meter. He didn't want Tav's bike towed the only day he let Micah ride it. That would be bad.

Wendy rolled in five minutes later. Micah slid into the shotgun seat. She stared at him. "Aren't you going to insist on driving?"

"No."

"Good."

She pulled around the front of the establishment and into traffic. Micah asked, "Why meet here?"

"Off-street parking. And none of the cops bother to ticket the machines."

"That's good to know."

"You did feed the meter, though, right?"

"I am a Knight of the Octagon. We always feed the

meters. Except when legally we can't." Micah growled. The city had passed an ordinance making feeding someone else's meter illegal. They were losing valuable revenue, they said. Yeah, well…Micah had dropped a quarter or two in a machine that was near expiring. Maybe. Once. Not anymore. Integrity.

Wendy was dressed in slacks professional enough to make an impression. But Micah bet they were also loose enough to be active wear…like for running or fighting or anything else needed. All-purpose attire.

Wendy navigated without Micah's help to the address on Harcourt. She cruised around the block before pulling across the street and parking. She eyed the dilapidated building for several moments before glancing across at Micah. "I don't think you should be here."

"Then you shouldn't either. We go together or not at all."

Wendy sat back in her seat. "Why do you have to be so frustrating?"

He smiled. "Just my nature, I guess. I'm the tenacious one."

"Among other things."

He drew back. "Good things, I hope."

She ducked her head from side to side. "Yes, good things. I like you, Mick. That's why I'm not happy you're here."

Micah motioned toward the building. "They're not going to be happy we're here if we don't get out and do something."

She looked out the window. "Who?"

"The residents. They're going to get suspicious. We need to either go and knock or leave."

"Fine. We'll knock. But you let me do all the talking."

"Always. You're in charge."

"So you say."

"What's your cover story?"

"Same as before. I'm a journalist looking to write a story on the Magary treasure hunt, looking for Quinn Magary. Found this address in the file left by my former colleague and thought I'd chase it down."

"Go for it."

They got out. Micah followed Wendy across the uneven pavement, marked by patched blacktop that patched nothing. The gutters were pitched and pockmarked, and the sidewalks non-existent. Trees had long since overgrown their demarked area to create ruts and furrows in the ground. In short, the site had seen better days.

Wendy located the correct door and knocked. They heard music coming from inside, but no one came to the door. Wendy knocked a second time.

The door creaked open. "What do you want?" a male voice sneered. Cigarette smoke billowed from the room. Micah hoped it was only cigarette smoke. Smelled like it.

Wendy put on her professional persona. "I'm Wendy Smothers with Regal News. We're doing a story on the Magary Quest from two years ago. My colleague tragically passed away last month and had this address in her files. I wonder if you have information about the Chase? Or if you know Quinn Magary?"

The door flew open. Micah recognized the face immediately. Race. The man who had dogged the footsteps of Micah and his team all during the Magary Chase. The man who planted trackers in Grace and Chay Painter's backpacks. Who cheated, lied, and did everything possible to steal the treasure from its rightful winners.

Race snarled, "Magary? Yeah, I know Quinn Magary. That lying, cheating…" He ranted off a string of expletives

Micah scrubbed through his Holy Spirit filter. "He stole my winnings."

Micah shifted his weight to bump against Wendy. Would she get the hint?

"Really? Tell me about it." She made half a step forward.

Obviously not.

Race jerked his head. "Come on in, and I will."

Micah stepped down on Wendy's foot lightly. He motioned with his head ever so slightly to leave.

She ignored him. "Thank you. I'd love to hear it."

Micah lowered his head in hopes Race wouldn't get a good look at him. And might have forgotten him. At the time of the chase, he did, after all, have a week's growth of beard and mustache. And bruises and cuts on his face.

Not unlike now. But no beard. And no shaggy hair. Maybe it would be enough. Maybe. He pulled his reading glasses from his pocket to add to the disguise. If being clean-shaven was a disguise. *Lord, blind his eyes, please.*

Wendy led the way into the house. A tarp covered the picture window. Straight-backed chairs circled a gray metal table that sat in the living room. The kitchen looked equally dim and dingy. Trash lined the counters and overflowed the garbage can. A sad existence.

Race motioned to the chairs. "Sit. Sorry, I can't offer you anything to drink. My deliveries have been interrupted lately."

Wendy took out a notepad and pen. "Tell me what you want our readers to know. When did you see Quinn Magary last?"

"When he ordered me off the federal reserve land after I found the treasure."

Wendy reacted with surprise. "He ordered you off the property?"

"Yeah. Me and a friend located the treasure. Quinn and his bunch showed up immediately after. They were tracking us, you see? We were ahead of them, but they followed us the whole way."

"And you figured out where the treasure was?"

"Yeah. Then Magary comes along and says we can't have it because there's only two of us. He gave it to the group he had with him."

"Did you file a protest?"

"With who? He's a Magary. They set this whole thing up fifty years ago."

"How did you figure out the clues?"

"They were easy to follow. A blind man could have found the way there."

Wendy wrote in her notebook. "And you simply followed the clues. Why did it take fifty years to locate it if it was so easy to find?"

Race shrugged. "I don't know. Me and my buddy didn't have any trouble."

"Tell me about how the search started."

Race began creating a fantasy that Micah could have admired if any of it had been true. But it was all a lie. Race wasn't the leader of a group of four. Two of his people didn't get sick and go home, leaving him with no team. He failed to mention the tracking devices on the women's packs. He failed to mention Grace and Chay at all. Convenient.

He did, however, fill in a gap Micah had long wondered about. "Yeah, we knew there were people following behind us. So we set up a diversion for them. Fly, my partner, had some smoke bombs. He set them off in the hills. The explosions caused a hillside to slide but didn't affect anything."

Micah bit the inside of his mouth. The whole group:

Jeremiah, Tav, Luke, Chay, Grace, BB, and Ben were nearly buried in the avalanche. God's grace kept them alive. Micah breathed slowly. Breathe. Old news. Everything turned out fine.

Except Jeremiah died.

Micah couldn't lay that at Race's feet. Of all the offenses Race committed, murdering Jeremiah wasn't one of them. No, that was reserved for...

Move on. Move on.

Wendy continued to ask questions. "Have you had any contact with Quinn Magary since the contest ended?"

"Yeah. I looked him up."

"How did that go?"

How do you think it went? You know Quinn.

"I got in his face. He said I was right about winning. He'd make sure I got the prize." He gazed around his home. "Does this look like he's awarded me my million dollars?"

"No, sir, it doesn't. I'm sorry things have shaken out like this. We'd certainly like to interview Mr. Magary and get his side of the affair. And ask him why he hasn't come through for you. Do you know where we can reach him?"

Micah watched Race closely. The man's eyes narrowed. His face tightened. He reached behind the chair where he sat and pulled out a rifle. He lifted it toward Wendy and shouted, "You can reach him in—"

Wendy ducked before Race could level the weapon. She lashed out with her foot, knocking the gun sideways. The blast tore a hole through the window. Micah piled on Race, pinning the man's body under his own. He grabbed the rifle and slung it to Wendy. She kicked it aside and pulled her own weapon. She drew down on Race and ordered, "On your feet. Federal Agent. You're under arrest for attempted murder."

Police came. Race went. Reports were taken and filed.

Wendy and Micah were kicked loose at about three. Micah looked at the clock. "I've got time to get home before the boys get home from their friends."

Wendy lowered her head. "I nearly got you killed. I knew you were trying to get me to leave. I'm sorry."

Micah shrugged. "I remembered him. I figured there would be hard feelings. But maybe he knew something about Quinn's whereabouts. Was worth a shot."

"Considering you almost got shot, I'm not so sure. We didn't learn anything."

"No, but we know where Quinn's not. We'll find him. I swear we will."

Wendy sniffed. "I hope you're right."

"That's what I've got, Wendy. I've got hope." He hugged her quickly, then let her go. "Let's go, boss. I've got kids to wrangle."

"Yeah." They climbed into the car and drove off.

$* * *$

THURSDAY AFTERNOON

Micah returned Tav's motorcycle. "Nothing, brother. I rode it downtown. I rode it on your route. I rode it everywhere I thought you would be. No one even honked at me. I'm not sure whether to be offended or relieved."

Tav grimaced. "Relieved. At least no one knocked you off the bike."

"You really think it's your dad? And now, since Addison has joined you and Luke in the rebellion, you think he'll quit?"

"Either he'll quit, or he'll come after all of us. I don't know, Mick." Tav donned his helmet and jacket. "I know I'll have eyes in the back of my head the whole time I'm out here."

"Maybe you should keep the car." Micah jerked his head over his shoulder. "It gets good mileage."

"I know. But it makes for a bigger target. I'll have to work this out. Next time it happens, I'm going to confront Dad and tell him I know it's him. Maybe I can't prove it, but when Quinn gets back, Quinn will." Tav smiled, tight-lipped. "He's very good at things like that."

"If he gets back."

"He will. I have faith."

Micah patted Tav on the helmet. "Stay alive until then."

"I plan on it."

Tav rode off. Micah went into the house. BB asked, "Tav gone?"

"Yeah. We need Quinn."

"He's the one who started this whole mess." BB grabbed the ice cream from the freezer and a spoon from the drawer. Micah frowned at him. "What?"

"You know the example you're setting for Ben, don't you?"

"He's working on his homework with Mialma. We've got twenty minutes."

Micah shook his head. "Fine. Hand me another spoon." Together they emptied the container.

Micah's phone rang. He answered it. "Ms. Smothers. How delightful to hear from you. Long time no hear. How can I help you?"

Wendy sneered over the phone, then said, "I've got a lunch appointment with May Vaughn tomorrow."

"That was fast. How did you arrange to see her so soon?"

"I told her I'm with the university news. I'm doing an

article for the paper about Addison becoming the starter. She became very eager to talk about him."

Micah stared at the phone. "What do you expect to get from this, Wendy? Do you honestly believe she's going to accept you with open arms?"

"No." Wendy's voice softened. "No, I don't. But I have to try. I have to at least try."

"I hear you. And I understand. Maybe more than you know." His separation from his own mother remained a wound he could not heal. Healed in the Lord, but still, an emptiness to be filled.

"I'll call you when I'm done."

"Remember, when you talk to Mrs. Vaughn, don't use Tav but Taylor. Never use any name but Taylor."

"Gotcha. Okay, I'm out."

"Bye." Micah disconnected the call and stuffed the phone in his backpack. "Lord, whatever You are doing in all this, keep Your hands on all of us."

BB eyed Micah. "She talk with her biological mom, yet?"

"Tomorrow."

"She's not expecting good things, is she?"

"The Vaughns have always been hard to understand. They had three great boys but were never happy with who Tav, Luke, or Addison were. Always trying to make them something different, something more significant. And all to fill Mr. and Mrs. Vaughn's own needs. I can't understand parents like that."

BB grinned. "Unlike you, who is painfully easy to understand."

Micah eyed him sideways. "Yeah?"

"Yeah. You duck your problems. You eat ice cream to feel better emotionally and hide behind your brothers—"

Micah drove his shoulder into BB's middle. He wrestled

the boy to the couch. BB twisted and came up laughing. Micah went for the leg. BB feinted to the left, then came back right. Micah was ready for him and pulled him to the carpet.

Ben came running from the back, followed by a barking Mialma. Ben grabbed BB around his middle. BB yelled, "Get Dad! Get Dad!"

Ben caught Micah around the leg and forced him to the ground. Micah let the boy turn him over onto his belly. Ben straddled him and began bouncing. Micah yelled, "No bouncing in wrestling! No bouncing!"

Ben grabbed Micah around the shoulders. Micah reached out and snatched BB by the ankle as the teen tried to escape. Micah flipped him to his back, twisted, and came on top of Ben. He held BB by the leg, carefully bending it to keep the boy under control. Ben wriggled and giggled and tried to work his way out of Micah's grasp but to no avail. The free-for-all reached a standstill…

Until the doorbell rang. Micah released BB but pointed at him. "This isn't done, Mister. Not by a long shot!"

Ben switched to bouncing on BB. Micah rolled to his feet and answered the door.

"Ms. Phelps." He breathed hard and had to rearrange his shirt and jeans. "We were just having a wrestling session." He waved her into the living room. "Care to join us?"

The woman peeked her head in the door, saw BB on the floor with Ben on top of him, and smiled. "No, thank you." She eyed Micah. "Nice to see you none the worse for wear. I've had to report your activities of late." She ducked her head to the side. "Much as I hate to. But it is the procedure." She added, "But I'll be happy to report no new injuries or dangers. If you can keep it that way, it will be much to your advantage when the adoption is ready to be decided." She looked at BB and asked, "I believe this is not the best time to ask if you've made a further decision about guardian versus father, is it?"

BB rolled over, caught Ben around the middle, and stood, holding the boy off the ground. "Not yet. But I'm leaning more and more."

"Which way?"

"I'll let you know when the time comes. I want to keep my options open." He grinned at Micah. "In case I need some leverage between now and then."

Micah shook his head. "Put your brother down and go get ready for dinner."

BB slung Ben over his shoulder and carried him out of the room. Micah caught his breath. "Would you care to stay for dinner, Ms. Phelps?"

She shook her head. "No. I appreciate the offer, but I will pass." She smiled. "I have clients who are far more questionable I need to supervise. You three seem well-suited to life together." She turned and headed out the door. She stopped. "No more injuries, though. Right?"

Micah nodded. "None I could prevent. Just common, everyday accidents."

She glared at him but with a twinkle in her eye. "Those would be preferable. Have a good evening, Mr. Andres."

"Good night, Ms. Phelps."

He closed the door, leaned against the wall, and let out a long, low breath. "Thank You, Lord. That could have been bad. I feel like she wants to be on our side. But I never am one-hundred-percent certain. Don't let me mess this up, please. Keep me in Your will. Always."

Now. What could he fix for dinner?

Waffles.

* * *

THURSDAY EVENING

Wendy and Jen played darts. Each throw became a dagger to the heart of a problem or problematic person. No one kept score.

Until Mom came in. "What's going on in here? I heard a dart hit the door."

"Sorry. A friendly game of stress reduction."

"Keep the stress on the board, please. No holes in the doors."

They sing-songed, "Yes, Mom." Then kissed her from either side. Mom shook her head. "You two are up to something. You want to talk about it?"

Wendy equivocated. "Not yet. Soon."

Mom pointed at her. "I'll hold you to that." She glanced at Jen. "You?"

"Like she said. Not yet."

Mom reached in and kissed both girls. "I love you, you know."

"We know. Thanks, Mom."

Mom closed the door. Wendy stepped forward and stuck a dart directly into the center of the bullseye. "That's what we have."

"Yes, we do." Jen sighed. "Come on. You tell me your secret, and I'll tell you mine."

"Deal. Except you go first."

"Why me?" The girls curled on the floor, leaning against Wendy's bed.

"You're older, and it's my room."

"Fine."

Jen leaned back. "There's this guy. Really great guy. Super guy. Straight-up gorgeous."

"I get the picture. And you like him."

"Yeah. A lot. A whole lot. A 'spend the rest of my life with him' lot."

"And the problem is?" Wendy shifted on the floor to remove the bed leg from her back.

"The problem is, he has these strong beliefs. Very strong beliefs."

"I know what you're saying."

Jen nodded. "What do I do, Wenders? Do I run while I can? What if I spend all this time with him and find out I don't want to accept his Jesus?" She shifted on the floor. "It's not like there's anything not to like, from what Tav tells me. Except the total commitment part. Total commitment is concerning."

"Like marriage wouldn't be concerning?"

Jen tilted her head and eyed her sideways. "I hadn't thought of it that way."

Wendy ducked her head to the side. "It just occurred to me. It is like a marriage. You have to go into matrimony determined to make it work. You don't look for an 'out' or 'backdoor' if things don't go right off the bat. That's why we consider marriage long and hard before committing to someone. No matter how much they say they love you."

"We're nowhere near that level yet."

Wendy grinned. "Yet."

Jen lifted her chin. "And where are you and Micah, hmm?"

"We're friends. He'd like to take it further, but I'm hanging back. The God-thing scares me." She shook her head. "He says I'll understand it when I'm ready. I don't know if I'll ever be ready."

"For marriage either?"

Wendy fell silent. Finally, she raised her head. "I don't know. I guess I should figure it out, as well."

"Probably. But maybe not tonight."

Wendy laughed. "Truth." She stretched. "You want to talk to Mom first, or should I?"

"Why don't we save time and talk to her together? We've got the same issues. Maybe she has answers for both of us that match."

Wendy chuckled. "That'll be a first."

"Yeah, well, she's Mom. She's allowed."

Together they rose and headed for the dining room.

* * *

THURSDAY LATE EVENING

The phone rang. "Yeah. Speak to me."

"I'm not paying you to play tag. I want the problem eliminated."

"You only said you wanted it sidelined."

"Now I want it eliminated."

"That'll cost you more."

"How much more?"

"Ten grand."

Silence.

"You still there?"

"Too high for one."

"What are you suggesting?"

"Two eliminations."

"Money up front."

"Half the money up front. Other half when the job is finished. And verified."

"Same meeting place?"

"Same."

"See you tonight."

* * *

FRIDAY MORNING

Wendy stared at the receipts and shook her head. She needed a second opinion. A Micah Andres opinion. He'd known Quinn longer. He might be able to make sense of what her boss was doing.

She dialed. "Mick. I need another set of eyes to look at some receipts I've got from Quinn. Can you meet me for brunch?"

"Where and when, and I'll be there."

"Burrito Billy's and ten. I've got lunch with May Vaughn at one."

"You pick all the good places, don't you?"

"What's wrong with Burrito Billy's?"

"Nothing. Nothing at all. I'll be there. With my antacids."

"Wimp."

"Sadist."

"Bye." She grinned. There was something about Andres she really appreciated. And needed to know more about. Day by day, right? One crisis at a time. Wendy stuffed the receipts into the atlas and set it aside. Other cases needed attention. None as pressing, and none as interesting. But they did need her attention.

Wendy pulled the first file from the holder. "Who do we have here? And why?" She opened the file and got to work.

* * *

At ten, she sat outside Billy's storefront. Mick strode quickly up the pavement and joined her. She looked at her phone. "You're late."

"I'm early."

She grinned. "Hi."

They ordered the breakfast burritos with extra cheese. Wendy ordered hers with extra salsa. Micah passed on the salsa. She cocked her head. "You aren't kidding about hold the heat, are you?"

"Nope. No stomach for spice. Love it. Doesn't love me. I figured I'd better pass since I have more work today. When I have the afternoon to recover, I'll eat to my heartburn's content."

Wendy waited until the food had been delivered to pull out her atlas and the receipts. "Help me make sense of this. I have a receipt for a rental car. But he picked it up in Seattle."

"Seattle? How'd he get from Hanford to Seattle? And then rent a car? You don't have any airline receipts, do you?"

"No. That's the weird part. Best I can figure, he took the train."

"Quinn took the train from Hanford to Seattle?" Micah's jaw dropped open.

"According to the receipts, yes."

"But why?" Micah swallowed one of his burritos.

"That's what I need you to tell me. What is he doing? Look at these other receipts. Port Angeles. Long Beach. Depoe Bay." Wendy shook her head.

Micah held up a hand. "Wait. Wait. Where are these receipts coming from? How current are they?"

"Current. And I busted into his email. No, he hasn't written anything I can trace down. But these gas receipts are coming in from all over."

Micah stared at the last one. "Depoe Bay is in Washington State." He reached for the atlas. "I'm glad we still have paper maps sometimes. Here. Look at this." Micah traced a route from Seattle along the sound to the coast.

"He's driving the coast."

"Alone? Why?"

"What else have you got?"

"Port Orford. Trinidad. Fort Bragg."

"Those are all along the west coast. He's driving the Pacific Coast Highway the length of the state."

"But why?" Wendy felt her frustration growing. "I see what he's doing. But I don't understand why."

"Sightseeing?"

"Quinn has lived here all his life. He can see any part of this state—or any other state—any time he wants, with anyone he wants. How does this make sense? He just up and takes off and decides to drive the length of California for the fun of it?"

"Remember what Mr. Smalls said about Quinn needing to make a decision? And it being the most important decision of his life? Maybe he's taking the time to make up his mind."

"Mick, if you have a big decision to make…say, you want to marry someone. Are you going to drive off into the sunset to think about it? Or are you going to ask the people close to you?"

Micah studied his plate, then raised his head and fixed his gaze on Wendy. "I do both. I talk to my closest friends, I ask their counsel, and I listen to it. Then I go off by myself. I get alone with God, and I ask Him what HE thinks. And what He wants. And what His will is. Then I make my decision."

Micah shook his head. "Would I drive the length of California? Maybe. Maybe not. I'm not Quinn. I don't know how he makes his life-altering decisions."

Micah finished his second burrito and went in for the third. "How far down the coast did he get?"

"The last receipt I have is from Santa Cruz. He dropped the car off at the airport in San Jose."

"That's not too far from Mt. Diablo. Where Grace's camp is." Micah chewed, swallowed, then said, "I have a theory." He rubbed his cheek. "But I'm not going to share it yet. I'd need more proof." His eyes gleamed. "But I have an idea." He finished his brunch. "I'll tell you this much. I think Quinn is fine. I think he's taken some of his free days, and he's figuring something out. And he's fine."

Wendy eyed Micah sideways. "You sure about this?"

"Yeah. Am I sure I'm right? No. But I'm sure it's a theory. We'll know in a few days when he gets back from wherever he is."

"And is Grace part of this?"

"My guess is yes. But again, it's only my guess. Which I'll keep to myself for now." He put his napkin on the table. "Are you ready for lunch today?"

"As ready as I can be." She frowned, but a straight-lipped frown. "Back to work. Both of us."

Micah stood as well. "Question: do you really work for Homeland Security?"

Wendy cocked her head. "Why would you think I do?"

"You told Ms. Phelps you were 'DHS.' Department of Homeland Security, right?"

Wendy grinned. "Ah, the beauty of acronyms. They can mean anything, and people will jump to the most fantastic conclusion. DHS could mean 'Dig here, stupid.' Or 'Department of Horse Stables.' I don't have to fill in the blanks. The hearer will do it for me."

Micah chuckled. "So what does it stand for?"

"I'll never tell. Quinn's first rule: keep 'em guessing."

"He does."

A quick hug, a parting, "See you tonight," and they went their separate ways.

* * *

FRIDAY LUNCH

Wendy sat across from Mrs. Vaughn. The outdoor café had a crowd. Wendy was grateful and surprised she could obtain a reservation this late. But a cancellation left an open table. What a coincidence, right? Uh-huh. I hear you, Mick. I hear you, God.

Mrs. Vaughn finished her first glass of wine before the entrees arrived.

Wendy decided she better get to her interview while the woman was sober and alert. If she ever was. "Thank you for meeting with me. I truly appreciate the time."

Mrs. Vaughn twisted her wine glass around. "You said you needed information about Addison. And you wanted to do an article about him for the paper?"

"Yes, ma'am, I do. He's going to be the starter this weekend."

"How is that possible? Chris, his father, said he would terminate Addison's support."

"I don't know anything about your husband and his dealings with Addison. I do know Addison is paid up through the end of the semester. The school will do what it can to keep him enrolled. Losing one's funding doesn't automatically mean the end of schooling."

"Addison never qualified for assistance. Chris made too much money. Even with Chris not supporting him, Addison wouldn't qualify. There's no way Addison can remain in school."

"Apparently, some private individuals offered him support for the remainder of the year. They will also pay for the next three years if he continues in school. Money includes tuition, books, and housing."

Mrs. Vaughn sat back. Her flat tone belied her words.

"Good for Addison. I'm thrilled for him. He deserves to be in school." She paused, then added, "Chris always said since the other two didn't go, he could pay for Addison without a problem. I never believed he would cut Addison off." She took a sip of her drink. "I wouldn't put it past him to set up this scholarship as a ruse. He'd pay for Addi, but Addi wouldn't know it was actually from his father."

Wendy thought it over, then said, "The scholarship has been in existence for two years. I doubt your husband could anticipate these events so far in advance."

Mrs. Vaughn shrugged. "You never know." Her tone ended all debate.

The entrees arrived. Mrs. Vaughn had the tuna salad served in a tomato cup on a bed of green lettuce. Wendy had a three-cheese toasted cheese sandwich and bisque tomato soup.

Mrs. Vaughn started in on her salad. "You said he was going to be the starter this weekend? I thought he had to wait until next year. There were two men ahead of him."

"True. But Henri, Blake, and half the team came down with food poisoning. Severe cases, so it's said."

The older woman lifted her chin. "How horrible." She bit into her salad. "That's terrible for those two men, but it's wonderful for Addison. I always knew he should be the starter. Now everyone will see what a great player he is. His father worked so hard to make him the man he is. He should be grateful."

Wendy swirled her soup with her toasted cheese sandwich. "He is grateful, Mrs. Vaughn. He'd love it if you and Mr. Vaughn came to the game to watch."

Mrs. Vaughn shook her head. "That will never happen. After what Addison and Luke did? Walking out on their father? Chris will never attend anything Addison or Luke participate in. Ever."

"That's very sad. All three men love their father. They love you as well, Mrs. Vaughn. They want nothing more than to be a family again."

"Chris has too much pride. Taylor and Luke hurt him by leaving." Mrs. Vaughn glared at Wendy.

"I heard Luke was told to leave." Wendy bit off the end of her sandwich.

"Yes, but Chris didn't mean it. Not this time, and not the first time." Mrs. Vaughn's eyes narrowed. "I blame Taylor for that. He stole Luke away from us. Chris only wanted the best for Luke. Maybe he didn't say it in the kindest way, but he tried to build Luke up. To make him the player Chris knew Luke could be. Luke pushed back, and then Taylor swooped in. Taylor practically kidnapped Luke right out of the house. Then he brainwashed him into saying his father abused him. As if Chris would ever hurt anyone."

The woman downed her wine and poured another glass. Wendy's opportunity drained quickly. "Mrs. Vaughn, I have a question for you about Addison. I'm going to be writing an article about the game this weekend. Addison gave me some background, but I'd love it if I could get more from you."

"What kind of background?"

"Growing up. Maybe back to when you had him. What about your time in the hospital? How long were you in labor? Who stayed there with you?"

"He was my third boy and the biggest of them all. Nine pounds-twelve ounces. Twenty-four inches long. My big baby." May smiled at the memory.

"Were you in labor long?" *Every woman talks about her labor. I refuse to be one of them.*

"Oh, hours and hours. I wanted a C-section, but Chris wouldn't hear of it. His boys needed to fight their way out. Makes them strong, he said. After ten hours, the doctor said they should operate if Chris wanted a live baby. I think he's always been a little disappointed in Addison for not fighting more."

"Mr. Vaughn puts a lot on his boys, doesn't he?"

The older woman tossed back half her wine. "No more than any father. He wanted to make men of them."

Wendy poked around her soup, ate more of the sandwich, then dabbed at her mouth. She pulled a paper from her purse. "I've got another question about Addison. He gave me his birth certificate to copy the information about where and when he was born. But I saw an unusual detail. The certificate says he is 'four of four live births.' But there are only the three of your boys. Is there another child?"

Mrs. Vaughn's face drained of color. She stuttered, then finished off her glass. "He had no business giving it to you."

"Maybe not. But he did. Who was the other child? And what happened to it?"

"That's none of your business. I think I'm done here." May stood but had to grab the table to stand without wobbling.

"Sit, Mrs. Vaughn. Please. Let me tell you about the child."

The woman sat. She bit her lower lip. Her eyes were guarded.

Wendy laid the birth certificate on the table. "A week-old baby girl was left in a 'safe box.' The place where unwanted babies can be surrendered, no questions asked. The baby had been wrapped in a blanket from the hospital. She had this partial family tree pinned to the blanket. First names only and the father's name had been crossed off. Emphatically."

Wendy held Mrs. Vaughn's eyes. The woman did not

look away. Wendy continued her story. "The baby girl went into the foster program. Because there existed some uncertainty about parental rights, no one could adopt her for a full year. A family who fostered many children took her in. They already had a little girl the same age as the baby, but they loved her so much they decided they should adopt her when the time came.

"She grew loved and wanted and cared for. She has wonderful parents, loving siblings, and a great career. The only thing that would make her life more complete is to have a relationship with her biological parents. Or her mother." Wendy drew out the family tree and handed it to her. "Does this look familiar?"

Mrs. Vaughn reached out, her hand shaking. Fear washed her face. She touched the paper, laid it on the table, then read the names. No sound. Only her lips moved.

She glanced at Wendy. "How did you get this?"

"It was pinned to my blanket. My parents kept it. They gave it to me when I turned sixteen. I've held on to it on the one-in-a-million chance I would ever find a match. And guess what?" Wendy dipped her head. "I found it."

"Where?" she whispered.

"Micah Andres knows the man I work with. Micah introduced me to Taylor and Luke." *Taylor. Never Tav. Always Taylor. Poor guy.* "Long story, but I went to their house, saw the family tree, and thought it resembled mine." Wendy played her ace. "We did a DNA match. They're my brothers."

She swallowed and pressed ahead. "Which makes you my biological mother."

Mrs. Vaughn's eyes lost focus. She stared off into space. "I wanted a daughter. To share all the woman things, you know?" The older woman came back to the present and met Wendy's eyes. "Dresses and boyfriends and dances and secrets." She looked sad. Wistful. Lonely.

"Chris was so sure you would be a boy. He was too much of a man to have girls, you know? He'd never have anything but a boy. But then the baby was a girl. I held you for a whole week. Then Chris said we couldn't afford another baby so close to Taylor. We would have to give you up for adoption. Give you away. Be rid of you."

Tears cascaded from the corners of Mrs. Vaughn's eyes and dripped onto the front of her blouse. The woman ignored them. "I got so angry. But what could I do? Chris said it. That ended it. I took you to the safe box. But I put the family tree with you. I never thought you'd happen on the real one. Never."

Wendy reached out and touched her hand. Touched it. Not held it. Emotions were too precarious. The wrong move could destroy her progress. "Mrs. Vaughn...I..." She stopped, then started again. "I love my brothers. Addison is a kick, and Luke is a joy to be with. Taylor—"

Mrs. Vaughn jerked her head. "Taylor is not my son. I disowned him. He destroyed our family. I want nothing to do with him. Not until he apologizes for all the hurt he has caused. And even if he does, I will still not accept him as my son. Luke and Addison are welcome any time." She stopped. "Unless their father is home."

Wendy nodded. "I understand. You believe Mr. Vaughn would be unhappy to meet me?"

"He will want nothing to do with you." She lifted her chin. "Unless you renounce Taylor, I will have nothing to do with you, either."

Wendy stared at the woman. "I have never seen this kind of hate before. Not in a family. It's killing you, Mrs. Vaughn. This vendetta against your son has robbed you of all your children. Is that what you want? To be alone?"

"No. I want Luke and Addison. Only them. No one else."

"But they want Taylor and me, too."

"They can't have you or Taylor. Not and have me. I will make certain of it. I know my sons. I can make them hate you and Taylor. I will. You watch."

Wendy lowered her eyes. "I'm so sorry you feel that way. You won't make Luke or Addison hate anyone."

Mrs. Vaughn stood. "I'm done here." She grabbed Addison's birth certificate and Wendy's family tree. She ripped it to shreds in front of Wendy. "This is what I think of your claim. You're no child of mine, and you never will be."

The older woman stormed away from the table, leaving Wendy to pay the bill. She shook her head. "That poor woman. My poor brothers."

Wendy went back to work and looked at the receipts.

Her phone rang. Mick. She debated whether to ignore the call or not. Integrity. Honesty. Right. She picked it up. "Hey, Mick."

"How'd it go?"

"Like I expected. She wants nothing to do with me."

"I'm sorry, Wendy. I am. Are you okay?"

"Yeah." She paused. "I am. I hoped it would be different, but I never really believed she'd accept me. I didn't expect the hate, though. She is so full of animosity. I can't understand her. Tav is her son. He's never done anything except what was best for Luke. But she refuses to see it."

Micah's voice was soft. "I know. She changes the facts to fit her reality. I'm sorry. I ask again. Are you okay?"

"I will be. I've got hours of work ahead of me, so I can bury my sorrow in paper." She laughed. "Maybe I'll pick up Quinn's trail again."

"That would be a miracle. I'll talk to you later, Wendy."

"See ya." She hung up and went back to her files.

* * *

Two hours later, she received a call. Mrs. Vaughn.

"Wendy, I was wrong. Please, forgive me."

Wendy looked at the caller ID to make sure it was Mrs. Vaughn. She found her voice. "Of course. It's understandable. This is hard for everyone."

"Yes. I couldn't get past the shock. But I've done some deep soul-searching. I want to meet with you again. And Chris wants to meet you as well."

Wendy stared at the phone. "Mr. Vaughn wants to meet me?"

"Yes. We spent time talking and realized how wrong we were to give you away. I know we can't change the past, but we can start a new relationship. If you still want."

"I do. Where and when do you want to meet?" Wendy scribbled on a sheet of paper.

"I'd love it if you'd come to the house. It will make things easier. I can show you all the baby pictures of the boys and them growing up. You can bring your photos, too, if you like. One day we'll meet your family. Your *real* family. I know we're not. But we can be close."

"What time?" She looked at her calendar. Nothing.

"If you can come today, say, for dinner? About six?"

Wendy raised her eyebrows. This wasn't right. Too soon. Way too soon. "Give me the address, and I'll be there."

"123 Windsor Place. And please, don't tell the boys about this. Chris and I want to make amends with them. We will, but we want to start with you."

Nope. All wrong. All of it. "Thank you, Mrs. Vaughn."

"Call me May, please. We're going to be friends. And I'll see you tonight."

Wendy hung up. "'Don't tell the boys.' If that's not a red flag, I've never seen one. Quinn, you trained me too well for such a trick." She punched in Micah's number. "Mick, need a backup."

"For what? You got it, but what's going on?"

"Mrs. Vaughn invited me over for dinner. She wants to make amends and have a relationship, after all. And Mr. Vaughn is in accord with her."

A long silence met the revelation. "I don't like it. This is wrong."

"Exactly what I thought. I'll go over, but I want you to know I'm going. In case I don't come back." She wrote *Dinner. Vaughn. 123 Windsor Place.* In case. Others could find her whereabouts. If.

"How about if I come along?"

"A little suspect, don't you think?" She circled the address.

"I can show up. It's been a long time since I've seen the Vaughns. It will be odd, but not impossibly so."

Wendy shook her head. Which she knew he couldn't see. "You think just dropping in out of the blue won't look strange?"

"I used to do it all the time when Tav and Luke still lived at home. I've done it once or twice since then. It's not totally out there, Wendy. And what are they going to say? Go away? Not with you there."

"But she invited me for dinner."

"Fine. I show up after. But not so long after, you can get in trouble. It'll work, Wendy. Trust me."

"Fine." It came out flatter than she wanted it to. She corrected herself. "I appreciate the concern, Mick. And the backup."

"What time are you supposed to be there?"

"Six."

"I'll see you at seven. Leave your keys under the mat in the backseat."

"Do what?" She stared at the phone.

"It's a Quinn trick. If someone tries to hide your car, they won't be able to start it if you don't have the keys on you. And no one looks in the backseat for keys."

"Hmm. Quinn failed to teach me that dodge. I like it. I'll do it."

"Be careful, Wendy."

"I will. No heroics."

"Me? Never. I'm the quiet one, remember?"

"Who gets the snot beat out of him all the time." She grinned.

"Yeah, well, I'm lucky, I guess."

"Maybe you should talk to your God about being used as a punching bag."

"Oh, we have. It's usually a short conversation. I ask why, and He reminds me He's God and I'm not. When I have His position, I can do things differently."

"Give me one good reason why you getting beat up achieves something significant."

"Well…if I hadn't been smacked by Mr. Tilley, you wouldn't have ever been at Tav's apartment and seen the family tree. I'd say that could be called a significant outcome."

Wendy frowned. "Wise guy. I'll give you one."

"I don't know all the whys, Wendy. Why is way above my pay grade. My job is to be the Micah Andres the Lord wants me to be. Which is basically myself with Him living through me."

Wendy dropped her eyes. "So much to learn."

"And plenty of time to learn it."

"Except now. I've got to get some work done, then be at the Vaughn's at six."

"Yeah, I should do some work, too. Gotta pay the bills. Someone should."

"Talk to BB."

"He's paid his dues. He gets to be a kid. I'll be the adult."

"Good of you."

"Goodbye, Wendy."

She laughed. "Bye, Mick."

* * *

FRIDAY EARLY EVENING

At six-forty-five, Micah arrived at the Vaughn's house. He tapped at the back door as had been his custom.

Mrs. Vaughn peeked out through the curtains, then threw the door open. She hugged Micah. "Oh, Micky. It's so good to see you! What are you doing here?"

Micah moved into the kitchen. "I had a job in the neighborhood. I couldn't be this close and not stop and see you. Not after you called the other day."

Mrs. Vaughn turned her head in surprise. "I called you?"

"Yes, remember you asked me where Tav and Luke lived?"

Mrs. Vaughn threw up her hand. "Oh, of course. I completely forgot. So much has been happening lately."

Micah looked toward the dining room. "Am I interrupting dinner?"

"Of course not. Never. Come on in, Micky."

She led the way to the dining room, where Wendy sat across the table from Mr. Vaughn. The man appeared perplexed and a little perturbed. But he covered it when Micah extended his hand to him. "Mr. Vaughn."

"Micah. Good to see you, boy. Nice someone remembers we used to be part of their lives."

Mrs. Vaughn laughed. It held a false note to it. A sense all might not be as well as it should be. "Now, dear. Micky kindly came to visit. He's not responsible for our sons."

She motioned to Wendy, "You know Ms. Smothers, right?"

Micah nodded. "Yes, I do. Her boss is a friend."

"That's wonderful. Ms. Smothers told us about some family connections."

Wendy eyed Micah. "Yes, I did. And this isn't a good time to be interrupted." She smiled, but her eyes didn't. "Get out, Andres. This is my time with the Vaughn's."

"I won't stay long. I wanted to tell Mr. and Mrs. Vaughn Addison is starting quarterback on Saturday." He glanced from husband to wife. "You really should go."

Mr. Vaughn snorted. "Why would I want to do that?"

Mrs. Vaughn answered for him. "Because he's our son, and we want to see him succeed." She gave Micah a warm pat on the back. "But I think Ms. Smothers is right. You should come back another time. We can have a long, lovely chat. And you can tell us all about what you're doing these days."

"You'll have to meet my boys, BB and Ben." Micah grinned. "They adopted me."

"I'm sure it's a fascinating story. Oh, Micky, can you help Chris get a box out of the garage? It's on a top shelf, and I'm afraid to let him get it alone."

"I can do it myself, May. I don't need anyone's help."

Micah shrugged. "I'm here. Won't take a second. Which box is it?"

The garage was attached to the kitchen. Access came through a windowed door. Chris rose and led Micah to the back. As they entered the garage, Chris muttered, "This isn't my idea."

Micah side-eyed Mr. Vaughn. The man pointed to an

oversized box stuffed precariously on a top shelf. "The one there. That's the one she wants."

Micah moved ahead of Mr. Vaughn to see if he could lift the box. He stretched as high as he could.

Behind him, he heard Chris mutter again, "Not my idea."

Micah went to turn, but a blow to the back of his head stopped him cold. Micah crashed to the floor. He heard Mr. Vaughn say, "Remember what I said."

Micah didn't lose consciousness. The room went dark. But he could hear and feel everything going on. Mr. Vaughn taped his mouth and eyes shut. Then taped his hands behind him. Finally, he secured his feet and knees together, placed Micah in a fetal position, and wrapped him again. Trussed like a Christmas turkey. He was going nowhere.

Something substantial was dragged in beside him. He heard tape being ripped off and applied. Grunts accompanied the activity. Mrs. Vaughn's voice ordered, "Take them out to the car and put them in the trunk. You can drive them to the dump tomorrow."

"Not my idea, May. You'll never get away with this."

"Dead bodies will be just more trash. No one will know."

"What about the cars? How will you dispose of those?"

"I know a guy. He'll take care of them for us. I will have my sons back. Luke and Addison belong here. They will come back. Once Taylor is taken care of, they will have no reason not to return."

"And you think that will make them want to come back?"

"What choice will they have? You cut off Addison's money. Tav supports Luke, so with Tav gone, Luke has nothing. Where else will they go?"

"What about the scholarship?"

"Pshaw. There's no scholarship. The woman lied. You'll see. He'll be let go from the team once they find out there's no tuition. He may play this weekend, but it will be the only time he does."

"You've got this all figured out. What if I don't want them back?"

"You want them. They're your sons. You always wanted sons. I gave you sons. Only sons. We got rid of the girl. You said we had to, and we did. All we have is our boys. I will have them back."

"Or what?"

"Or I know a guy."

Silence.

"Are you threatening me?"

"We will be a family, Chris. I will have my boys back."

"Fine. I'll move these out. You'll have to help put them in the trunk. I can't lift them alone."

"Leave them here until the morning. I'd say we put them in the dumpster, but the container would be too heavy to lift. You'll have to take them to the dump and drop them off."

"Get your guy to get rid of these cars tonight."

"Did you take Micky's keys and phone from him?"

"I got them."

Keys and phone. Keys and phone. Why was that always the only thing they were concerned about? What about his wallet and ID? Did they think to take those? Should he remind them of it? Probably not. Couldn't if he wanted to.

"Go on in the house. I want to double-check these bindings, then I'll be in." The light footsteps said Mrs. Vaughn complied. Mr. Vaughn muttered, "I'll be back for you in the morning. I'll get you somewhere safe. She's crazy. But I don't want her hurt."

Footsteps. Micah heard the light switch. A door closed.

Quiet followed.

Micah struggled. Stretched. Flexed. Did everything possible to get himself free. He rolled into cabinets. He smashed his face against the floor and ground the side of it against a shop table leg. Nothing worked. The one consolation was he could feel Wendy moving as well. She was alive. Trapped but alive.

Vain escape gave way to prayer. He prayed for Wendy. Prayed for Tav and his would-be killer. Prayed for Mr. and Mrs. Vaughn. Luke. Addison. Jen. His dad. His mother. Quinn. Grace. Chay. A thousand other people he knew. *Lord, if this is Your way of telling me I need to spend more time in dedicated prayer, I hear You. And I will when this is over. If I'm still alive. Until then, be with Mike and Leslie, Pat and Larry, Sue and Jerry, and....*

The list went on.

* * *

SATURDAY EARLY MORNING

So did the night. Micah prayed for the refugees in Turkey. The Central African Republic. Haiti. A door opened. A light switch clicked. Footsteps came near. Mr. Vaughn muttered, "She wants to ride with me to the dump. I'll have to take her."

Something clinked on the floor beside Micah. Mr. Vaughn humphed. "Dropped my knife. Great little knife. I'd like to get it back." He pushed the tool into Micah's hand. "Don't lose it. And remember, I did this." Footsteps walked away. The light went out. The door closed.

Micah began working on his taped hands. The knife felt razor sharp. Micah spent more time slicing his hands than he did the bonds. The blood made the instrument slippery and harder to wield. He stopped at intervals to refocus. Cut the tape. Cut the tape.

The door opened. Micah palmed the knife, hiding it as best he could. If Mrs. Vaughn examined too close, the ruse would be over. Micah prayed earnestly for blinded eyes.

Mr. Vaughn spoke. "I'll take the back. You get the front end."

Hands caught hold of Micah. Groans and complaints followed. His head smacked into the fender of the car. Rear fender, Micah figured. If it mattered.

They dropped him into the trunk, face down. His nose smushed against a carpet. He wiggled and shifted to leave himself room to breathe. Breathing mattered.

So did cutting his bonds.

Another weight was dropped beside him. Then the engine started, and the car began moving. Micah worked on cutting his bonds. He worked throughout the ride. Then palmed the knife once again when the car stopped. The trunk opened. Someone grabbed him by his arms, pulled and rolled him from the car's back end, and dropped him to the ground.

A horrendous stench filled his nostrils. Rotting food. Dead animals. Human waste. Everything reeked. The only salvation was the early morning hour. By midday, the aroma would be choking.

Mrs. Vaughn touched Micah's shoulder. "I really am sorry about this, Micky. But you made your choice. You supported Taylor. He'll be followed from the game today. This time, my man won't let him go. Taylor will die, and I'll get my boys back." She lifted her hand. Micah heard footsteps. The car door close. The vehicle drive away. They were alone.

Back to his hands. Cut the tape. Cut the tape. Nothing else mattered. Cut the tape.

* * *

Wendy lay on the ground and cursed the darkness. She cursed everything and anything else. She cursed until she ran out of curses, and then she started again.

But cursing didn't change anything. Neither would rolling, stretching, contorting, kicking her toes against the ground, digging her fingers into her backside... Nothing gained her freedom. She would die here, tossed out with the garbage.

So?

So she wasn't ready to die. Didn't want to die. Wanted to live.

For what? Why?

Because she wasn't ready to meet her Maker. Not yet.

Why?

Because I don't know him. Or Him.

Don't you?

I know what Micah's said.

And you trust Micah. You trusted him with your life. Do you trust what he says?

Usually.

You do, or you don't. One of the other.

I trust him.

Then what has he said?

That I need to ask God to save me. To commit my life to Him.

And?

And I don't get it. What does God want with me? I'm nothing.

The fosters your mom takes care of. What does she want with them?

Nothing. To take care of them. To show them they are loved.

And?

And nothing. She cares because that's who she is....

God loves because that's Who He Is. He loves you. He wants to save you.

From death?

From Death.

There's a difference?

One is physical. Here and now. One is eternal. Forever after.

But if I accept God, will He save me from dying now?

From Dying, yes. From dying…maybe.

And Dying is worse?

Think of the depravation and degradation you've seen in life. Multiply it a million billion times. That's what Dying is about. That's what living without Jesus is about.

Wendy let a few of the more depraved moments she'd experienced float through her memory. She shuddered. Beside her, Micah grunted. She could feel his body straining against hers. *Give it up, Mick. We're not getting out of this one.*

Says who?

You didn't promise we would get out.

Didn't promise you wouldn't. Said maybe. You have this chance to avoid Death. You may have this chance to postpone death. One is forever. The other is temporary.

But what does He want with me?

What does your mother want with her adoptees or fosters?

Nothing. To give them life. A life they wouldn't have on their own.

Silence.

He wants to give me life I can't have on my own. In exchange for what?

The life you have now. All of it. The good. The bad. The ugly. Especially the ugly.

And I get what in return?

His life of love and joy and peace and patience and glory and mercy and grace…all of it. And more. Much more. You give Him everything, and He gives you more.

This is hard. Mick says it takes faith. I'm not someone who walks by faith.

You want to see it to believe it. Test Me.

Test you? Really? Like, name something wild?

Test Me.

We ride out of here in a blue...a light blue pickup truck. In the front, not the back.

Done.

* * *

SATURDAY MORNING

Micah cut the tape. And his hands came free. Of one another. But his arms were still taped to his sides, and his sides taped to his thighs. He would have to contort to reach the next set of bonds.

No movement brought him closer to freeing himself.

Himself. What about Wendy? If she was still alive, if she was awake, she could help. First, he had to get to her.

Micah rocked back and forth, rolled and pushed, scooted, and lurched until he nestled beside the trapped agent. He rested his head against her back to listen for a heartbeat.

Wendy struggled beside him. He knocked his head against her back, trying to soothe her. It made her more frantic. Micah grabbed hold of her arm and squeezed. Not hard. Firm.

She caught the message and stopped fighting. Micah tapped her arm twice lightly. She leaned against him. Micah squirmed into position, then placed the knife in her hand so she could feel it. He didn't let go, but he did allow her to acknowledge he had a knife.

Her body bounced once. Micah began to saw at the bonds around Wendy's hands. He prayed he would have more success with hers than with his own. Fewer misses, fewer wounds, less blood. And a lot shorter time.

Three out of four isn't bad. It took as long to slice Wendy's hands free as it had himself. But only because he took more care not to cut her. Finally finished, he rolled free of her to allow her room to wiggle her fingers. Like him, her arms were still taped to her sides and her thighs. With only one hand free, trying to cut away at the tape around the eyes would be ignorant. No. More body parts had to be freed first. Micah pressed the knife into Wendy's hand. She would have to cut him free. One-handed. Better she do the slicing on him than the other way around. She could stab at the bonds that held his arms to his sides.

Even with one hand free, it still took time. Precious time. The day passed, and Micah didn't know how fast. Tav's life depended on them.

His arm came free. Wendy passed the knife back to him. Micah cut his other arm free, then cut the bonds holding his chest to his legs. He sat up, ripped the tape off his eyes and mouth, and breathed.

Micah reversed the order of freedom for Wendy, stripping the tape from her mouth and eyes, then cutting her loose. He put the knife in his pocket. "Thank you, Mr. Vaughn."

They had to wait for the circulation to pump blood to their extremities. Micah pounded with his fists, forcing blood flow back into his legs. He welcomed the pins-and-needles sensation. It meant he could feel life again. Let it hurt. He'd take pins over deadness any day.

Once Micah and Wendy were whole, Wendy whispered, "What now?"

"Call the police."

"And prove what? Kidnapping? Illegal restraint?"

"Attempted murder." Micah scowled at Wendy.

"I want her on the conspiracy to commit murder. I want to nail her for paying to have Tav killed. That's the one she won't be able to slide out of. We need to find out who the associate is."

"How do we catch her?"

"We bust the associate in the act. He fingers her, she gets convicted."

"How often does it really work out?"

"More often than you think. We have to get back to town first."

"You have your super-secret phone?"

"Not this time. They crushed it when they dropped me out of the car. We'll have to walk to the office."

Micah made his first attempt at standing but sank back to the ground. "I don't think the legs are ready yet. You?"

Wendy rolled forward, put tentative weight on her feet, then shook her head. "Not yet."

"We'll crawl." Micah edged forward.

Wendy moved with him. "Did I stab you much?"

"I don't know. I couldn't tell. I was too numb."

"You're not numb now. How bad is it?"

"When we get to civilization, I'll check. Until then, we keep moving."

They crawled another five minutes by Micah's estimation. He rolled to a sitting position. "Stop. I need a hand."

Wendy copied his motions. She sat and waited. Micah put both legs in front of him, grabbed her arms, and pulled. Wendy rose with him. They hugged for support until both sets of legs seemed to be able to hold weight. Micah broke first. Much as he preferred holding Wendy to walking in trash, they still had a killer to deal with.

They slogged forward. In the distance, they could see an office surrounded by seagulls. Flocks rose, glided, fought, and dived around the dump. Micah blanked his mind from thinking about birds attacking people. Stupid movie. He waved off one that dipped too close.

The smell while crawling had been rank. Standing

proved no better. Wendy gagged, covered her mouth, and kept walking. All that mattered was walking.

After an interminable segment of time, they reached the office. A man in a hazmat suit came out and shouted, "You can't be here."

Micah shouted back, "We don't want to be here. We were kidnapped and dumped. We need the police."

"I'll call them right away." The man slipped into his office. He came back out with clean towels and water for their hands. Micah took both. "Thanks."

"Police will be here—"

Wendy interrupted. "—when they get here. I know the drill. Can we sit in your office?"

"Yeah. Go on in."

A truck pulled to the door and honked. The clerk went out to direct the newcomers where to go.

A half-hour passed. Cars came. Cars went. Trucks came and deposited more loads of smelly trash. What didn't come were the police.

At the one-hour mark, Wendy stood. "Can I use your phone?"

"Sure."

Wendy punched in a number. "Jen? What are you doing right now?" She listened. "No. We're good. I'll find someone else. Yeah. Need a ride. No, you can't. Stay with the babies. We'll get someone to pick us up."

A light blue pickup drove to the window. A large man of color with tattoos covering his face called, "You need a ride?"

Wendy stared. Blood drained from her face. Micah didn't understand it but nodded to the stranger. "Yeah. Back to town would be great."

"Sure. Let me dump my load." He drove off to the designated area for old mattresses and futons. He returned a few minutes later. "Hop in."

Micah made to get in the bed of the truck, but the man stopped him. "No. Upfront. Not legal back there."

"Yeah, but we smell."

"I'll roll the windows down. Get in."

Micah and Wendy climbed into the front of the truck. The man stretched out his hand to shake theirs. "Sam."

"Micah."

"Wendy."

Sam eyed their hands. "Those look bad. You want me to take you to the ER?"

"No." Wendy curled her hands in her lap. "I don't want to put you to any trouble."

"You look like you already ran into a mess. Least I can do is help you out."

Wendy lowered her head. Micah didn't understand the reaction but picked up the conversation. "Thanks, we do appreciate it. If you could drop us at the closest police department, we'd appreciate it."

"You in serious trouble?"

"We were kidnapped."

Sam pulled his truck over to the side. "Let me clean your hands. I got a first aid kit under the seat. I don't like the idea of you riding with those hands."

The man refused to take "no" for an answer, and Micah didn't feel like fighting with him. Sitting on the side of the road, he washed and bandaged their hands. Sam even patched Micah's hip where Wendy had inadvertently stabbed him. Then he stopped along the way, bought food, and insisted they eat and drink before he drove them to the nearest police precinct. He asked, "You want me to hang around, so I can take you home if they don't get right to you?"

Micah shook his head. "No, Sam. You've been great.

More than great. Thank you."

Sam handed Micah a twenty. "Take this. In case you need it. I've been down on my luck before. Someone helped me."

Micah grinned. "Someone got a name?"

"They call Him Jesus."

Micah caught hold of Sam and hugged him. "My brother."

Sam smiled wide. "Glad to help."

Wendy lowered her head. "Thank you. We owe you."

"Pay it forward."

Sam let them out, and the two walked into the police station. Wendy walked to the front desk. The deputy asked, "What can I help you with?"

"We want to report a kidnapping, attempted murder, and a conspiracy to commit murder. And we need a phone to call and warn the intended victim NOT to take his motorcycle this afternoon."

"Sure. Let me get some information."

* * *

Tav took the call from BB. "Mick didn't come home last night. He went to be Wendy's backup at dinner with the Vaughn's. Left here at about six and never came home. I called his phone, but there was no answer. His 'FindMyBuds' app is still moving, but he's not answering."

"Did you try calling Wendy?" Tav looked at his watch. He needed to be at the field at nine. He had permission to watch practice with the team. Seeing Addison start, with Luke out on the wing as a receiver...what could be more special?

Now Mick was missing.

"No, I didn't call her. It felt weird."

"I understand. I'll call Jen and see what she knows."

He heard BB's laugh. "Yeah, I bet you will."

"Don't get smart with me. I'll leave your anatomy home." He stopped. "If Mick isn't there, how will you get to the game?"

"Chay is still in town. I'll call her."

"Good thinking. I'm sure Mick got delayed somewhere. He won't miss seeing Addison start, trust me."

"Yeah, I know. We're all excited. Ben's been wired all morning. He and Mialma have been running laps in the backyard. I'm not sure which one will get tired first."

"Don't forget Ben's earmuffs when you come."

"I have them in his backpack. Took out the rope he stole from Luke's trunk. I still gotta wonder what Mick and Wendy used to get Mick out of the hole."

"They're not saying. I don't think they ever will." Tav grinned. "Of course, you could have Ben ask, and Mick will tell Ben. Then Ben can tell you."

"Is that what brothers do? Sneak around behind each other?"

Tav laughed. "All the time. Until we became Knights, then such despicable conduct was beneath us. But it's still a viable interrogation technique."

He heard the wheels turning. "I'll try it. One of these days."

"If Chay can't pick you up, call me back. I'll call you if I hear anything from Mick or about Mick. You do the same."

"Right. Love you, brother."

"Love you too." Tav hung up and called Jen.

He beamed as he heard her voice. "Good morning, Tav. Why aren't you at the stadium?"

"I'm leaving in a few minutes. Have you heard from Wendy this morning?"

"Why? Is she missing?"

"Mick didn't come home last night. It's unusual for him

to leave the boys alone. Especially with Ms. Phelps prowling around making pop inspections."

"Wendy didn't come home last night, either. But it's not unusual when she's working. She may disappear for a few days, then show up and not be able to talk about where she had been."

Tav pulled on his Red Raider jersey. "Okay, then maybe it's just Mick missing. I thought they were together last night."

"They had brunch, but I didn't know anything about being together last night." Jen's tone sounded concerned.

Tav slipped into his shoes. "I'm sure it's a communication thing. They're fine. And they'll be at the game. None of us are going to miss seeing Addison and Luke play." He adjusted his belt. "I'm saving a whole section in case more than you, BB and Ben, Chay, Mick, and Wendy come."

"Like who?"

"Your folks. My folks, though I'm fairly certain that won't happen. It would be fantastic. Mick's dad said he'd come. We could have half the stadium."

Jen laughed. Her excitement sounded genuine. She wasn't coming just because he wanted her to. He hoped. "I think this will be a good game. It's fun to watch the bench players get thrown into the fire. It'll give the coaches some real insight into what kind of team they have coming up."

"Which is all good, but tough to see it at this point in the season. This game could determine if we play for the championship or not."

Jen growled. "Teams can't win every game every year. You expect perfection of these players."

Tav intercepted the protest. "Not perfection. Consistency." He heard her disagreement with his assessment. "Okay, we'll argue about the fairness of the

Championship Determination Rules later. Right now, we're just going to watch my brothers play."

Jen's tone lightened. "Right. And I'll be there about eleven. I'll see you then." She hesitated, then added, "I'm looking forward to seeing you, Tav."

"Same here, Jen. Bye."

He disconnected the call, then punched in Micah's number. No answer. He left a message. "Mick. Call in, brother. We're missing a Knight."

Tav put the phone away. He knelt beside the couch. "Lord, You know my heart. You know everything. I'd love to see Addison play well. I'd love the team to win. But only if it is in Your will. I can think of a million ways it would bring You glory if they do. But You have Your will, and it doesn't always match mine. You are God. I am not. Your will is what matters. But You said to bring our requests, so I bring 'em. Keep my brothers safe from harm. Let them have a good game. Be with Jen and me as we deepen our relationship. And close the door if this is not from You. I want Your will in all my life, Lord. In Jesus's Name, amen."

He stopped, then added, "And be with Mick. And Wendy. And Mom and Dad. Work it all out as only You can. And You can do anything. I love You, Lord."

Tav grabbed his Red Raider hat and stuffed it in his pants. He pulled on the motorcycle helmet and leather jacket before heading out the door. Safety first. He'd need to get another coat without the cuts and scrapes soon. But not today.

He rode to the stadium without incident and joined Addison and Luke in the locker room. Addison stuffed Tav's jacket and helmet into his locker. "You can get it after the game. No chance of someone walking off with it, and you won't kick it when Luke drops a pass."

Luke shoved Addison. "You throw the ball. Anything in

my direction, I'll catch. Anything else, you're on your own."

Together they ran out on the field. As it had always intended to be.

* * *

Before the game started, Tav and Addison went into the stands and joined Jen and Chay, BB and Ben. BB's face bore concern. "Still nothing from Mick."

Tav nodded. "He'll be here. I promise he'll be here."

Addison tilted his head. "Mick's missing?"

Tav shook his head. "He's late. He and Wendy. They'll be here."

Addison lowered his head. He looked at the helmet he carried and swore. "Sorry. Someone's got my helmet. I've got to go back to the locker room and get it." Tav jumped the stanchions with him. Addison waved him off. "I'll get it and be right back."

As he reached the room, he heard the phone ringing in his locker. He grabbed it. Micah. "Hey, Mick. What's happening? Why aren't you at the game? Tav even got to come down with the team."

"Shut up and listen."

Addison jerked back from the phone and stared at it as if he could see the speaker. Micah continued, "Do not let Tav ride his bike home under any circumstances, you understand? He's not to leave the stadium on his bike, period. At all. Never. Am I clear?"

"What's going on, Micah?"

"Your mom has paid someone to kill him. To not just run him off the road but to kill him. Until the police track the guy she's hired, he's not safe. "

"Mom would never—"

"I heard her say it, Addison. As you love your brother, keep him off the bike this afternoon."

"I hear you, Mick. I understand." *Not sure I believe you, but I hear you.* "I won't let Tav ride his bike."

"Thanks. Wendy and I will be at the game as soon as we can. We've been at the police station since this morning. We'll have to go home to clean up, but we should be there by half-time. We want to see your first start and you and Luke play together."

"Police station? What for?"

"Long story. Very long story. We were kidnapped and dumped at the landfill. But we were able to get free by God's grace. Now we're taking care of the paperwork."

"Kidnapped? By who?"

"I said, it's a long story. I'd rather tell it in person. So go be with the team, tell Tav not to ride, don't let Luke ride for him, and you stay off the bike yourself. You hear me, Knight?"

"I hear you, Mick. I'll see you after the game. Go Red."

"Go Red." Micah hung up the phone.

Addison set the phone back in the locker, in his brother's motorcycle jacket. Tav could collect it after the game.

Convenient. Convenient for Addison. Mom would never stoop to murder. She wanted her sons back, yeah. And she wasn't above some crazy schemes. But murder? Never. Never. Addison would never believe it. And he would prove it. Addison would take the bike, ride it to the house, and show Mick his mom was not a murderer. He'd show all of them.

Addison grabbed his helmet and ran to the squad room. Tav waited. "Anything wrong? I thought you were going to grab your stuff and come back."

"Nothing's wrong. Couldn't find it. Some lineman must have grabbed it. But he probably tossed it behind the bench after he tried it on. Took me a moment to find it, that's all.

Come on, big brother. Let's go join the team."

Arm-in-arm Addison and Tav caught up with the remainder of the squad.

* * *

SATURDAY AFTERNOON

The offense huddled. Addison took the call from the sideline and relayed it to the players. "Halfback sweep right. On two."

The ball snapped back to him. Addison handed it to the halfback, who surged to the right for four yards before being tackled.

Huddle. "Fullback sweep right. On four."

Another four yards.

"Halfback sweep right."

Three yards and a first down.

"Tight end sweep right."

Five yards.

"Quarterback sweep."

* * *

In the stands, Jen asked, "Are they going to call other plays besides sweep right? We're better than this."

Tav chuckled. "I know Coach. When their defense figures out how to stop the sweep, he'll call something else. But until then, he'll keep piling up the yards." He'd heard the speech too many times to doubt it.

Jen smiled. "You miss it, don't you?"

"Do I miss getting hammered by three-hundred-pound linemen? Miss getting stepped on and ground into the turf by 'accident?' Miss six a.m. workouts and eating six meals a day?" He shrugged. "Some days. God had a different plan for me. I accept it. And thank Him." Now.

"But you didn't at first, did you?"

"It took time. When I blew out the knee the first time, I thought He was teaching me perseverance. And I learned well. But when I blew it out the second time, I knew it wasn't about character as much as direction. He had a different plan for my life."

"And you're okay with it? Just 'everything is fine?'"

Tav shifted on the bleacher. "It wasn't 'just everything is fine.' But yeah, I'm okay with it." He took hold of Jen's hand. "If I were on the field being the quarterback, I couldn't be in the stands with a woman who's as lovely on the inside as she is on the outside."

Jen beamed. "That's sweet. Thank you."

* * *

The Blue Bombers called a time-out. Addison and the offense huddled with the coaching staff. Coach Wiggins's eyes beamed. "Go deep." He patted Addison on the shoulder. "Throw it deep. Don't care who's open. Don't care if you miss. Just throw it deep. We'll scramble their collective brains."

Addison nodded. Luke saw the...uncertainty? fear?...in his brother's eyes. Afraid he'd throw an interception and lose the starting spot? Afraid of looking foolish when the run still worked? Luke laid his hand on Addison's shoulder. "Pitch and catch. Just like we used to do when Dad drilled with Tav. Throw it, and I'll run under it. We're good, bro."

Luke held his brother's eyes for several seconds. At last, Addison ducked his head. Once. Luke patted his shoulder. "Let's do this."

The team ran back onto the field. Luke lined up in the slot position. He could read the eyes of the man across from him. He had murder written all over him. And his eyes were laser-focused on Addison. Luke yelled, "Fresno thirty."

Addison didn't look. He called "Bench thirty. Bench thirty." The outside lineman shifted to the right. Luke would say "imperceptibly" but no movement of a two-hundred-eighty-pound lineman is imperceptible. The shift was enough to take out the blitzing opposition. And leave Luke free to fly downfield.

The center hiked the ball. Luke broke free and ran for all he could down the sidelines. He looked over his shoulder to see the ball going over his head into the end zone. But if he leaped...if he stretched...if he could coax one more inch from his frame....

The ball hit his fingertips and rebounded into the air. Luke went after it, muscling the defender to the side. He would not let this pass hit the ground. Not his brother's first pass. He would not...

And he didn't. Luke pulled the ball into his chest, cradled it, then hit the ground. The defender tried to rip the ball out, but Luke refused to let go. Not Addison's pass. No way. Too many tears...and blood...had been shed to let this go.

The impact knocked the wind from his lungs. His head slammed against the turf. But he held the ball. All the way to the ground. Addison's first throw. A touchdown.

Luke laid still, unable to move. The fans went quiet. Teammates surrounded him. A trainer ran out and sat him up. He massaged Luke's back, forcing him to gasp and bring in air. Life-giving air. He breathed. And breathed. And breathed. Only after breathing became second nature did he take the arms of the trainer and stand to his feet.

Addison pushed through the crowd and grabbed his brother. "Luke!"

Luke put his arm around Addison and handed him the

ball. "For your trophy case."

The crowd lost its mind.

* * *

Tav held his breath until Luke came to his feet. Then Tav jumped and began cheering and screaming. "My brother! Those are my brothers!"

Jen grabbed him and hugged him, leaping up and down in excitement.

Wendy and Micah threaded their way into empty seats. BB and Ben rose and made way for Micah and Wendy to join the group. Micah dropped on the chair two places from Tav, leaving room for Jen and Wendy to sit. Tav studied both, and his excitement fell into a hole in his gut.

Both had deep scratches on their faces. Micah's hands were bandaged. His friend appeared pale, except where the road rash had colored his cheeks and forehead. As the spectators sat, he asked, "What happened to you?"

Wendy hugged Jen. Jen stared aghast at her sister. Micah ignored the question and asked, "Did Addison give you the message?"

His tone was terse, pained. Bad things had happened. "What message?"

Micah cursed. Actually cursed. Tav's mouth flew open. "Obscenity jar!"

Wendy eyed Micah from the side, shocked.

Micah lowered his head. "Forgive me. I lost it." He lifted his head again. "The message you're not supposed to ride your bike home this afternoon. Or any time in the near future until the police catch the for-hire killer who is after you."

Tav had to shout over the cheers of the crowd. "You want to tell me what's going on?"

"No. I want to watch the rest of the game. Then when

it's over, we fall back to my place, and we can discuss the last twenty-four hours."

"You okay, bro?"

"No, but I will be." Micah fell silent, glanced at the field, and yelled, "Get him!"

Tav noted a Blue halfback ran down the sidelines with the ball. Two Red defenders chased after him. Tav screamed, "Stop him!"

The thrill of the game resumed.

* * *

SATURDAY LATE AFTERNOON

Two hours later, the game ended. The crowd filtered out. Micah, Tav, Jen, Wendy, BB, and Ben waited until most of the spectators in their area left before climbing down to join the team milling around the field. Tav read the scoreboard: Red: 45. Blue: 40. Tense game. Not a lot of defense on either side of the ball. But the offenses played well.

He sought Luke and Addison and hugged each one jointly and severally. He couldn't stop beaming as he shook Addison by the shoulders. "I knew you had it in you. I knew you did."

He turned and caught Luke. "Your catch! Your catch!"

Luke grinned. "I wasn't going to drop Addison's first collegiate pass. And his first touchdown."

Addison glowed. "You nearly killed yourself, but what's more important?"

"The ball. The ball." Luke laughed. Tav saw the smile fade from his brother's face as he studied Micah.

Micah laughed with them, however. "Yeah, your dad always warned you: never let the quarterback look bad.

Makes 'em surly."

Tav nodded. "No one wants a surly quarterback."

Ben was passed around from player to player, pleased to be part of the celebration. BB congratulated as many as he could, getting signatures on his jersey. Jen pulled around Tav's waist. "Where are we going to celebrate?" She sparkled and laughed.

Addison jumped in. "Team's meeting at Lindy's house. We're going to celebrate the third-string victory. Before the regulars come back." He held Luke's eyes. "Sober, man. Only sober."

Luke grinned. Addison grabbed his gear and headed to the locker room.

Luke looped his index finger around to indicate the others. "I'd be a fifth wheel."

Tav shook his head. "We're only going back to Mick's house. He's got some information to give us."

Luke eyed Micah. Micah gave him a thumbs up. "You can miss it for now."

"I hate reruns. I'll come with you. Wait for me." He, too, grabbed his gear.

Tav motioned to Micah. "I'll leave the bike here and ride with Luke. Jen drove separately."

Micah's face was drawn again. Tired. Whatever had happened had taken everything out of his friend. But he rallied enough to promise, "We'll stop and get shakes for everyone. Winning tradition."

Tav pumped his fist. "Shirley's for the win!"

"Always." Micah and Wendy left the crowd.

Luke caught Tav's arm. "What happened to Mick?"

"That's what we're going to his place to find out." Arm over shoulder over shoulder, they walked to the locker room.

* * *

SATURDAY EVENING

Addison didn't shower. Yeah, he'd tighten and regret it tomorrow. But right now, he needed to prove his mom was not a murderer. Or even thinking of murder. He grabbed Tav's jacket and helmet from his locker. Donner, one of the receiving corp, passed by him. Addison caught his attention. "Donner. Need a favor. Take this phone to my brother. Luke. The one they called E.L. Have him give it to Tav. Tell them I have the jacket and will get it back to them after the party."

"You going to the party, man?"

"No. I got something I need to do. Don't forget."

"I won't. Killer game, man. Killer."

Addison frowned and nodded as Donner walked away with Tav's phone. "Let's hope not."

He went to the garage and found Tav's motorcycle. The bike Tav had owned less than a week. The replacement for the bike which had been wrecked when Tav got run off the road. Before someone blew up the restaurant he ate at.

Addison sat still on the bike for several moments. Was he really sure about this? Was it even a good idea? What if he was wrong? With Tav's helmet, jacket, and bike, he'd be a ringer for Tav. A dead ringer.

But Mom… Could she really? Would she? Not in her right mind. Not clean and sober.

Except she hadn't truly been sober for months. Maybe years. Maybe six years since Tav and Luke left. Or were thrown out. Luke's version of events looked truer the way his dad had reacted the other night. And if true, and Mom didn't defend her sons…well, maybe.

One way to find out. Addison started the engine,

revved it, and pulled to the parking garage exit. He muttered into the wind, "Let's go. Let's get it over with. Catch me if you can." He accelerated down the ramp.

* * *

SATURDAY EVENING MICAH'S

Seven frozen milkshakes (three vanilla, two chocolate, two strawberry) later, the group at Micah's had partied sufficiently to turn to serious business. Tav took the lead. "So what happened? You and Wendy have obviously been through major trauma. Tell us."

Ben sat on the floor at Micah's feet. He hugged Mick's legs and didn't let go. Tav noted Micah wince as he adjusted his weight in the chair. But the man said, "I want to start with prayer. If no one objects."

Tav glanced around the room. He didn't expect an objection. Neither did Mick, to be honest. But he would ask.

Receiving no "nay" votes, Micah closed his eyes. "Lord, thank You for saving Wendy and me today. That was all You, Lord. Thank You for sending Sam to take us back to town. Thank You the police listened and all the right moves were made. Please, be with May and Chris Vaughn. Whatever You have in mind for them, be with them. Help Tav, Luke, and Addison to see Your hand and give You glory. This is hard, Lord. Hard and deep, and only You can make it make sense. Keep us in You. In Jesus's Name, amen."

Micah opened his eyes. He squeezed Wendy's hand. "Wendy and I were kidnapped by Mr. and Mrs. Vaughn last night. We were dumped at the landfill this morning."

A knock sounded at the door. Jen jumped and went to open it. She turned and called over her shoulder, "It's Ms. Phelps."

Micah dropped his head to his chest. "Let her in." He did not rise as she entered.

Ms. Phelps had on Red Raider attire, head to foot. She beamed with joy. "I had to stop in and say congratulations on a great game! What a wonder—"

She trailed off as she noticed Micah and Wendy. Her eyes widened in shock, then narrowed. "Mr. Andres. What happened? I thought—"

Wendy climbed to her feet and interrupted. "Ms. Phelps. I appreciate you came here for fun and to be part of the celebration. For that, you're welcome. But don't you say one word to this man or any of his friends about their life choices. You essentially threatened Micah you would pull your support for the adoption if he got into trouble again. And now you see him torn up again. What you don't see is the reason for his condition. I asked Micah to help me locate a missing friend. One to whom Micah owes a deep debt of gratitude. Without Quinn Magary, BB and Ben wouldn't be with him today. Without Quinn Magary, none of this group would be here today. So Micah felt a duty to help find him.

"At the same time, if not for BB and Ben, Micah wouldn't be here. Dueling loyalties. And if there is one thing this man has in abundance, it is loyalty. To a fault, he is loyal. You put him in an either/or situation. He could be faithful to Quinn, or he could be devoted to BB and Ben. I know this man, and he would sooner shred himself into pieces than let down either friend. His sense of duty and loyalty put him in his condition."

Wendy stopped to take a breath. She held Ms. Phelps's gaze. "And I'm tired and hurting, and I should have kept my mouth shut. Disregard everything I just said." She plopped on the couch and hung her head. Tav reached over and touched her hand. She didn't look up. He could guess how she felt.

No one said a word. Ms. Phelps cleared her throat. "Um…I came by to say, 'Great game.' And on that, I'll let you go back to celebrating." The corners of her mouth twitched. "And Ms. Smothers, I value loyalty whenever I see it. Have a good evening." She turned and walked out.

BB closed the door. He walked over, leaned down, and kissed Wendy on top of the head. "Will you write my next school paper for me?"

Wendy shook her head. She continued to stare at the floor. Ben walked over, crawled under Wendy's head, reached up, and hugged her around the neck. He kissed her on the cheek, hugged her again, then moved over to sit at Micah's feet once again.

Mick's eyes were haunted. He picked up where he'd left off. "Mrs. Vaughn intended us to die. She felt we were coming between her and Luke and Addison. If we were gone, they would come back to her."

He swallowed hard, then continued. "It gets worse. She hired 'a guy' to kill you, Tav. That's why you weren't supposed to ride the bike. The man knows what you look like, knows your motorcycle, and is supposed to run you off the road and kill you. Then Luke and Addison are sure to come back to her."

Micah's voice trembled. He held Tav's eyes. "Your mom's gone over the edge. The police are looking for her and your dad now."

Luke's voice strangled. "What about Dad? Was he in on it?"

Wendy squeezed Micah's hand in return. "Yes and no. He helped, but he also helped us get away. He gave Mick a knife to cut the bonds. But he helped dump us at the landfill. He insisted he had nothing to do with the plan to kill us. It wasn't his idea."

Luke stood and walked out of the room. Micah's eyes

cast down, and tears streamed over his cheeks. Tav rose, squeezed Mick's shoulder, then went in search of his brother.

He found him on the back porch. His face empty of emotion. Drawn. Blank. Luke turned to Tav and asked, "How? How could she do this? How could she think this?"

Tav shook his head. "I don't know, Luke. Except she's not in her right mind. She can't be."

"What will happen to her? And Dad? Are they going to prison?"

Luke's façade shattered. He began crying. "She's Mom. Our Mom. She bakes cookies. She washes my jerseys. She doesn't kidnap my friends or hire killers."

"That was Mom before the blow-up. Who knows who she became after."

"Addison knows." Luke lifted his face. "I need to talk to him. Now. I need to know what happened to her." He pulled out his phone and speed-dialed his brother.

The call went to voice mail. Luke stared hard at the phone. "Where is he?"

"If he's at the party, he may have his phone off. Be present where you are, remember?"

"But I need him." Luke dialed again. "Addison. Call me. I need to talk to you. I need you to come to Mick's. Please." He begged. "Please, bro. I need you."

He disconnected the phone and hung his head. "I'm sorry. I can't accept this. I can't. Not without knowing what happened. You don't go from Mom to monster. You don't."

Tav kept his tone light. "You think Mick is lying?"

Luke jerked his head. "No. No. I believe him. I believe she did all those things. But I have to know why. I have to know what changed her."

"You're not to blame, Luke."

Luke managed a weak grin between his tears. "No, you

are. Apparently."

Tav nodded. "Yeah, well, I've got broad shoulders. I'll carry the blame."

Luke put an arm around Tav's shoulders. "No blame, brother. No blame. We were gone, and not by choice." Luke chuckled. "I know. Let's blame Addison. He was there the whole time. It's his fault."

"Yeah, that works." Tav shook Luke. "Let's go back to the others."

"Right."

The two brothers rejoined the group in the living room.

* * *

Addison watched his rearview mirror. A car followed him out of the parking garage. Not surprising. It turned left as he did. Also not unusual. There were only two choices, after all. Addison accelerated down Main and turned on Pike. The white sedan followed him. No plates on the front. Maybe not a big deal.

Addison rode down Pike for three miles. Traffic was heavy. Saturday at the university after a big game. Typical. The sedan stayed with Addison, three cars behind him. Whenever Addison changed lanes, the sedan did as well. Just in case Addison decided to turn? Or intimidation?

The road curved ahead. Addison watched the light. The left turn signal remained yellow. Gunning the engine, Addison crossed two lanes, caught the light, and made a U-turn.

The sedan copied Addison, except blew through the red light. Wheels squealed, and horns blared. The sedan swerved and dodged, missed sideswiping two vehicles, and raced to catch the motorcycle. Addison glared. "Game on, man." He took the right on Putzer and headed to the country. He could shake him there. He accelerated past the speed limit, weaving over the hills and around the curves. He could see the car in his mirror. Falling behind but still in pursuit.

Where did the road split? Where could he jump off and hide, then double back?

Tunnel Road. He could shoot through the tunnel, hide behind the exit, and then return home. It would work.

Too much thinking. The sedan closed in. Addison sped up, straightening the road by driving across the yellow lines. As long as he could see ahead, he'd be fine. He would.

Where are the cops when you need them? Never around.

Fear mounted in him. He could die out here. Die for doubting Micah. For not wanting to accept what he already knew to be true. Knew but didn't want to believe.

Die protecting Tav?

No, Tav wouldn't have come out on the bike. Addison owned this one. His fault.

Well, Mr. Sedan still had to catch him. Addison lowered his head to eliminate the drag from the wind. He flew—literally—over the small humps in the road. He pushed the speed to a hundred...a hundred and ten...one-fifteen. Still, the sedan stayed in his rearview mirror. Tunnel Road lay ahead. Could he pull out and whip around without being seen?

Maybe he should go off-roading. The tunnel crossed an aqueduct that ran between two farm fields. He might have to dodge cows, but he'd have the advantage over the sedan. Addison could jump the aqueduct and be home free. The sedan couldn't.

Addison gunned the motorcycle as fast as he could make it go. He didn't bother looking in the mirror. All he knew: go fast. The tunnel loomed ahead. Addison felt more than heard the sedan catching him...pulling beside him…crowding him into the wall. The bike hit the embankment and cartwheeled. Addison's body flung sideways into the concrete side of the tunnel. He heard flesh and fabric shredding as he tore along the passage. His helmet cracked. His neck whipped up and down, bouncing with the force of the collision. Blackness filled his vision. His last thought…

"Mom."

* * *

"Where is he? I'm going to go find him." Luke grabbed his jacket.

Tav nodded. "I'll go with you." *No way I'm leaving you alone right now, little brother. Your head's not straight.*

They left Micah and company to hold the fort and call if Addison showed up. Luke and Tav climbed into the car and pulled out of the driveway. Tav reminded Luke, "No speeding. God has him. Wherever he is, speeding—"

"I know, I know. God has him. And we're going to find him."

They drove to the location of the after-game party. Addison's car wasn't on the street. Considering how many cars there were, finding his would be nearly impossible. Luke led the way into the meeting hall. He grabbed the first player he saw. "Addison? Where is he?"

The man shrugged. "Haven't seen him. Check with Chewy."

Tav searched over the heads of the crowd looking to see if he could spot Addison. No luck.

Luke caught the next man by the elbow. "Addison? Do you know where he is?"

Same response. "Haven't seen him. Check with Bill."

And on and on. No one had seen Addison. Luke speed-dialed his brother's phone. Still no answer.

Tav made his way to the DJ at the front of the hall. "Call for Addison Vaughn. Tell him to report now."

The DJ complied. After the song ended, he broadcast, "We have a special request. Addison Vaughn, front and center, please."

Laughter filled the hall. People began looking around to see the quarterback dragged from wherever he hid...or whoever he hid with.

But Addison didn't show. The DJ repeated, "Addison Vaughn. Come on, man."

Silence poured over the crowd. Followed by murmurs and variations on a theme: "Did you see him?"

Luke caught Tav's eye. "This is wrong. Something bad's happened."

Tav grimaced. He strode outside and typed, "FindMyBuds." Tav tapped on Addison's icon. The GPS signal indicated the phone was out of town. Way out of town. And not moving.

Tav dialed 911. "I need police to respond to a possibly endangered or injured person..." He detailed what he knew, what he suspected, and where to find the phone. And hopefully, Addison.

Luke grabbed his arm. "Let's go. We can beat the police."

"Or take them with us when they pull us over. I'm driving."

The brothers raced to the car. Tav put it in gear and wove his way around the parked cars. Only after he hit the freeway did he open the engine. He pushed past eighty, and it still felt too slow. His brain and his heart battled.

God has him. Go the speed limit.

He's hurt. He may be dying. We have to go.

God has him.

We can save him.

God has him.

Tears blinded Tav. He slashed them away and focused on the road.

Luke bounced his leg. Bounced his whole body. "Clear on the left. Go."

Tav whispered, "I'm sorry, Lord." And pushed the accelerator.

If you die trying to save him, what have you accomplished?

Tav breathed hard. He slammed his hand into the steering wheel. Reduced his speed.

Luke glared at him, then closed his eyes. After a moment, he breathed out. "You're right. Drive."

Lights and sirens appeared in the rearview mirror. Tav pulled to the side of the road.

To be passed by two police cars flying by. Tav sagged. He looked at Luke. "God has him. You know He does."

"Right."

They drove to Tunnel Road. Arrived to find two police cars, an EMS squad, and an ambulance. A patrolman waved them down as they approached the tunnel. "Turn around. This is closed."

Tav pulled to the side of the road. The police officer yelled, "This is closed. Turn around."

Tav and Luke spilled out of the car. Tav yelled in return, "That's our brother!"

The officer stared at them. "Show me some ID."

Both men dug in and pulled out licenses. The officer examined them, then jerked his head to let them pass. He yelled, "Family. Let them through."

Addison lay on the stretcher. Blood spattered everywhere. Luke and Tav stood in silence, letting the professionals do what they could. The brothers tried to get as close as possible without interfering with the life-saving—or life-prolonging—measures.

Numb. There was nothing else.

Tav asked, "Can I ride along?"

He knew the answer. "No. They'll escort you."

"Where?"

"CRMC. It's the only level-one trauma hospital around."

"Don't let him die."

"We'll do our best."

Tav tapped the stretcher as they loaded it into the ambulance. Luke grabbed Addison's foot and squeezed it. The doors shut. The wagon made a wide Y-turn and headed back to town, lights, and sirens blazing.

A police officer motioned to Tav. "Follow us. Behind us, got it?"

Tav nodded. Numb. Obey directions. Drive. *That should have been me.*

In the car, Luke pounded the dashboard. "She did it. She did it. She wanted you killed."

Tav gritted his teeth. Narrowed his eyes to focus on the police escort in front of him. All that mattered was getting to the hospital while Addison lived. Everything else would wait until his fate had been decided.

Everything but the prayers.

* * *

SUNDAY AT HOSPITAL

At the hospital. Long hours in the ER waiting and waiting for word. Knowing the medical personnel were doing all they could to save Addison's life. Once, someone came out to tell them he was alive. He could lose the arm. Or the leg. But he still breathed.

Then the monitors in the emergency bay went crazy, and the attendant disappeared back behind the curtains. The wait continued. Luke paced. Tav paced. Addison was moved to surgery.

Micah, Jen, Wendy, BB, and Ben showed up. They took seats along the wall. Micah prayed. Luke and Tav prayed. Jen prayed. BB prayed. Ben prayed in his silent way.

Wendy prayed. "Lord, You can do anything. You worked for me. You proved Who You Are when You didn't have to. Please, heal Addison. Bring him back to us. Leave him with us a little longer. Let me get to know my baby brother. Please. But...but You know what is best. Do it, Father."

She stared at the floor. Finally, she lifted her head and added, "In Jesus's Name, amen."

Tav cocked his head. "Wendy?"

She looked at her hands. "I haven't had time to tell you. Friday night, during the time Mick and I were being held captive, I had a long talk with God. Long talk. I challenged Him." Tears covered her face. She lifted her head. Her voice trembled. "He said to test Him. Test God. Test Him and see He is good. And faithful and true." She smiled a tight-lipped smile. "So I did. I said I'd surrender if he sent a guy in a blue truck—a *light* blue truck—to save us. And who pulls up? Sam Martin, the owner of a light blue Chevy truck. The police didn't even come, but Sam Martin dressed our wounds, drove us to town, bought us coffee, then gave us money for food."

Wendy tossed her head and sniffed. "I'm a heathen, but even I know the story of the Good Samaritan. And God reenacts it there in front of me." She chewed her lip. "So yeah, I gave Him my life. How could I not?"

Tav and Luke put their arms around her. They held a joy-filled family union. Then Wendy went back to sit with Micah again. She took his hand. He squeezed hers.

Time passed.

The elevator door opened. Mr. and Mrs. Vaughn spilled into the hallway. Mom appeared white as a ghost. She grabbed hold of Tav. "The college called us. The police say Addison has been in an accident. They said they don't know his condition. He's in surgery. What's going on?"

Tav gritted his teeth and yelled, "Your assassin took him out! He tried to kill the wrong son. Your plan worked but on the wrong man."

Mom's eyes went wide. She stared at the blood on Luke's jacket. The blood on Tav's coat. She backed against the wall. "No. No. It's not true."

Luke snarled, "We were there. We saw it."

She stared at the floor, not comprehending. She glanced up, her eyes wild. "No. No. It didn't happen." She swallowed hard, then turned to Tav. "Addison, I'd never hurt you or anyone. Taylor had the accident. You're right here. You're fine."

Tav froze. He gave her a side-eye. "I'm Taylor."

She laughed. Lightly. "Oh, Addison. You always pretended to be Taylor. You wanted the attention Taylor got from your dad. But you were my baby. I'd never do anything to hurt you. Never."

Luke caught Mom's arm. "He's Taylor. Tav. Addison is in surgery, fighting for his life." He turned to Dad. "Tell her. Tell her this is Taylor."

Dad kept his head down. "May. It's Taylor."

"No, no, no." Again she laughed. "It's a great joke, but I know my son. All my sons. And you are Addison." She hugged him. "My Addi."

Tav pushed her away. He breathed heavy, his heart breaking. "You killed Addison. Tried to. Maybe he's going to make it. Maybe he's not. But pretending I'm him isn't going to change anything."

He motioned to Luke. "Get one of the police officers from the lobby. Tell them what's going on. They're looking for these two for attempted murder." He looked over at Wendy and Micah. "Three attempted murders. Have them check their files."

Mom continued to insist, "Addison, this isn't funny anymore. Admit it. You're Addison. Taylor is the one in the accident. I'd never hurt you. Never."

A police officer came and took Mom by the arm. "Ma'am, you're under arrest for attempted murder, conspiracy to commit murder, and kidnapping."

She jerked away and yelled, "Addison! Tell them who you are! Tell them!"

Tav lowered his eyes. He turned his back on Mom. Dad brushed past him and muttered, "Sorry. She's lost it."

Tav didn't respond. Dad walked out with the officers. May continued to cry out, "Addison! Addison!"

Luke stood beside Tav. Wendy came to her feet and joined the two men. Micah, Jen, BB, and Ben rose as well. Together they closed ranks around the grieving.

They huddled together until the surgeon came out to address them. He surveyed the group. "Family?"

Tav nodded. "All of us."

"Blood family?"

Tav pointed to Luke, then included Wendy. "Us."

"Your brother will live. We've closed the major wounds and stabilized his neck and spine. The right arm and leg will need multiple surgeries. But if we're good, if he works hard, if he has some encouragement, he may retain the use of both of them. That's a lot of ifs. We'll do the best we can."

He glanced over his shoulder. "They'll take him to recovery, then to a room in ICU. You can see him there." The corners of his mouth moved upward half an inch. "Family only."

Tav shook the doctor's hand. "Thank you, sir. Thank you for saving my brother."

"You're welcome." The surgeon moved away to the locker room.

Tav sighed. Luke and he collapsed into chairs. Tav let out a loud and relieved, "Praise the Lord!"

An echoed "Amen" came from the locker room the surgeon had just entered. Tav chuckled. And chuckled. And laughed. And it felt good.

* * *

TUESDAY

Two nights later, the crowd gathered as usual at Micah's. He grumbled as he passed the kitchen, "Someone in this group needs to buy a house of their own."

Luke grinned and tossed a wadded-up napkin at him. "You love us. You wouldn't know what to do with yourself if you didn't have us around."

Micah humphed. "I'll never find out, will I?"

He limped to his chair in the living room. Jen, Tav, and Ben sat on the couch. Luke lounged in the rocker. Chay sat at his feet. Wendy sat in the winged-back chair. BB had the ottoman. Micah's hands still bore the bandages from his escape. Wendy had two on her hands as well. Micah and Wendy's faces were raw with the road rash they'd accrued. Tav and Jen had burns on their faces and arms. Micah looked around at the gathering of Knights and shook his head. "This looks like a hospital ward."

Mialma barked and raced to the back door. Ben ran with her. Micah cocked his head, waiting to see who would enter.

Quinn and Grace sauntered into the room, Ben holding hands with both of them. He bounced and jumped.

Quinn stopped short as he took in the occupants of the room. His mouth dropped open. He closed it, narrowed his eyes, and focused on Micah. "What in the world happened here?"

Tav asked, "Lead?"

Luke offered, "Mick."

The vote was swift and unanimous. Micah didn't rise but drawled. "Oh, we were looking for you."

"Me? Why?"

Wendy glared at him. "You're missing."

Quinn did a round-the-world examination of the room. "I'm not missing."

Micah took back the conversation. "You were. You had a three-day assignment in Hanford. Your intern became concerned when you didn't show up within another five days. Her superiors told her not to worry unless you were gone more than thirty days. Your intern thought that excessive."

Wendy nodded. Quinn shrugged. "Policy."

"The intern contacted Kurt Andres, who, in turn, suggested she contact us. Which she did. And since we've been looking, we have solved two cold-case missing persons. Both were at your dig site, Grace. One was a murder, one a lost soul who became entangled in a cavern with his liquor bottles and never found his way out."

He pointed to Tav. Tav took the baton. "There were multiple attempts on my life, including the fire-bombing of the restaurant where I ate with this..." Tav stopped. He grinned. "I have too many descriptors I want to put in that sentence, but I'll leave it with 'this young woman.'"

Micah added, "From Tav and Jen's descriptions, the police were able to catch the man who set the place on fire. Insurance fraud."

Luke picked up the story. "Addison and I bonded. Addison got to start the game Saturday because the other two quarterbacks came down with food poisoning. And no, it was *not* deliberate on anyone's account." He grinned and added, "Addison threw his first touchdown."

Quinn raised his eyebrows. "And you caught it."

Luke gave a single Ben-nod. "Yes, I did."

Micah finished. "Wendy and I were kidnapped and left to die at the landfill. An actual real-life Good Samaritan helped us back to civilization. We brought charges against the perpetrators. But the police weren't able to arrest them at the time. One of the perpetrators put a hit out on Tav. Addison impersonated Tav and got run off the road into the tunnel at the aqueduct. They nearly killed him. The doctors think they can save his arm and leg. It's going to be touch and go. But he's going to live."

Micah pointed to Wendy. She drew in a deep breath. "I discovered I am directly related to Tav, Luke, and Addison. They're my brothers. Mrs. and Mr. Vaughn were behind everything. Mrs. Vaughn couldn't come to terms with nearly killing Addison and is being evaluated for her mental state. Mr. Vaughn is complicit but also aided us in our escape."

Quinn turned to BB. BB held up his hands. "Don't look at me. I was in school or taking care of the little guy. I had nothing to do with this."

Quinn bent and held Ben's eyes. He frowned deeply. "Ben, you promised me you would take care of this bunch. What happened?"

Ben turned his head to look one way around the room. Then he turned in the opposite direction. Finally, he raised both hands, palms up.

Quinn chuckled and hugged the boy. "Can't blame you. They're the adults."

Wendy demanded, "Where were you?"

Chay glared hard at her mother. "Where were *you*?"

Quinn and Grace found seats side by side. Quinn

looked at Grace. She smiled. She lay her hand on his arm. Quinn smiled. "Grace and I decided to get married. Spur of the moment decision we've been talking about for months. I had some days off coming, so I swooped in, dashed her off her feet. We ran away to Hawaii and got married."

Micah hung his head. Wendy covered her eyes. Luke and Tav crowed. Micah lifted his face. "Congratulations. We're very happy for you. All of us."

Wendy sagged. "Why didn't you tell us? Any of us?"

"We weren't certain until we stepped off the plane in Maui."

"And you couldn't have called home?" Chay demanded angrily.

"I did. I left a message on your landline, Mick." He eyed the room. "Don't suppose anyone bothered to check it, now, did they?"

Eyes rolled all around the room. Quinn walked to the phone, pressed the button, and his voice came over the speaker. "Mick. Quinn. I'm picking up Grace." Quinn shut it off.

Eyes closed around the room. One by one, Knights rose, walked across the room, and bopped Micah on the head, then went back and sat down.

Quinn swallowed a smile before asking, "Did anything else happen of note?"

Micah stood. "No. I ran across an old friend of yours. James Tilley."

Quinn sucked in a breath. "Ooo...so sorry. What did he have to say?"

"He gave me a message to give to you...verbatim."

All eyes focused on Micah. Would he do it? Would he not? Integrity? Honesty? Self-preservation? What would win the day?

Quinn held up his hand. "Give it to me exactly as he

said it."

Micah stepped in front of Quinn. He lifted his fists...

...and dropped them. "I can't. I can give you my interpretation of what he said. But I can't deliver it the way he did. I just can't."

Quinn grinned. "Oh, give it your best shot."

"My best shot pales in comparison to what Mr. Tilley said." Micah tapped Quinn in the eye, in the side, and in the jaw. "You'll have to imagine the rest."

Quinn laughed. "I'm sorry you had to carry the message." He glanced around the room. "Anyone else have messages to deliver?"

Heads shook in the negative. Quinn grinned. He rubbed his hands. "Well, then, I've got a favor to ask. I've got a case I'm working on..."

Eight bodies scattered.

Quinn looked at Grace. "What did I say?"

Grace kissed him. "Nothing, dear. Young people, you know. So flighty."

Quinn nodded. "I'd noticed. Let's go home."

They patted Mialma as they went out the door. She woofed her approval. And closed the door behind them.

If you enjoyed **Knights of the Octagon,** sign up for Colleen Snyder's newsletter to keep up with new books and projects. It will also give you a place to talk to the author directly. And she loves to talk to her readers. Trust me!
Emails will NOT be sold, shared, or used for any other purpose. Promise.
Go to: **colleensnyderauthor.com** and leave your email to sign up.
Also connect with her at Facebook, **Colleen K. Snyder, Author**.

COMING SOON: Book Three in the *Knights of the Octagon Series: QUAKE.*

THURSDAY

They heard the crack from the backyard. Almost like an explosion but deeper. More resonance. Micah jerked his head up. Mialma, the black lab, jumped from the cot and barked frantically. Another clap sounded almost immediately after. It came from the hills. Micah stared hard, looking for movement, smoke, anything that would tell him the cause of the noise.

Nothing. Two air-reverberating crashes and nothing else. What did it mean?

Micah calmed Mialma. "Shh, girl. It's okay. Whatever it was is over now. Shh."

Mialma quieted but paced around the yard before settling. She laid her head on her paws and watched Micah.

BB stuck his head out of the kitchen door. "Did you hear that?" The lanky teenager leaned against the doorframe.

"Yeah. Weird. Not an explosion. It came from the hills." Micah continued to survey the area for a source of the noise.

"What do you think it was?" BB's voice carried more curiosity than concern.

"I don't know. Check the news. See what the buzz is about." BB disappeared back into the house to comply. Very little rattled BB. Adopting him was an easy call, despite there being only eight years between them.

Micah pulled out his phone and scanned the news sites

to see if anyone else heard or knew anything. Nothing. No mention of the noise at all.

Local neighborhood sites mentioned it but dismissed it as construction blasting. Not that there was any in the vicinity, but what else could it be? Had to be construction. Yeah, we'll go with that.

Micah's senses all said no. This was something else. He didn't know what, but he would catalog it for more research.

Nine-year-old Ben came out of the house. He tip-toed to his dad's side and stepped in front of Micah. The boy reached out for a hug. Micah gave him one. Ben didn't let go. Micah held him until the child released him. Ben looked up at Micah, searching his face. Micah smiled. "It's okay, buddy. Just loud noise. Like thunder. It comes, it makes noise, it goes. Can't hurt you."

Ben hesitated, then nodded. He hugged Micah one more time, then went back inside the house. Too thin. Two years with Micah as his adopted son, and the boy still hadn't put on enough weight. Not to Micah's mind. But the doctors all agreed the boy was fine. Let him grow.

Micah followed Ben in, along with Mialma. BB sat at the kitchen table surfing the news on his phone. "So far, it's construction, it's the quarry blasting, it's the aliens, it's a precursor to an earthquake, it's the government, it's rifles, it's jet engines backfiring...pick your theory."

Micah nodded. "Aliens. Has to be the aliens."

BB snorted. "That was my guess, too." He laid the phone down and stretched.

"Unless something more happens, I say we forget it and move on. What have you got planned for tonight?"

"Kenmore and Lutz are coming over to jam for a while if that's okay with you."

Micah nodded. "Sure. Long as you keep it street legal

and everyone goes home at midnight."

BB grinned. "Sure thing, Dad. We'll keep it down to the dull roar you're always telling us about."

Micah put a hand on Ben's shoulder. "Ben and I will go bowling for a couple hours." He knelt and asked, "Would you like that tonight?"

Ben bounced up and down on his toes. "Yes."

Micah smiled. "Should we invite Tav and Jen to come, too?"

More bouncing on the toes. Beaming face. "Yes!" Ben loved Tav. Tav loved Jen, so Ben loved Jen as well. Worked well.

"And should we invite Wendy?"

Ben's head dropped, and he stood still. He didn't move, but Micah read the emotion. And heard the voice. "No."

"You don't want Wendy to come?" Micah kept his tone soft. Even. Avoid the frustration.

Ben turned his body left, then right. Once.

Micah sighed. Quietly. He needed to break through this wall. "Okay, buddy. This time it's just you and me. Next time we'll invite Wendy, okay?"

Ben continued to hang his head. Micah looked into Ben's eyes. "Wendy is Tav's sister. Tav loves her. So does Luke. And Addison. It's not fair to Tav to say we don't want Wendy around. That will make Tav feel bad. He won't want to come around, either. Do you understand?"

Ben nodded, then shook his head again. Micah squeezed Ben's shoulder. "We'll still invite Tav and Jen." Maybe if Tav talked to Ben, it would help. Nothing Micah had to say mattered.

The boy loved Wendy in the beginning. Last year. But as Micah and Wendy spent more time together—making sure to keep Ben in the picture—Ben had become more jealous of Micah's time. And less tolerant of Wendy. Micah wanted to give the boy time to "work it out." But six months, and they were no closer to resolving Ben's issues with Wendy. Counselors, teachers, pastors...no one had the magic answer to Ben accepting Wendy as anything but a rival for Micah's time. Just "give it time."

He made the text. *Bowling? Kensies? Seven?*

Jen out. Luke okay?

Micah grinned. *Your date. I got Ben.*

No Wendy?

Not yet.

Bummer.

Yeah. I know.

See you.

BB passed in the hall. "You want me to keep the little guy so you and Wendy can go out?"

"Thanks, but no. Jen is out, so it's Luke and Tav. Ben will be fine with us." Micah tapped fists with BB. "I appreciate the thought, my man."

"You got it. I may need the favor one day."

"And I'll remember it."

BB grinned and went to the back to set up the gear for his friends.

Micah looked at the clock, then pointed it out to Ben. "We will meet Tav and Luke at seven. What should we do until then?"

Ben grabbed a menu from the drawer. "Pizza."

"Maybe not pizza since they have it at the bowling alley. Maybe something different?"

"Pizza."

"Ben..." *Pick your battles.* "Pizza it is." Nothing says Micah couldn't have a salad. Not everything had to be a test of wills. Not yet.

* * *

ABOUT THE AUTHOR

Colleen K. Snyder has always had a passion for writing. She authored two previously published books: *Journey to Amanah: The Beginning* and *Return to Tebel-Ayr: The Journey Continues* (B&H Publishing). In 2020 she published the first book in the *Collin Walker* series: *Verdict at the River's Edge*. There are now seven books in the series. She lives on a "ranchette" in California and is the juniorest ranch hand. She serves on her church prayer team, and exercises a ministry of intercessory prayer. She has worked as a factory line worker, pharmacy technician, USAF missile systems analyst, janitor, nanny, teacher, accounting manager and anything else the Lord required. Her son, Bear and his wife Krystal, their two daughters, Mara and Kaylynn, and her daughter Katie all live in Ohio.

Colleen's story is for His glory, always.

Read on to learn more about Colleen's books in the *Collin Walker* series.

The Collin Walker Series

Six books of action and suspense for your reading enjoyment. Follow Collin Walker as she follows the Lord into murder, intrigue, mayhem...you know, Life.
Available on Kindle, KindleUnlimited, and in paperback.
(Also hardback, but why??)